Praise for

DEVIL MAY CARE

"*Devil May Care* is a delight. The over-the-top villain, the massive weapons, the grandiose plans and schemes, Bond's ability to bounce back from the most savage beatings, and the collisions and explosions are all on display.... Well done, Mr. Faulks. It is indeed good to see Bond back." —*Forbes*

"Smart and enjoyable.... Among the now thirty-three post-Fleming Bonds, this must surely compete with Kingsley Amis's for the title of the best."
—*The Guardian* (UK)

"Considerable fun.... Best of all, there's retro charm when Bond swims into enemy territory wearing only a swimsuit and—nice touch—a commando knife strapped below the knee." —*Entertainment Weekly*

"Well-written [and] entertaining.... The tension ratchets up." —*The Wall Street Journal*

"Where would 007 be without his Bond girl? Faulks provides a fresh spin." —*The Charlotte Observer*

"The biggest literary thrill of [the year]."
—*The Observer* (UK)

"It's Faulks's expertise at crafting inner lives that gives his Bond the character and persona we know and love. The story line is equally well-turned, a nicely calibrated distillation of Fleming's oeuvre."
—*Minneapolis Star Tribune*

"Deftly done. . . . Everything you want from Bond."
—*The Sunday Telegraph* (UK)

"Goes down as easily as one of 007's bon mots."
—*The Christian Science Monitor*

"Faulks is a graceful writer with a bracing cold streak and a sharp eye for period detail."   —*Time*

"[*Devil May Care*] comes commendably close to the original and . . . provides some real, retro pleasure."
—*The Dallas Morning News*

"[Filled with] admirable style and verve."
—*The South Florida Sun-Sentinel*

"This is vintage Bond. . . . A ripping yarn."
—*The Times* (UK)

"So satisfying was Sebastian Faulks's new James Bond novel that I felt obliged to celebrate by making myself a vodka martini, very dry, shaken, not stirred."
—Fritz Lanham, *Houston Chronicle*

DEVIL MAY CARE

DEVIL
MAY CARE

The New James Bond Novel

SEBASTIAN FAULKS
writing as IAN FLEMING

SEAL BOOKS

Seal Books and colophon are trademarks of Random House of Canada Limited.

DEVIL MAY CARE
Seal Books/ published by arrangement with Doubleday Canada
Doubleday Canada hardcover published 2008
Seal Books edition published May 2009

ISBN: 978-1-4000-2607-4

Printed and bound in the USA

Seal Books are published by Random House of Canada Limited.
"Seal Books" and the portrayal of a seal are the property of
Random House of Canada Limited.

Visit Random House of Canada Limited's website: www.randomhouse.ca

10 9 8 7 6 5 4 3 2 1

To the memory of

Ian Fleming
&
to Fali Vakeel

who, when he and I were schoolboys,

first introduced me to Bond

DEVIL MAY CARE

1. THE WATCHER WATCHED

It was a wet evening in Paris. On the slate roofs of the big boulevards and on the small mansards of the Latin quarter, the rain kept up a ceaseless patter. Outside the Crillon and the George V, the doormen were whistling taxis out of the darkness, then running with umbrellas to hold over the fur-clad guests as they climbed in. The huge open space of the place de la Concorde was glimmering black and silver in the downpour.

In Sarcelles, on the far northern outskirts of the city, Yusuf Hashim was sheltered by the walkway above him. This was not the gracious arch of the

Pont Neuf where lovers huddled to keep dry, but a long, cantilevered piece of concrete from which cheap doors with many bolts opened into grimy three-room *appartements*. It overlooked a busy section of the noisy N1 and was attached to an eighteen-storey tower block. Christened L'Arc en Ciel, the Rainbow, by its architect, the block was viewed, even in this infamous district, with apprehension.

After six years of fighting the French in Algeria, Yusuf Hashim had finally cut and run. He had fled to Paris and found a place in L'Arc en Ciel, where he was joined in due course by his three brothers. People said that only those born in the forbidding tower could walk its airborne streets without glancing round, but Hashim feared nobody. He had been fifteen years old when, working for the Algerian nationalist movement, the FLN, he took his first life in a fire-bomb attack on a post office. No one he had ever met, in North Africa or in Paris, placed much value on a single life. The race was to the strong, and time had proved Hashim as strong as any.

He stepped out into the rain, looking rapidly back and forth beneath the sodium light. His face was a greyish brown, pocked and wary, with a large, curved nose jutting out between black brows. He tapped the back pocket of his blue *ouvrier*'s trousers, where, wrapped in a polythene bag, he carried twenty-five thousand new francs. It was the largest amount he had ever had to deal with, and even a man of his experience was right to be apprehensive.

Ducking into the shadows, he glanced down for the fifth or sixth time at his watch. He never knew who he was looking out for because it was never the same man twice. That was part of the excellence of the scheme: the cut-out at each end, the endless supply of new runners. Hashim tried to keep it equally secure when he shipped the goods on. He insisted on different locations and asked for fresh contacts, but it wasn't always possible. Precautions cost money, and although Hashim's buyers were desperate, they knew the street value of what they dealt in. No one in the chain made enough money to be able to act in absolute safety: no one, that is, except some ultimate, all-powerful controller thousands of miles away from the stench of the stairwell where Hashim was now standing.

Sticking a soft blue pack of Gauloises to his mouth, he wrapped his lips round a single cigarette and drew it out. As he fired his cheap disposable lighter, a voice spoke in the darkness. Hashim leaped back into the shadow, angry with himself that he'd allowed someone to observe him. His hand went to the side pocket of his trousers, where it felt the outline of the knife that had been his constant companion since his childhood in the slums of Algiers.

A short figure in an army greatcoat came into the sodium light. The hat he wore looked like an old kepi of the Foreign Legion, and water ran from its peak. Hashim couldn't see the face. The man spoke in English, softly, in a rasping voice. "In Flanders fields," he said, "the poppies blow."

Hashim repeated the syllables he had learned by sound alone, with no idea of what they meant: "Betveen de crosses, row on row."

"Combien?" Even that one word showed that the dealer was not French.

"Vingt-cinq mille."

The runner laid down a brown canvas bag on the bottom step of the stairs and stood back. He had both hands in the pockets of his coat, and Hashim had no doubt that one would be clasping a gun. From the back pocket of his blue trousers, Hashim took out the polythene-wrapped money, then stepped back. This was how it was always done: no touching, and a safe distance maintained. The man bent down and took the money. He didn't pause to count it, merely inclined his head as he stowed the package inside his coat. Then he in turn stood back and waited for Hashim to move.

Hashim bent down to the step and lifted the bag.

The weight felt good, heavier than he had known before, but not so heavy as to make him suspect it was bulked out with sand. He shook it up and down once and felt the contents move soundlessly, with the satisfying heft of packed dry powder. The business was concluded, and he waited for the other man to move off. That was the routine: it was safer if the supplier didn't see which way the receiver even started his onward journey, because in ignorance was security.

Reluctant to move first, Hashim faced the other man. He suddenly became aware of the noise around them—the roar of the traffic, the sound of rain dripping from the walkway on to the ground.

Something wasn't right. Hashim began to move along the wall, furtive, like a lizard, edging towards the freedom of the night. In two strides the man was on him, his arm across Hashim's throat. Then the unpainted wall smashed into his face, flattening the curved nose into a formless pulp. Hashim felt himself thrown face down on the concrete floor, and heard the click of a safety catch being released as a gun barrel pressed behind his ear. With his free hand, and with practised dexterity, the man pulled Hashim's arms behind his back and handcuffed them together. Police, thought Hashim. But how could they . . .

Next, he was on his back, and the man dragged him to the foot of the stairwell, where he propped him up. From his coat pocket, he drew out a wooden wedge, about four inches at its deepest. He smacked it into Hashim's mouth with the heel of his hand, then hammered it home with the stock of his gun, to the sound of breaking teeth. From his coat pocket, he took out a large pair of pliers.

He leaned over Hashim, and his yellowish face became momentarily visible. "This," he said, in his bad French, "is what we do to people who talk."

He thrust the pliers into Hashim's mouth, and clamped them on his tongue.

René Mathis was having dinner with his mistress in a small restaurant near the place des Vosges. The net curtains on their brass rail obscured the lower half of the view from the window, but through the upper light Mathis could see a corner of the square with its red brick above the colonnades, and the rain still running from the eaves.

It was Friday, and he was following a much-loved routine. After leaving work at the Deuxième, he took the Métro to St. Paul and made for his mistress's small apartment in the Marais. He walked past the kosher butchers and the bookshops with their scriptures and seven-branched candelabra, till he came to a battered blue *porte-cochère* where, after instinctively checking that he had not been followed, he tugged the ancient bell-pull.

How easy it was for a secret agent to be a successful adulterer, he reflected happily as he glanced up and down the street. He heard footsteps on the other side of the door. Madame Bouin, the stocky concierge, opened up and let him in. Behind her thick glasses, her eyes gave their usual mixed signal of conspiracy and distaste. It was time he gave her another box of those violet-scented chocolates, thought Mathis, as he crossed the courtyard and climbed to Sylvie's door.

Sylvie took his wet coat and shook it out. She had prepared, as usual, a bottle of Ricard, two glasses, a carafe of water and a plate of small toasts from a packet, spread with tinned *foie gras*. First, they made love in her bedroom, a hot bower of floral curtains, floral cushion-covers and flower prints on the walls. Sylvie was a good-looking widow in her forties, with dyed blond hair, who had kept her figure well. In the bedroom, she was skilful and accommodating, a real *poule de luxe*, as Mathis sometimes affectionately called her. Next—following the bathroom, a change of clothes for her and the *apéritif* for him—it was out to dinner.

It always amused Mathis that so soon after the abandon of the bedroom, Sylvie liked a proper conversation, about her family in Clermont-Ferrand, her sons and daughter, or about President de Gaulle, whom she idolized. Dinner was almost over, and Sylvie was finishing a fruity clafoutis, when Pierre, the slim head waiter, came regretfully to the table.

"Monsieur, I'm sorry to disturb you. The telephone."

Mathis always left numbers at his office, but people knew that Friday nights were, if possible, sacrosanct. He wiped his mouth and apologized to Sylvie, then crossed the crowded restaurant to the wooden bar and the little lobby beyond, next to the door marked WC. The phone was off the hook.

"Yes." His eyes travelled up and down over the printed notice concerning public drunkenness. *Répression de l'Ivresse Publique. Protection des Mineurs.*

No names were exchanged in the course of the conversation, but Mathis recognized the voice as that of the deputy section head.

"A killing in the *banlieue*," he said.

"What are the police for?" said Mathis.

"I know. But there are some . . . worrying aspects."

"Are the police there?"

"Yes. They're concerned. There's been a spate of these killings."

10

"I know."

"You're going to have to take a look."

"Now?"

"Yes. I'm sending a car."

"Tell the driver to come to the St. Paul Métro."

Oh, well, thought Mathis, as he gathered his damp raincoat and hat from the hook, it could have been worse. The call could have come two hours earlier.

A black Citroën DS21 was waiting on the rue de Rivoli beside the entrance to the station with its engine running. The drivers never switched off because they didn't want to wait while the hydro-pneumatic suspension pumped the car up again from cold. Mathis sank into the deeply sprung back seat as the driver engaged the column shift and moved off with an unrepentant squeal of rubber.

Mathis lit an American cigarette and watched the shop fronts of the big boulevards go by, the Galéries Lafayette, the Monoprix and the other characterless giants that occupied the bland Haussmann thorough-fares. After the Gare du Nord, the driver switched into smaller streets as they climbed through Pigalle. Here were the yellow-and-scarlet awnings of Indo-Chinese restaurants, the single lights of second-hand furniture shops or the occasional red bulb of an *hôtel de passe* with a plump and bare-legged *poule* standing beneath an umbrella on the corner.

Beyond the canals and criss-cross traffic systems of the old city boundaries, they went through the Porte de Clignancourt and St. Denis on to an elevated stretch of road that nosed between the upper floors of the tower blocks. It was here that Paris shunted off those for whom there was no house in the City of Light, only an airless room in the looming cities of dark.

The driver swung off the N1 down a smaller road and, after two or three minutes' intricate pathfinding, pulled up alongside the Arc en Ciel.

"Stop," said Mathis. "Look over there."

The Citroën's directional headlights, turned by the steering, picked out the foot of a stairwell, where a single uniformed policeman stood guard.

Mathis looked about the desolate estate. Stuck to the walls at what appeared to be random intervals were "artistic" wooden shapes, like something from a Cubist painting. They had perhaps been meant to give the buildings colour and character, like the rainbow they were named after. Almost all had now been pulled down or defaced, and those that were left made the façades look grotesque, like an old crone with badly rouged lips.

Mathis walked across and showed the policeman a card. "Where's the body?"

"In the morgue, Monsieur."

"Do we know who he was?"

The policeman took out his notebook.

"Yusuf Hashim. Thirty-seven. *Métis, pied-noir*—I don't know."

"Record?"

"No, Monsieur. But that doesn't mean anything. Not many people here have records—even though most of them are criminals. We seldom come to these places."

"You mean they're self-policing."

"It's a ghetto."

"How did he die?"

"He was shot at close range."

"I'm going to look up there."

"Very well, Monsieur." The policeman lifted the rope used to close off the stairwell.

Mathis had to hold his breath as he climbed the pungent steps. He went along the walkway, noting the chains and padlocks with which the residents had tried to reinforce their flimsy front doors. From behind one or two came the sounds of radio and television, or of voices raised. In addition to the foul stairway smell there was the occasional whiff of couscous or merguez.

What a hell this was, thought Mathis, the life of the *métis*, the half-caste or the *pied-noir*, the French of

Algerian birth. They were like animals, not fenced in but fenced out of the city. It wasn't his job to set right the inequalities of the world. It was his business to see if this Hashim was anything more than a cheap one-shot killing and, if so, what it might have to do with the Deuxième.

The head of his section would require a written report, so he had better at least get a feel for the Arc en Ciel and what went on there. Back in the office, he would look up the files on similar killings, check with Immigration and see if there was a pattern, or a reason for disquiet. An entire section of the Deuxième was devoted to the fallout of the French colonial wars. The eight-year struggle for Algerian independence had brutally divided not only Algeria but France itself and caused one political upheaval after another, finding a resolution only with the astonishing return to power of the wartime leader, General de Gaulle. Mathis smiled for a moment as he thought of Sylvie's reverent look when she mentioned the great man's name. And at the same time, even more shaming in an international sense, had been the defeat of the French army in Indo-China—or what now called itself Vietnam. The humiliation of the battle of Dien Bien Phu had burned itself into the soul of France, leaving a scar that had been hastily covered over.

The only consolation, thought Mathis, was that

the Americans now seemed hell-bent on meeting the same catastrophe. For him and his colleagues, however, Algeria and Indo-China had meant uncountable thousands of immigrants, embittered, violent and excluded, many of them criminals and some of them committed enemies of the Republic.

Mathis methodically noted the layout of the block and the angle at which the killer might have approached the stairwell. He made other rudimentary observations more suited in his mind to the procedure of a local gendarme.

He lit another cigarette, and went back down the stairs. He thanked the policeman and walked across the waste-ground to where the Citroën's engine was still idling. "Take me to the morgue."

As the big car turned slowly, its headlights for a moment picked out a single figure in a ground-floor doorway. He wore a Foreign Legion kepi, and as the Citroën rejoined the road, he moved off swiftly, as though he'd now seen all he needed.

At the morgue, Mathis waited for the attendant to gain authorization to show him in. He told the impassive driver to wait.

"Monsieur," the man grunted, and returned to the car.

The attendant came back with a pathologist, a senior-looking man with gold glasses and a neat black moustache. He shook hands with Mathis and introduced himself as Dumont.

Checking and rechecking the numbers on the attendant's sheet against those on the fridge drawers, Dumont eventually found what he wanted and hauled with both hands on the thick metal handle.

It was a moment that had never ceased to give Mathis a frisson of excitement. The cadaver was already greyish, cold, and although it had been cleaned up, the face was a mess.

Hashim looked like thousands of young Algerians who had come to a bad end. And yet . . .

"Cause of death?" said Mathis.

"Single bullet, fired up through the roof of the mouth."

"But why the damage to the nose?"

"He must have been beaten up first," said Dumont. "But it's not just the nose. Look at his right hand."

Mathis lifted Hashim's clenched fist. There was a bloody piece of meat sticking out of it. "What the—"

"It's his tongue," said Dumont.

Mathis lowered Hashim's arm. "Why mutilate

16

him when he's dead? Some code or signal, do you think?"

"They didn't do it when he was dead," said Dumont. "I'm almost certain they did it when he was alive. Must have ripped it out with pliers or something."

"God."

"I've never seen anything like it."

"Haven't you?" said Mathis. "I have. It rings a bell. I've come across it somewhere . . . Somewhere. Anyway, thank you, Doctor. You can put him back now. I have work to do."

He strode down the corridor, through the lobby of the building and out into the rain. "Turn that awful Piaf racket off," he said, as he climbed into the car, "and take me to the office."

The driver said nothing, but switched off the radio, pushed the gear lever up into first and moved off with the inevitable squeal. It was just past two a.m.

2. A VOICE FROM THE PAST

It was a bright Sunday morning, and the pilgrims had gathered in their thousands in St. Peter's Square to hear the Pope address them from an upstairs window.

James Bond dallied for a moment among the faithful. He watched their credulous faces crane towards the distant balcony and the light of joy that came into them when the old man spoke a few words in their own language. He almost envied them their simple faith. He shook his head and moved off through the pigeons.

Not even the supposedly universal tongue of

Latin had been able to make an impression on Bond, a disconsolate figure as he walked off past the squat Castel Sant'Angelo and crossed the Tiber into the via Zanardelli, where he stopped at a bar and ordered an americano—a pungent espresso that lasted two sips instead of the single one of the regular *caffè*. The place was filled with people taking a leisurely late breakfast, talking animatedly, and of waiters cheerily calling out their orders to the bar. One or two middle-aged women had brought their pet dogs and fed them morsels of pastry beneath the table. Bond stood at the bar to drink his coffee, left a few coins and wandered off again into the street.

His three-month sabbatical, enforced by the medical people back in London, still had two weeks to run. It had been pleasant enough to begin with. An old friend of M's had fixed him up with a cottage in Barbados where he'd been able to swim and snorkel most of the day before eating dinner on the terrace, cooked and served by a plump female islander called Charity. She did marvellous grilled fish and rice dishes, with home-made ice-creams and piles of sliced mango and papaya to follow. At the medics' insistence, Bond had drunk no alcohol and retired to bed no later than ten o'clock with only a paperback book and a powerful barbiturate for company.

He kept up a fitness regimen to no more than

75 percent of his potential. In addition to the swimming, he ran three miles a day, did pull-ups on a metal bar on the beach and fifty press-ups before his second shower of the day. It was enough to stop him going stale, but little more than that.

However, he had also been given honorary membership of the local tennis club, and in the early evenings, instead of drinking cocktails, he walked down to play with Wayland, an impressively quick youngster from the local police service. Bond, who, since his schooldays, had played tennis only a dozen times, and then without great enthusiasm, found his competitive instinct aroused by Wayland's booming serve-and-volley game. Tennis was not, it turned out, a game of cucumber sandwiches and sporting pleas to "take two more"—not how Wayland played. It was a lung-searing, shoulder-wrenching battle of wills. Bond was horribly out of practice, but his co-ordination was exceptional and his will to win even more so. It wasn't until the fifth encounter that he managed to take a set from the younger man, but as his own game improved he began to exploit the mental weaknesses in Wayland's play. It became an encounter neither wished to lose, and they generally stopped at two sets all for a long drink on the veranda.

After four weeks M's friends inconveniently

required their house back, and Bond, more or less banned by his boss from re-entering Britain, took himself off to the South of France. His plane landed in Marseille one hot evening in May, and he thought that, with time so heavy on his hands, he would take dinner in the port and stay the night rather than head straight off down the coast. He asked the taxi driver to take him to a place where they did the best *bouillabaisse*, and half an hour later found himself beneath an orange awning, sipping a chaste *citron pressé* and looking over at the ships that lay at anchor in the port.

A man who travels alone has time to reflect and observe. A man, furthermore, who has been trained by the most rigorous and secret organization in his country and whose instincts have been honed by years of self-discipline will see things other travellers barely register.

So it was that Bond, perhaps alone of all the diners on the *quai* that night, asked himself why the two men in the black Mercedes 300D Cabriolet did not fit in—even here, in a port loud with commerce and people of all nationalities.

The car pulled up beside the dock, where the smaller of the two men, who wore a short-sleeved bush shirt with a kind of French military kepi, climbed out and began to inspect some of the vessels. Eventually, he went up the gangway of one and disappeared on board.

Bond found himself looking at the man's companion, who remained in the open-topped car. He was about Bond's own age, of possibly Slavic or East European origin, he judged, from the high cheekbones and narrow eyes. His straw-coloured hair was oiled and driven back straight from his forehead without a parting. He was dressed in a beige tropical suit, probably from Airey and Wheeler, with a pale blue shirt and scarlet tie such as one sees in the windows of Jermyn Street. The carriagework of the car shone with a deep black gleam and the burgundy leather seats had been buffed to a factory finish. But what held Bond's eye was the fact that the man affected a single driving glove.

Even when he took a silver case from his pocket, manoeuvred a cigarette out and lit it, he kept the glove on. Was it Bond's imagination, or did the glove seem remarkably large, as though the hand it encased was bigger than the other?

More interesting than any physical peculiarity was something the man gave off—a kind of aura. He exuded arrogance. The attitude of his thrown-back head, the set of his lips and the movement of his wrist as he flicked ash on to the cobbles conveyed contempt for all around him. But there was something else—a sense of burning, zealous concentration. This was a man with a mission of such consuming urgency that he would trample anything before him. Perhaps, Bond thought, that was why he held himself so aloof—because he feared that being exposed to the demands of other people might corrupt the purity of his purpose. But how many years, and what bitterness or reverses, must it have taken to create such a creature?

His colleague returned to the car, carrying a bag, his face in shadow beneath his strange kepi. In the boutiques of the King's Road, Chelsea, near his flat, Bond had seen the new fashion for military uniforms among the young, who sported coats and tunics with coloured braid. But this man was no "hippie" or "child of peace." Though short of stature, he moved with the speed and agility of an army scout or tracker. There was a functional brutality about his movements as he climbed into the driver's seat, threw the small canvas bag into the back and started the engine. This was a man of action, the NCO fanatically loyal to the overbearing officer beside him.

He turned the big Cabriolet round in a single sweep and accelerated hard. A small dog ran out from one of the cafés, barking at a seagull on the dock. It was caught by the front wheel of the car, and flattened. While the animal lay squealing in its death throes, the Mercedes drove off without stopping.

Bond travelled listlessly along the Côte d'Azur. He spent a couple of nights at the Eden Roc on the Cap d'Antibes, but rapidly grew tired of the clientele. Although his work had often forced him to mingle with the rich and he'd developed expensive tastes of his own in liquor, cars and women, he found it enervating to be always in the company of men who'd made a paper fortune by sitting on their backsides in a bourse, and women whose looks were kept precariously alive by the surgeon's knife and the resources of the hotel beautician.

At Monte Carlo he made a modest killing at the *chemin de fer* table, but lost at poker. Neither game excited him as once it might have done. Did he need an opponent of the calibre of Le Chiffre or Hugo Drax, he wondered, to make the game worth the candle?

One evening in the early-summer twilight, he sat at a café overlooking the Mediterranean at Cannes, hearing the chatter of the tree frogs in the pines. How wonderful this little fishing town must have seemed to its first English visitors, with the softness of its air, the fragrance of the breeze and the simplicity of life exemplified in its food—grilled fish, salads and chilled wine. It was turning into a version of Blackpool now, Bond thought, with the cheap hotels, the crowds, the youths on noisy scooters and two-stroke motorcycles. Soon they'd put a ferris wheel on the promenade.

Bond caught himself thinking in this way too often.

In his hotel room he took a vigorous shower, first as hot as he could bear it, then freezing cold, letting the icy needles pierce his shoulders. He stood naked in front of the mirror and looked into his face, with a distaste he made no attempt to soften.

"You're tired," he said out loud. "You're played out. Finished."

His torso and arms bore a network of scars, small and large, that traced a history of his violent life. There was the slight displacement of his spine to the left where he had fallen from a train in Hungary, the skin graft on the back of the left hand. Every square inch of trunk and limb seemed to contribute to the story. But he knew that it was what was in his head that counted.

That was what M had told him. "You've been through a lot, James. Much more than any human being should. If you were a normal man—even if you were another double-O—I'd just move you on. Put you on a desk job. But because it's you, James,

I'm going to let that decision come from you. Take three months' sabbatical, full pay, then come and tell me what you've decided."

Bond put on clean underwear, dress shirt and white dinner jacket with a black cummerbund. At least everything fitted. For all Charity's home cooking and the occasional delights of the restaurants along the Riviera, he hadn't run to fat. Tennis and not drinking alcohol must have helped. But his mind . . . Had his *mind* run to fat?

Tired of the South of France, wishing the days would pass more quickly, Bond had come to Rome and searched out a hotel on the via Veneto of which Felix Leiter, his old friend in the CIA, had spoken warmly when he called him from Pinkerton's, where he now worked. Felix was a good man, and he'd picked the best. Bond was able to sit on his balcony with a cigarette and a glass of fresh blood-orange juice while he watched the film stars—the real and would-be—parade up and down between the cafés in their evening *passeggiata*. "It's a bit close to the US embassy for my taste," Leiter had warned him. "All those Yalies with their button-down shirts and cocktail parties. But I'm sure it'd be fine for a stuck-up Limey like you, James."

On the Sunday evening after he'd been in St. Peter's Square, Bond, in a simple woollen jacket, charcoal trousers and black loafers, decided to walk down to a traditional Roman restaurant in the via Carrozze near the Spanish Steps. As he crossed the lobby, a young woman wearing an expensive Dior suit brushed past him. Her evening bag fell noisily to the floor and Bond bent to pick it up, noticing the slim ankles, sheer nylons and elegant court shoes as he did so.

"How clumsy of me," she said.

"It was my fault," said Bond.

"No, no, I wasn't looking where—"

"All right," said Bond, "I shall let you take the blame, but only if you allow me to buy you a drink."

The woman glanced at her watch. She had black hair, cut short, and wide-set brown eyes. "All right," she said. "Just one. My name is Larissa Rossi."

"Bond. James Bond." He held out his hand and she took it gently. "I knew another Larissa once."

"Did you?" Her tone was noncommittal.

They were crossing the marble-floored lobby. "Yes," said Bond. "But she was a blonde. A Russian blonde."

Larissa smiled as they entered the bar. "And I suppose she was a business connection. A translator, perhaps?"

"No. She was a professional seductress."

27

"Goodness." Larissa laughed, but she seemed amused more than shocked, Bond thought. Good.

"It's not a story I've ever told," he said. "Now, what can I get you?"

"A dry martini, please. They do a very good one here. You should try it."

Bond smiled grimly and ordered tomato juice for himself. The trouble with not drinking alcohol was that all soft drinks were more or less repellent.

They took their glasses to a table in the corner, away from the piano. Bond watched enviously as Larissa stirred the viscous fluid with the olive on its cocktail stick. She lit a Chesterfield and held out the packet to him. He shook his head and took out one of his own. He had long ago finished his supply from Morland's, but had managed to find an enterprising tobacconist at the foot of the via Condotti who had made him up five hundred Turkish of passable quality.

"What are you doing in Rome, Larissa?"

"I'm with my husband. He's a director of one of those large insurance companies whose offices you see on via Veneto." Her voice was interesting: low-pitched, educated English with a hint of something more cosmopolitan.

"And has your husband abandoned you for the evening?"

"I . . . Perhaps. And what are you doing here, Mr. Bond?"

"James, please. I'm on holiday. I'm in the export business."

"On holiday alone?"

"Yes, I prefer it that way. I find one gets to see more sights."

Larissa raised an eyebrow and crossed her legs. It was a way of bringing them to his attention, Bond knew, and he couldn't blame her. They were long, with a supple shapeliness and elegance: not the result of exercise or dieting, Bond thought, but of breeding, youth and expensive hosiery.

An hour later they were at dinner in the via Carrozze. A telephone call from the hotel by Larissa had apparently secured her husband's permission for the innocent date and one by Bond had added a second person to his reservation.

The restaurant was wood-panelled and traditional. The waiters in their short white coats were all Romans of a certain age who had spent a lifetime in their chosen profession. They were swift and precise in their movements, polite without being deferential.

Bond watched as Larissa chatted over ravioli glistening with truffle oil. She told him her father was Russian, her mother English, and that she'd been educated in Paris and Geneva before going to work in Washington, where she'd met her husband. They had no children.

"So of course my husband does a good deal of travelling," she said, sipping a glass of Orvieto. "Our base is in Paris, and I travel with him some of the time. To the better places."

"Let me guess," said Bond. "Rome, New York, Singapore, Hong Kong—"

"No, I can't bear Hong Kong. I stay at home when he goes there. I'm quite a home girl, really."

"Of course you are," said Bond.

Early thirties, bored, he thought, part Jewish on her father's side. She had a beautiful mouth whose upper lip occasionally stiffened into something almost like a pout. Her skin had a light honey glow, but her air of innocent respectability was a front. There was an unrepentant wildness in her eyes. She would have to pretend that it was all an aberration, that she was "not like that," but that would only make it more exciting for both of them.

"You look distracted, James."

"I'm sorry. Do I? I blame the two Bs."

"And what are they?"

"Brainwashing and bereavement."

"Goodness. Tell me more."

For a moment, Bond was tempted to confide in this animated and beautiful girl—to tell her about his wife of a few brief hours, Tracy di Vicenzo, and how Blofeld's men had killed her, how he himself had fallen into their clutches, the whole Japanese nightmare and his part-redemption in Jamaica. But confidences were unprofessional. He had already allowed his strange, distracted mood to let him say more than he should.

"Another time," he said. "When we know each other a little better."

He steered the conversation back to Larissa, noticing as he did that his evasiveness had made him more interesting to her. Reluctantly at first, but then with increasing self-absorption, Larissa took up the narrative of her life.

When they arrived back at the hotel, she stopped outside the front door and placed her hand on Bond's forearm.

"My husband has had to go to Naples for the night," she said, looking down at her feet and licking her lips a little nervously as she spoke. "He told me when I called him earlier. You could come up to our suite for a drink if you like."

Bond looked down into the large brown eyes as the full lips parted in an expression of modest excitement. Then he heard himself utter three words that in all his adult life had never, in such a situation, left his mouth before. "No, thank you."

31

"What?" It seemed as though she truly hadn't heard.

"No, thanks, Larissa," said Bond. "It's better this way. I—"

"No explanations," she said. She stretched up and kissed him on the cheek. "Thank you for a lovely evening."

He watched her as she walked over to the desk, collected her key and made for the lift. As she stepped in, she hesitated, turned and waved.

What a girl, thought Bond. He lit a cigarette and went outside to smoke it.

Perhaps this was the sign he'd been waiting for. A couple of years ago he wouldn't even have waited for coffee at the restaurant before getting her back to his room at the hotel. Although there had been times when he'd tired of the game, even been repelled by it, he'd been sure it would be a lifelong compulsion.

Yet tonight . . . Now he knew for sure that an epoch had ended and he knew what he would have to tell M when he returned to London. It was over. He was resigned to a life of interdepartmental meetings and examining cables at his desk, with only his shared secretary, Loelia Ponsonby—now mercifully back at her post after giving birth to two healthy boys—to distract his eye occasionally from the paperwork.

After the business with Scaramanga in Jamaica, Bond had spent eighteen months—it seemed longer—pushing paper round his desk before M despatched him on his "make-or-break" sabbatical, after which he alone was to decide whether Bond would ever return to active duty. Without Loelia, office life had been drab indeed: a succession of mousy matrons had occupied the desk, relieved only for a couple of months by a delectable and super-efficient blonde called Holly Campbell, who had been swiftly promoted by M.

Bond chucked the end of his cigarette moodily into the street and went back into the hotel. As he collected his key, the clerk gave him a message. It read simply: "Call Universal. Urgent."

He went out again and walked down to a telephone box. Universal . . . He was secretly pleased that after various experiments the Service had reverted to its old cover name. No other word had such curious power over him. There was a heavy echo and delay on the telephone line, then a long low hum—a sign that he was being diverted.

At last, he heard the voice—distorted, distant but unmistakable—of the man he most respected in the world.

"Bond?"

"Sir?"

"The party's over."

"What?"

"We need you back. Take the first flight tomorrow."

"Sir, I thought—"

"One of our sales force is reporting exceptional activity."

"Where?"

"The Paris branch. Though imports from the Middle East are looking up as well."

"What about my sabbatical? It doesn't end till—"

"To hell with your sabbatical. We can talk about that in the office. Got that?"

"Yes, sir. I'll see you tomorrow."

"Thank you. And bring some of those little chocolates in the blue-and-silver paper, will you?"

3. THE MONKEY'S HAND

May, the Scottish "treasure" who looked after Bond's flat in Chelsea, was trying frantically to complete her house-warming preparations when she heard the cab from the airport drop him outside the front door in the quiet street.

"Could you no' have given me a wee bit more warning, Mr. Bond?" she said, as he let himself in and dropped his crocodile-skin suitcases in the hall. "The bed's not been aired properly, we've none of your favourite marmalade in and the laddie come to do the cupboards in the spare room has left the most fearful mess."

"Sorry, May. Duty called. Rather late at night."

"Would you like me to make you some lunch?"

"No, thanks. I'm just going to have a quick shower, then I must go into the office."

"Well, at least there's some clean towels on the rail. I'll have some coffee for when you're out."

"Thanks. Black and strong, please."

"And some orange juice?"

"Fresh oranges?"

"Of course, Mr. Bond."

"May, you're a marvel. I'll be ready in ten minutes. Please ring for the car to be brought round."

As he dressed after his shower, in clean shirt, navy worsted suit and knitted black tie, it felt almost like getting back into uniform, Bond thought. He had shaved before leaving the hotel in Rome at six that morning and had had a haircut only the week before. He might not be quite his old self, but at least he looked presentable.

In the sitting room, he flicked through the worst of the accumulated mail and was able to shovel almost half of it straight into the wastepaper basket. He sipped May's scalding black coffee and took a Balkan Sobranie cigarette from the box on the coffee table.

"Now then, May," he said, "tell me what's been happening while I've been away."

May thought for a moment. "That elderly feller got back from sailing round the world all on his own."

"Chichester."

"Aye. That's his name. Though don't ask me what the point of it all was. And him a pensioner as well."

"I suppose men just feel the need to prove themselves," said Bond. "Even older men. What else?"

"Those pop singers have been arrested for having drugs."

"The Beatles?"

"No, the ones with the hair down to their shoulders who make such a racket. The Rolling Stones, is it?"

"And what was the drug? Marijuana?"

"It's no use asking me, Mr. Bond. It was drugs, that's all I know."

"I see. There's a lot of it about." Bond ground out his cigarette in the ashtray. "When I've gone, will you call Morland's and ask them to send another box of these as soon as possible. I may be travelling again before long."

"Travelling?" said May. "I thought you were going to—"

"So did I, May," said Bond. "So did I. Now, was that the car I heard outside?"

It took Bond almost ten minutes to get the "Locomotive," the Bentley Continental he'd had rebuilt to his own specification, as far as Sloane Square.

London seemed to have gone slightly off its head in the time he'd been away. Every zebra crossing on the King's Road was packed with long-haired young people, ambling across, standing and talking or, in one remarkable case, sitting cross-legged in the road. With the convertible hood down, Bond could smell the bonfire whiff of marijuana he'd previously associated only with souks in the grubbier Moroccan towns. He blipped the throttle and heard the rumble of the twin two-inch exhausts.

Eventually, he made it to Sloane Street and up through Hyde Park, where the speedometer touched sixty as the Arnott supercharger made light of the car's customized bulk. Bond turned the car into the right-hand bend on the racing line and just missed the apex he was aiming for as he came out of the left-hander. He was out of practice, but it was nothing serious. This is more like it, he thought, an early-summer day in London, the wind in his face and an urgent meeting with his boss.

All too soon he was in Regent's Park, then at the headquarters of the Service. He tossed the car keys to the startled doorman and took the lift to the eighth floor. At her station outside M's door sat Miss Money-penny, a tailored Cerberus at the gates of whatever underworld awaited him. "James," she said, failing to keep the elation from her voice. "How wonderful to see you. How was your holiday?"

"Sabbatical, Moneypenny. There's a difference. Anyway, it was fine. A little too long for my taste. And how's my favourite gatekeeper?"

"Never better, thank you, James."

It was true. Miss Moneypenny wore a severe black-and-white hound's-tooth suit with a white blouse and a blue cameo brooch at the throat, but her skin was flushed with girlish excitement.

Bond inclined his head towards the door. "And the old man?"

Miss Moneypenny made a sucking noise over her teeth. "A bit cranky, to be honest, James. He's taken up . . ." She crooked her finger in invitation to him to come closer. As he inclined his head, she whispered in his ear. Bond felt her lips against his skin.

"Yoga!" Bond exploded. "What in God's—"

Moneypenny laughed as she raised a finger to her lips.

"Has the whole world gone raving mad in my absence?"

"Calm down, James, and tell me what's in that pretty red bag you're carrying."

"Chocolates," said Bond. "M asked me to bring some from Rome." He showed her the box of

Perugina Baci in their distinctive blue-and-silver wrapping.

"Do you know what *baci* means in Italian, James? It means 'kisses.' "

"I suppose they must be for his wife."

"James, you b—"

"Ssh . . ."

Before she could protest any further, the heavy walnut door swung open quietly, and Bond saw M standing on the threshold, his head to one side.

"Come in, 007," he said. "It's good to see you back."

"Thank you, sir." Bond followed him in, pausing only to blow Miss Moneypenny a last tormenting kiss before he closed the door.

Bond sat down in the chair across from M's desk. After a long sequence of struck and abandoned safety matches, M finally had his pipe going to his satisfaction. The small-talk about Bond's sabbatical was over, and the old sailor peered briefly out of the window, as though somewhere over Regent's Park there might be enemy shipping. Then he swung round to face Bond.

"There's something I need your help with, 007. The details are a little hazy at the moment, but I sense that it's going to be something big. Very big indeed. Have you heard of Dr. Julius Gorner?"

"You're not referring me to another medic, are you, sir?" said Bond. "I thought I'd satisfied you on—"

"No, no, it's an academic title. From the Sorbonne, I believe. Though Dr. Gorner also holds degrees from Oxford University and Vilnius in Lithuania, which is one of the oldest universities in Eastern Europe. At Oxford, he took a first-class degree in modern greats—that's politics, philosophy and economics to you and me, Bond—then, rather surprisingly, switched to chemistry for his doctorate."

"A jack-of-all-trades," said Bond.

M coughed. "Rather a master-of-all-trades, I'm afraid. This academic stuff is merely background, and he's said to have acquired it pretty easily. He volunteered under age in the war and had the distinction of fighting for both sides—for the Nazis initially, and then for the Russians at the battle of Stalingrad. This happened to quite a few people in the Baltic states, as you know, according to which country was occupying theirs and compelled them to fight. The odd thing with Gorner is that he seems to have changed sides of his own free will—according to who he thought was the likely victor."

"A soldier of fortune," said Bond. He found his interest piqued.

"Yes. But his real passion is business. He studied a year at Harvard Business School, but left because

41

he found it insufficiently stimulating. He began a small pharmaceutical business in Estonia, then opened a factory near Paris. You'd think it would be the other way round, having the office in Paris and the cheap labour in Estonia. But nothing about Dr. Gorner is quite what you'd expect."

"What sort of pharmaceuticals?" said Bond.

"Analgesics. You know, painkillers. Then in due course they're hoping to develop neurological medicines, for Parkinson's disease, multiple sclerosis and so on. But of course he was in a very big league there, what with Pfizer, Johnson and Johnson and the other giants. Some of them have been around since the last century. But this didn't deter our Dr. Gorner. A mixture of industrial espionage, cost-cutting and strong-arm sales techniques gave him a big market presence. Then one day he discovered the poppy."

"The poppy?" Bond wondered whether the yoga had addled M's thought processes. Perhaps he'd been standing on his head—though it was hard to imagine him in a dhoti.

"Source of the opiate class of drugs, which are widely used in hospitals as anaesthetics. All our infantrymen carry morphine in their packs. If half your leg's been blown off by a shell you need something powerful and fast-acting. Heroin was first legally marketed by the German company Bayer as a cough cure. Recently, of course, since people have come to understand the problems of addiction, there's been tough legislation about such things. There's a legal trade in opium derivatives destined for medical use, and there's an illegal one."

"And which is our man involved in?"

"The former, certainly. But we suspect the latter, too, on an increasing scale. But we need to know more, much more."

"Is this where I come in?"

"Yes." M stood up and walked over to the window. "In some ways what I want from you is a simple fact-finding exercise. Find Gorner. Talk to him. See what makes him tick."

"Sounds rather psychological," said Bond.

"Indeed." M looked uneasy.

"Is that what you have me down for now? I thought it was going to be my choice as to whether I returned to active operations."

"Well, yes, James, it is."

Bond didn't like it when M called him "James" rather than "Bond" or "007." The personal note always preceded some disappointing news.

"I want you to have some more tests with the medics and then a talk with R."

"The head-shrinker?" said Bond.

"The psychological-fitness assessor," M corrected

him. "I've recently appointed an assistant therapist in his department. You will have a course of breathing and relaxation techniques."

"For heaven's sake, sir, I—"

"All the double-Os are doing it," said M stiffly. "009 reported immense benefits."

"He would," said Bond.

"Which reminds me. I've appointed a new double-O. To take the place of 004, who, as you know, unfortunately—"

"Yes. Under an East German train, I gather. And when does the new man start?"

"Any day." M coughed again. "Anyway, they're all doing it and I'm not going to make an exception for you."

Bond lit a cigarette. It was pointless to argue with M when he had one of these bees in his bonnet. "Is there anything else I need to know about this Dr. Gorner?"

"Yes," said M. "I believe he could turn out to be a major threat to national security. That's why the Service has been called in. The Government is panicking about the amount of illegal drugs coming into this country. There are already three-quarters of a million heroin addicts in the United States. We're heading the same way. And the trouble is that it's no longer just tramps and so on. It's our best young people who are at risk. Drugs are becoming respectable. There was a leader in *The Times*—*The Times* of all places—asking for lenience in the case of these wretched pop singers. If drugs become embedded in a nation's culture, it quickly becomes a third-world country. They sap the will to live. Look at Laos, Thailand, Cambodia. Not exactly superpowers, are they?"

"It reminds me of Kristatos and that Italian operation," said Bond.

"By comparison," said M, "that was chickenfeed. Weekend smuggling. So was that little job in Mexico just before you met Goldfinger."

"And where do I find Gorner?"

"The man crops up everywhere. One of his hobbies is aviation. He has two private planes. He spends a good deal of time in Paris, but I don't think you'll have much difficulty in recognizing him."

"Why's that?" said Bond.

"His left hand," said M, sitting down again, and staring Bond squarely in the eye. "It's a monkey's paw."

"What?"

"An extremely rare congenital deformity. There's a condition known as *main de singe*, or monkey's hand, which is when the thumb makes a straight line with the fingers and is termed 'unopposable.' Being in the

45

same plane as the other digits, it can't grip. It's like picking up a pencil between two fingers." M demonstrated what he meant. "It can be done, but not very well. The development of the opposable thumb was an important mutation for *Homo sapiens* from his ancestors. But what Gorner has is something more. The whole hand is completely that of an ape. With hair up to the wrist and beyond."

Something was stirring in Bond's memory. "So it would be larger than the right hand," he said.

"Presumably. It's very rare, though not unique, I believe."

"Does he travel with a sidekick in a Foreign Legion hat?"

"I've no idea," said M.

"I think I may have come across him. In Marseille."

"At the docks?"

"Yes."

M sighed. "That sounds all too feasible."

"Is he about my age, strongly built, straight oily fair hair a bit too long at the back, Slavic—"

"Stop there," said M, pushing a photograph across the desk. "Is this the man?"

"Yes," said Bond. "That's him."

"It looks like your destiny," said M, with a wintry smile.

"I don't believe in destiny," said Bond.

"It's time you did," said M. "The best defector SIS has ever had was a colonel in Russian military intelligence. Penkovsky. One of their men spotted him in a café in Ankara looking depressed. That's all. Just a look in his eye. They took it from there. It was fate."

"And observation," said Bond, stubbing out his cigarette. "So does this mean I'm fully operational again?" he said.

"I have in mind a phased return," said M. "You do the reconnaissance. You do your course with R. Then we'll see."

An unpleasant thought occurred to Bond. "You haven't mentioned any of this to 009, have you? Or this new man, 004? I'm not going to do the legwork for another agent, am I?"

M shifted uneasily in his chair. "Listen, 007. This Dr. Gorner is potentially the most dangerous man the Service has yet encountered. I'm not setting you on the trail of some old dope peddler, but a man who seems intent on destroying the lives of millions and so undermining the influence of the West. I may use any number of operatives to stop him. I reserve that right."

Bond felt his boss's grey eyes boring into him. He was sincere, all right. M coughed again. "There is a Russian link as well," he said, "that the Government's particularly anxious about. A cold war can be waged in many ways. I need a report on my desk in six days' time."

There was no point in taking the discussion any further, Bond thought. "Are the Deuxième in on this?" he asked.

"Yes. Get in touch with Mathis as soon as you arrive in Paris. Miss Moneypenny's already booked your tickets and hotel."

"Thank you, sir." Bond rose to go.

"And, James, listen. You will be careful, won't you? I know that drugs don't sound like arms or even diamonds. But I have a bad feeling about this man. Very bad. He has a lot of blood on his hands already."

Bond nodded, went out and closed the door.

Miss Moneypenny looked up from her desk. She held up a sealed brown envelope. "You lucky boy," she said. "Paris in the spring. I've found you a lovely hotel. Oh, look, you forgot to give M his chocolates."

Bond put the red bag down on her desk. "You have them," he said.

"You are sweet, James. Thank you. Your flight's at six. You've just got time for your first session of deep breathing and relaxation exercises. I've made a booking for you at two thirty. On the second floor."

"You wait till I get back from Paris," Bond said, as he headed towards the lift. "Then I'll give you cause for heavy breathing."

" 'Deep breathing' was the expression, James. There is a difference."

"Or if you insist on splitting hairs I shall have to resort to something firmer. A good spanking, perhaps. So you won't be able to sit down for a week."

"Really, James, you're all talk these days."

The lift doors closed before Bond could come up with a reply. As he sank through the floors of the building, he remembered Larissa's puzzled face in the hotel doorway in Rome. All talk. Perhaps Moneypenny was right.

Bond passed forty-five minutes with a man called Julian Burton, who wore a collarless white shirt and instructed him on how to breathe from the pit of his belly.

"Think of a jug you're trying to fill with water. That's your breathing. Take it right down to the base of your spine and your kidneys. Feel that jug fill up. Now close your eyes and think about a pleasant scene. Perhaps a beach or a lovely stream in a wood. A special private place. Just shut out all the cares of your day and concentrate on that one lovely peaceful place. Now keep on breathing. Deeply in, right down to the small of your back. Shut out all other thoughts, just keep yourself in your one special place."

The "special place" to which Bond's thoughts kept returning was not a sylvan retreat but the skin on Larissa's throat and neck he'd noticed in the hotel bar. Perhaps there was life in the old dog yet . . . At the end of the "session," Bond promised Julian he'd do his deep-breathing exercises every day. Then he ran down the steps, rather than take the lift, to the front desk. He'd left it too late to achieve full operational fitness, but every little bit helped.

He could feel the old juices begin to flow again at the thought of Dr. Julius Gorner. He had never taken such a profound dislike to anyone at first sight. There was also something particularly underhand in trying to attack a country through the gullibility of its young people rather than through guns and soldiery.

He found himself anxious to impress M. After all he'd done, thought Bond, heading the Locomotive south off Bayswater Road and into Hyde Park, surely he had no need to prove himself. Perhaps it had been the mention of the other double-O agents that had made him uneasy. Of course there would always be others who were licensed to kill—indeed, the average length of time in the job before meeting a fatal accident ensured that recruitment and training was a continuous process—but Bond had always believed himself to be unique: the agent of choice. Perhaps M had deliberately withheld his full confidence on this occasion in order to concentrate Bond's mind. The more he thought about it, the more certain he became that that was what the old fox was up to.

Back in his flat, he found that May had already laundered and pressed his clothes from Italy. It was tea-time, but she knew better than to bother him with that old ladies' brew. Instead, she knocked at his bedroom door with a silver tray on which sat a soda syphon, a bucket of ice, a cut-glass tumbler and a full bottle of Johnnie Walker Black Label.

"For your health's sake, Mr. Bond," she said, placing it on top of the chest of drawers. "Here, let me pack those for you."

Bond had not quite completed three months on the wagon, but if in M's eyes he was fit to return to work, then . . . He poured a conservative two fingers of whisky into the glass, added a lump of ice and the same amount of soda.

"Your good health," he said, then tossed the whole lot down in a single gulp.

As Bond left Hammersmith and headed along the Great West Road, he became aware of a motorcycle in his wing mirror and instinctively hit the brake. These speed cops seemed to be everywhere, and his selfish, showy car was a natural magnet. However, the bike seemed to fall back at the same moment. Without signalling, Bond swerved left at the roundabout and took the road towards Twickenham, away from the main flow of rush-hour traffic leaving the capital. He changed down and kicked the accelerator to beat the first red light before checking his mirror again. The bike was still there.

Bond felt a mixture of irritation and excitement. It was galling to be followed in this amateurish fashion when he was on his way to deal with a problem as large and dangerous as that posed by Dr. Julius Gorner. Just before Chiswick Bridge he suddenly wrenched the wheel round to the right.

This time he had judged the line well, and the tyres held the road close. Bond checked his mirrors once more, and felt the first tremor of anxiety. There was not one but two motorcycles now—big BMWs—and no car can outsprint a bike. The riders put their heads down and twisted their right wrists. The roar of their Bavarian flat-twins filled the quiet Kew street.

In a few moments, the bikes were either side of Bond's Bentley. Now he had to take them seriously. He wished he was in the Aston Martin with the compartment beneath the seat for a Colt .45. He wasn't sure his Walther PPK had the power for the job at this range, but he had no alternative now. Before he could take the gun from its holster, there was a shattering roar as the glass of the front passenger window was broken by a bullet. Through the open space, Bond fired once, then braked hard. Braking was the one thing cars were quicker at than bikes, and he bought himself a momentary glimpse of the second motorcycle, which had now slightly overshot him. He leaned across the passenger seat, and through the broken window fired again with his left hand. He saw the rider jerk forward, hit squarely in the shoulder, while the snarling German bike slid away from under his body, showering sparks along the pavement.

The original motorcyclist was now alongside him on the off side, and Bond could see that they were nearing the end of the street, where it came to a right-angled junction. He estimated they were travelling at about fifty, and he needed to slow down if he was to complete the manoeuvre he had in mind. He saw the rider lift his left hand to fire, making himself vulnerable for a moment with only one hand on the handlebars and no control of the clutch.

Bond smacked the footbrake, dropped the wheel to his right, then hauled up the handbrake. This was not the standard handle below the dash, but a fly-off model fitted to his specification behind the gear lever. With a tortured squeal of tyres and a smell of burning, the big car juddered, then whipped its great tail round, straight into the front wheel of the BMW. Bond felt the impact of the bike's momentum as it hit, then crumpled, sending its rider head over heels up into the junction ahead. As he landed on his back, the man's gun went off once, impotently.

Bond checked his watch to see that he'd still be on time for his flight, put the car into first gear again and headed north, sedately, through the streets of Kew, where the commuters were returning home from work. Back on the Great West Road, he found that a favourite phrase of René Mathis had come into his head. *Ça recommence*, he thought.

4. "SHALL WE PLAY?"

Bond's hotel room was a typical Moneypenny booking: Right Bank, discreet and slightly unimaginative. Bond swept quickly through the bedroom, bathroom and small sitting room, looking for bugs. The Service changed its hotels so often that it was unlikely anyone could have known he was coming, but the motorbikes showed someone at least was on his tail. Personally, he was inclined to put the BMWs down to unfinished business from a previous operation. This Julius Gorner might be dangerous, but he couldn't, surely, be psychic. And, God knows, there were enough people who'd wanted him dead for years. Even the most successfully concluded operations left many with a grudge against him.

So far as he could tell, the room was clean. He closed the shutters, pulled a hair from his head and stuck it across the crack between the bathroom door and jamb. Then he opened the concealed compartment in the bottom of his case, took out some ammunition, refilled the Walther and replaced it in his shoulder holster, making sure no bulge showed beneath the coat of his suit. He shut the case and sprinkled a fine grey talcum over the combination lock. Then he left the hotel and went out on to the rue St. Roch to do battle with the French telephone system.

It occurred to him as he rotated the bevelled edge of the coin against his fingertip that he hadn't eaten since breakfast in Rome. But the one-hour time change had gone against him, so in Paris it was nearly nine and Mathis, it transpired, was not available. Out at dinner with his wretched mistress, thought Bond, as he was forced to leave a message with a surly telephonist at the Deuxième.

Bond had done enough eating out alone in the last few months and it was beginning to rain. He decided to return to his room, order an omelette from room service, then get an early night.

The porter handed over his key on its heavy brass

weight with a scarlet tassel. Bond strode across the marble lobby, pressed the lift-call button, changed his mind and ran up three flights of stairs. Deep in thought, he let himself into the soft Right Bank gloom of number 325, flicked up the light switch and tossed the weighty key on to the bed, where it bounced once, playfully. He crossed to the bedside table, took the phone off the hook and dialled zero. As he did so, he turned back to face into the room and saw the most remarkable sight.

Sitting in the uncomfortable gilded armchair beneath the imitation Louis XV looking-glass, her long legs demurely crossed and her empty hands folded in front of her breasts, was one of the most self-possessed young women he had ever seen. She had long dark hair, held back by a scarlet ribbon in a half-ponytail, then falling over the shoulders of her suit. Beneath it, she wore a white blouse and black stockings with low-heeled black shoes. Her lips were painted red and were parted in an apologetic smile.

"I'm so sorry to startle you, Mr. Bond," she said. "I had to make sure of seeing you. I didn't want to give you the chance of turning me down again." She leaned forward into the light.

"Larissa," said Bond. His gun was in his hand.

"I really can't apologize enough. This is not how I normally behave, but I was desperate to see you."

"Your hair. It's longer."

"Yes. I was wearing a hairpiece in Rome. This is me as I really am."

"And your husband . . ."

"I'm not married, Mr. Bond. And if I were ever to take that step I doubt it would be with a man who works in insurance. Now I have to tell you something else rather shameful. My name is not really Larissa."

"How disappointing. I had plans for Larissa."

"Perhaps this time you'll stay around long enough for me to give you my business card."

Bond nodded, watching the girl carefully as she stood up. He checked that there was no one behind the curtains. He took the proffered card, then pushed open the bathroom door with his foot, pointed the gun inside and made sure that, too, was clear.

The girl said nothing, merely watching as though this was no more than her bad behaviour had deserved.

Only then did Bond look down at the card. "Miss Scarlett Papava. Investment Manager. Diamond and Standard Bank. 14 *bis* rue du Faubourg St. Honoré."

"Perhaps I can explain."

"I think you'd better." Now that he'd recovered his composure, Bond felt an overpowering curiosity, tinged with admiration. This girl had nerves of iron. "Before you do," he said, "I'm going to order a drink from room service. What would you like?"

"Nothing, thank you. Unless . . . A glass of water, perhaps."

Bond ordered two large bourbons and a bottle of Vittel. If she didn't change her mind, he'd drink the second himself.

"All right," he said, replacing the receiver. "You have three minutes."

Miss Scarlett Papava, formerly Mrs. Larissa Rossi, sighed heavily and lit a Chesterfield as she sat down again in the hard armchair. At least her choice of cigarette had been genuine, thought Bond.

"I've been aware of who you are for a short time," said Scarlett.

"How long have you been a financier?" said Bond.

"Six years. You can have me checked with the bank. The headquarters are in Cheapside."

Bond nodded. Instinctively, he felt that most of the story "Larissa" had told him about her Russian father and her education had been true. But the way she'd deceived him about her husband was galling, and he felt the slight unease he had when he suspected he was in the company of a fellow agent.

"You look sceptical," said Scarlett. "Run whatever checks you like."

"So what were you doing in Rome?"

"Please, Mr. Bond. You're eating into my three minutes with your questions."

"Go on."

"I was in Rome to find you. I need your help. To rescue my sister. She's working against her will for a very unpleasant man. He effectively has her captive."

"I'm not a private investigator," said Bond sharply. "I don't rescue distressed damsels. I suggest you get in touch with Pinkerton's or their French equivalent. 'Cherchez La Femme' it'll probably be called."

Scarlett smiled demurely. "As a matter of fact," she said, "I did."

There was a knock at the door. It was the bell-boy with the bourbon. He poured two measures and retreated.

"Leave the bottle," said Bond, placing a folded note on the tray.

"Merci, Monsieur."

"Did what?" said Bond, when the waiter had gone.

"Call Pinkerton's," said Scarlett. "Eventually, I found myself talking to a man called Felix Leiter."

Bond nodded wearily. He might have guessed.

"Mr. Leiter said he couldn't do it himself—he only leaves America in exceptional circumstances—but he knew someone who might. He mentioned your name. He said you were in semi-retirement, on a lengthy paid sabbatical or some such thing. He said that, knowing you, you'd be itching for some action. He said, 'This is right up James's alley. Mention the broad and the 'coon'll be treed.'" Scarlett shrugged. "Whatever that means. Anyway, then he said he didn't know for sure where you were, but the last time he'd heard, you were on your way to Rome. He gave me the name of a hotel he'd recommended. I made some calls."

"How resourceful of you."

"Thank you. You took your time getting there, I must say. I spent a fortune ringing the hotel every day."

"Not from work, I hope."

"Certainly not. From my apartment in the rue des Saints Pères. I must stress, Mr. Bond, that this problem is nothing whatever to do with my work. It's entirely private."

"But of course," said Bond.

SIS usually placed its agents on the staff of the embassy under the guise of a chargé d'affaires or visa officer or some such thing. Bond disliked diplomats—men with soft hands sent abroad to lie to foreign governments—and he disliked the agents on their staffs even more. Few of them would have lasted thirty seconds in a fight. But it wasn't just the embassy that could be used as a front for these people. They used other jobs as well, and finance, with its requirements for up-to-the-minute information and international travel, was as good as any. Bond had never encountered a British female agent before, but it was just like SIS to think they must "move with the times."

"I know you must distrust me," said Scarlett. "You're quite right to, I suppose. But I'll gain your trust. I'll prove myself, I promise you."

Bond said nothing. He drained his bourbon and poured another glass.

"The thing is," said Scarlett hesitantly, "that I think I can help you find Julius Gorner. I can tell you where he'll be on Saturday morning. At the Club Sporting de Tennis in the Bois de Boulogne."

"I think you've had your three minutes," said Bond.

Scarlett crossed her legs in the way Bond had noticed in the bar in Rome. The girl's presence troubled him in more ways than one. She seemed to have shed some years. He would have put Larissa Rossi down as thirty-two, but Scarlett Papava looked more like twenty-eight.

She watched him closely, as though calculating her next move. "All right," she said. "I won't pretend. I know you've come to investigate Gorner."

"How?"

"My sister told me. She telephoned. She wanted me to warn you to keep away from him."

Bond lit a cigarette. "And your sister can only have heard it . . ."

Scarlett nodded. "From the horse's mouth."

Bond inhaled deeply. That explained the motor-bikes. The fact that Gorner knew there was someone taking an interest in him was not that surprising— not if he operated on the scale M had suggested. Such people relied on good intelligence. It was irritating, but it wasn't fatal to his undertaking.

"And your sister knew I was coming to Paris?"

"Yes. She rang this morning."

"And she knew which hotel?"

"No. I waited at the airport, then followed you in a taxi. I'm sorry. As for getting into the room . . . Hotel staff in Paris are used to unescorted women going up in the lift. Provided you look smart. I asked for your room number, then I gave a room-service boy in the corridor some money to open the door. I said I'd lost my key. It was all ridiculously easy."

"So Moneypenny booked me into an *hôtel de passe*. I must have a word."

Scarlett flushed. "I'm sorry this has all been so underhand. But I had to see you again and I couldn't take the chance you'd freeze me out. I knew if I just telephoned that you'd refuse to see me. Of course, what I meant to do was grab you in the morning in Rome and make a clean breast of it. But I was a bit put out by your . . . coldness. Then the desk told me you'd left at the crack of dawn."

"And now you have a second chance. I'm officially engaged to follow a man you wanted me to meet for your own private ends."

Scarlett smiled. "Do you believe in destiny?"

Bond said nothing. He kicked off his black loafers and propped himself up on the bed. He put his gun down beside the telephone and thought for a long time. He was amused. Lonely housewife, busy banker, lady of the night . . . Scarlett was undeniably intriguing. Her composure, as she sat there, her red lips half-parted in a self-deprecating smile, was remarkable. And the husband, Mr. Rossi, in insurance . . . What an improbable figure he now seemed. But he had to hand it to her, she'd managed it brilliantly in Rome, that air of frustrated-housewife boredom. Presumably she'd thought it unsafe to talk about her sister in the restaurant and was waiting till she got him up to her room. Or had she had another, more personal, motive?

It didn't matter. At such moments he relied on instinct and experience. Whatever the complications of her story, the signals that the girl gave off were good. Dangerous, perhaps, but interesting.

"All right, Scarlett," he said, "this is what we'll do. Today is Thursday. Tomorrow I shall meet up with an old friend. Just the two of us, in case you were thinking of dropping in. Depending on what he says, I will then go with you to the tennis club on Saturday morning. I'll call you on this number at six o'clock tomorrow." He held up her card. "Then you can make the introductions and—"

"No, I can't make the introductions. Gorner mustn't see me. It would put Poppy in danger. I'll point him out to you."

"All right. But you must stay at the club. I want you there. Until the moment I leave."

"As your security?"

"Securities are what you deal in, aren't they?" Bond eyed her sardonically. "Is it a deal?"

"Yes. It's a deal." Scarlett held out her hand.

Bond took it. "Larissa kissed me on the cheek," he said.

"Autres temps," said Scarlett, with a low laugh, *"autres moeurs."*

He watched her walk down the corridor to the lift, the skirt holding its elegant line along the length of her thighs.

This time there was no wave from the lift, but as the doors were closing, she called out, "How's your tennis? I hope it's good!"

René Mathis seemed anxious to meet early in the day. "Friday evenings, James," he said, "always so many loose ends to tidy up in the office. I'll buy you lunch. Come to Chez André in the rue du Cherche Midi. Not my normal *quartier* at all. So much the better."

Bond arrived five minutes early, as was his custom, and took a seat, away from the window, from which he could survey the room. He was pleased to see Mathis arrive, a little out of breath, complaining of the traffic.

"Just a little bistro, James. Nothing special. Have the dish of the day. It's mostly publishers and lecturers, people like that, in here. No one you won't want to see, I assure you."

Mathis spoke a fluent, lightly accented English. He ordered two Ricards before Bond could stop him.

"What do you know about Julius Gorner?" said Bond.

"Not much," said Mathis. "And you?"

Bond told him what he knew while Mathis listened, nodding intently. He often pretended to be more ignorant than he really was, Bond knew. It was a habit, but it didn't mean he couldn't be relied on.

"It sounds as though someone needs to get closer

to this man," Mathis said, when Bond had finished. "People who work on his scale seldom leave much trace of their activities. You need to close in very tight."

"I have a way in," said Bond, "but it's a slippery one."

"My dear James," laughed Mathis, "what other kind of *entrée* can there be in our line of business?"

The waiter brought terrine with cornichons and a basket of bread.

"You must break the habit of a lifetime and drink some wine," said Mathis. "No one can eat terrine without wine."

He ordered a bottle of Château Batailley 1958 and, having poured a half-inch into his own glass, filled Bond's. "It's a fifth growth," he said. "It comes from a few metres west of Latour but it's a fraction of the price. Try it."

Bond raised the glass circumspectly to his lips. The aroma was rich, though hard to define.

"Lead pencils?" said Mathis. "Tobacco? Blackberry? A hint of roast beef?"

Holding up a warning finger, Bond let the wine trickle back over his tongue. "Not bad," he said.

"Not bad! Batailley is a miracle. One of the great secrets of Bordeaux."

By time the waiter had cleared the plates with

what remained of the *lapin à l'ancienne* and replaced them with a cheeseboard, they were into the second bottle, and Bond was inclined to agree.

"Have you heard of a woman called Scarlett Papava?" Bond said.

"God, she sounds like a Russian," said Mathis.

"I think her father is, or was," said Bond. "Would you do me a favour? See if any of your colleagues have her marked down as SIS? Or worse?"

"SMERSH? KGB?"

"I doubt it," said Bond, "but with the Russian connection you have to be doubly careful."

"Is this urgent?"

"I need to know by five thirty." Bond passed Scarlett's card across the table. He'd memorized the phone numbers. "Take this."

"God, you never change, James. I'll see what I can do. Call my secretary. I'll leave a message. A simple code. Green, orange or red. Now what about some more wine?"

After lunch, Bond bought some tennis clothes and a Dunlop Maxply racquet, loosely strung in gut, from a sports shop on the boulevard St.-Germain, then took a cab back to his hotel. He entered his room more cautiously this time, with his gun drawn, though concealed in his coat pocket. He checked the powder and the single hair which he had replaced after the maid had cleaned the room. They were still in place. Then he read a *Newsweek* article on drug trafficking that Loelia Ponsonby had included in his secret briefing papers. At five thirty he went down into the street and found a telephone in the rue Daunou. He disturbed Loelia over a cup of tea in the office and told her to get the garage people out to the airport to replace his car windows.

"Not dangerous driving again, James, I hope?"

"Never you mind. Enjoy your tea, Lil."

"I've told you before not to call me that, it's—"

But it was too late. Bond was already dialling the Deuxième.

"Le bureau de Monsieur Mathis, s'il vous plaît."

"Un moment, Monsieur."

There was a series of hisses and clanks on the line, then the same abrupt female voice as the day before.

"Oui."

What a sour old biddy, thought Bond. What she needed was a good—

"Qu'est-ce qu'il y a?" she snapped.

"Il y a un message pour Monsieur Bond? James Bond."

"Attendez. Oui. Qu'un mot."

"Et?"

"Comment, Monsieur?"

"Le mot. C'est quoi?"

"C'est 'vert.' "

"Merci, Madame," said Bond. "And give my commiserations to your poor bloody husband," he added, as he replaced the receiver.

Something about the name of the street he was in seemed familiar. Rue Daunou. Yes, he had it. Harry's Bar. "Ask for Sank Roo Doe-Noo," as the *Herald Tribune* advertisement told its readers. Bond glanced at his watch. He had time for a bourbon and Vittel in the soft clubman's atmosphere of Harry's before telephoning Scarlett. As he sat in the leather armchair, smoking the last of the day's second packet of cigarettes, Bond had to admit he was starting to enjoy himself. The mission, the girl, the wine with Mathis and now the all-clear . . .

He threw a note on to the preposterous bill and went back to the call box. He was connected to Scarlett's office without demur.

"Scarlett? It's James Bond. Are you on for tomorrow?"

"Yes. Are you?"

"What time should we arrive?"

"About ten. Shall I pick you up from your hotel at nine? Then you'll have time to warm up for a few minutes."

"All right." He hesitated.

She was quick to notice. "Was there something else?"

He had been on the point of asking her to dinner. "No," he said. "Nothing else. Just remember. You're on probation."

"I understand. *À demain.*"

The line went dead.

Bond slept like a child in the quiet cocoon of his hotel room. A dinner of scrambled eggs from room service, three large bourbons and a hot bath made the barbiturate unnecessary.

In the morning, he exercised strenuously, pushing himself through sixty sit-ups and a variety of stretching exercises for the legs and back that Wayland had shown him in Barbados. The maid brought him breakfast as he was cooling down, and he ate it wrapped in a towel at the table in the window. The coffee was good, but he could never feel enthusiastic about croissants. At least there was something approaching marmalade.

After a shower, Bond changed into a sea-island cotton shirt, short-sleeved, charcoal trousers and a blazer. He wasn't sure what the dress code of the Club Sporting de Tennis would be, but in his experience such places in France generally tried to out-British the British in their display of checks and loud "club" ties. He put his tennis clothes in a small holdall and went down to the front door.

At one minute to nine, a white Sunbeam Alpine drew up with a squeak alongside him. The hood was down, and in the driving seat, in dark glasses and a distractingly short red linen dress, was Scarlett Papava.

"Hop in, James. You can push the seat back if you like."

Before he had had time to settle himself, she let in the clutch, and the little car sped off towards the place de la Concorde.

Bond smiled. "Are we in a hurry?"

"I think so," said Scarlett. "If we can manage to get you a game with Dr. Gorner, you'll need to be at your best. I suggest you have a little warm-up first. He's rather competitive."

Scarlett swept on to the Champs-Élysées and sank her right foot. "You have to take these chaps on," she said. "These French drivers, I mean. Play them at their own game. There's no point in being a shrinking violet."

"Why did you go for the Alpine, not the Tiger?" said Bond.

"My father found it for me. Second-hand. The Tiger's bigger, isn't it?"

"It has a V8 engine," said Bond, "but the Sunbeam chassis can't really handle that much torque. Anyway, you don't need it. Not the way you drive."

At the Étoile, where fifteen streams of traffic merge and battle for survival, Scarlett gave no quarter, and a few terrifying seconds later, in a barrage of hooting, they were on their way down the avenue de Neuilly. A small smile of triumph flickered round Scarlett's lips as the wind blew back her dark hair.

The Club Sporting was hidden off a discreet, sandy avenue in the Bois. Bond and Scarlett walked across from the car park, through the hissing lawns where hidden sprinklers played and up the steps into the enormous modern clubhouse.

"Wait here," said Scarlett. "I'll be back in a moment."

Bond watched the slim legs, bare to mid-thigh, as she walked away, with a slight rolling dip of the hips, towards the secretary's office. It was the walk of a confident girl, he thought, athletic and sure of herself.

He looked at the notices on the board: club tournaments, ladders, plates, knock-outs, seniors' and juniors' competitions. The names of the entrants included some of the best-known families in Paris. Towards the top of the second ladder, he saw the name "J. Gorner." If the top echelon was the first and second teams, men in their twenties of near-professional standard, that must mean Gorner was a formidable player. The equivalent in golf, a game Bond knew better, would be a player of a seven or eight handicap. Quite fierce enough.

"James!" He heard his name called, and saw Scarlett beckoning him over.

"The secretary says Dr. Gorner will be here in a few minutes, but has no game booked. You're in luck."

"How did you manage it?"

Scarlett looked momentarily ashamed. "I know from Poppy that Gorner likes a bet. I took the liberty of telling the secretary that you were a fine athlete who would give Dr. Gorner a good game and that you enjoyed a flutter yourself. I may also have led him to believe that you might not be quite good enough to win—but that you were a thorough gentleman who would pay his debts."

"I should think he must be salivating at the prospect," said Bond.

"Well, I think they find it hard to get the regular members to play against Gorner."

"I can't imagine why," said Bond. "How much am I in for?"

"Only a hundred pounds," said Scarlett, innocently. "Now I'm going to make myself scarce."

"You're telling me," said Bond. "But you're not to leave the premises."

"I wouldn't miss it for anything. I'm going to watch. From a discreet distance. Look. Isn't that his car arriving?"

Through the large glass doors Bond saw a black Mercedes 300D, driven by a man in a kepi. He watched it draw up at the foot of the steps, where the driver threw the keys to an attendant and went round to open the passenger door.

From it stepped the man in M's photograph, the same man he'd seen in Marseille. He wore a long-sleeved white flannel shirt and grey slacks with a single white glove on his outsized left hand. Bond turned to study the noticeboard as the men went past him towards the office. Scarlett had vanished.

Bond looked up to a bank of television screens on the wall, which showed the games in progress on the outside courts with a running scoreline updated from a courtside link by the players when they changed ends. Such technology was rare, Bond knew, outside a television studio and it must have cost the club—or, at any rate, the members—a hefty amount.

In addition to these games, there were indoor facilities in a basement complex immediately below the outside courts. Progress of these matches could be monitored from the indoor gallery that encircled them.

A minute later, Bond heard footsteps approach him. It was the man in the kepi.

"Excuse me," he said in English. "Mr. Bond? My name is Chagrin."

Bond turned to face him. He had yellowish skin, narrow eyes with the epicanthic lids of the Orient and flat, inert features. There was something half dead, or at least not fully alive, about him, Bond thought. He had seen that lifeless flesh once before, in a stroke victim. It sat oddly with the man's otherwise active demeanour.

"I think you play Dr. Gorner." Chagrin's accent sounded Chinese or Thai.

"If he's looking for a game," said Bond casually.

"Oh, yes. He looking. I introduce you."

Chagrin led the way past the spiral staircase that wound up to the extensive viewing area, bars and restaurant.

Gorner was staring through the plate-glass window at the nearer courts.

He turned and looked Bond in the eye. He held out his right, ungloved hand.

"What an enormous pleasure to meet you, Mr. Bond. Now, shall we play?"

5. NOT CRICKET

The changing room was on the lower ground floor, and included a large steam room, four saunas and enough colognes and aftershaves to have stocked Trumper's of Mayfair for a year. Bond, who was used to the club in Barbados (single shower stall, wooden bar with cold beer) or the shabby back rooms of Queen's Club in London, noticed that no amount of expensive scents had quite concealed a rancid under-smell of socks.

Gorner changed in a secluded cubicle, and emerged in new white Lacoste shorts that showed off muscular, tanned legs. He had retained the long-sleeved flannel shirt and the white glove on his large left hand. Over his right shoulder, he carried a bag with half a dozen new Wilson racquets.

Without speaking, as though he merely expected Bond to follow, Gorner led the way upstairs and out into the playing area, which consisted of a dozen immaculate grass courts and the same number again of beaten earth with a powdery red dirt dressing. The club was proud of the surface, said to give a fast but exceptionally regular bounce and to be kind to the joints of knee and ankle. At each court there was a raised umpire's chair, four smaller wooden seats for the players, a supply of fresh white towels and a fridge, which contained cold drinks and new boxes of white Slazenger tennis balls. Marshals in the club's striped green and chocolate colours moved busily between the courts to make sure the members were happy with their arrangements.

"Court Four is free, Dr. Gorner," said one of them, as he ran to meet them. He spoke in English. "Or Number Sixteen if you would prefer grass this morning."

"No, I shall take Court Two."

"Your usual court?" The man appeared anxious. "It's occupied at the moment, Monsieur."

Gorner looked at the marshal as a vet might inspect a spavined old horse to whom he is about to administer a lethal injection. He repeated, very slowly, "I shall take Court Two."

The bass-baritone voice retained a slight Baltic thickening of the vowels in the otherwise cultured English pronunciation.

"Er . . . Yes, yes. But of course. I shall ask the gentlemen to move to Court Four straight away."

"You will find Court Two a better surface," said Gorner to Bond. "And one isn't troubled by the sun."

"As you wish," said Bond. It was a beautiful morning and the sun was already high.

Gorner took a fresh box of tennis balls from the fridge, threw three to Bond and took three for himself. Without consultation, he selected the far end, though there was no obvious advantage that Bond could see. They knocked up for a few minutes and Bond concentrated on trying to find a nice, easy rhythm, hitting the forehand well in front of him with a good long swing, and slicing the backhand with a proper follow-through. He also kept an eye on Gorner's game to see if there were obvious weaknesses. Most players concealed their backhands in the knock-up, but Bond hit several wide to that side to give Gorner no chance. He chipped each one back to Bond's baseline without difficulty. His forehand, however, was not really a tennis stroke at all. He slashed downwards at it with heavy slice, so that it fizzed flat over the net. Either he could not play a regular forehand drive with topspin, thought Bond, or he was keeping it in reserve. In the meantime, Bond knew he must not let the awkward slice unsettle him.

"Ready," said Gorner. It was less a question than a statement.

He marched up to the net and began to measure it carefully with the metal yardstick that hung from the end. "You think I am wasting my time with this, Mr. Bond, but I invite you to consider. At our level, almost every shot passes only a few inches over the net, and perhaps once each game the ball will actually strike the netcord. Add in the 'lets' from services and the figure is higher. In a close match there are perhaps two hundred points and a typical winning margin of less than ten. Yet of those two hundred points perhaps thirty, including services, are affected by the net— more than three times enough to win the match! One should therefore leave nothing to chance."

"I'm impressed by your logic," said Bond. He swung his racquet a few times to loosen his shoulder.

Gorner adjusted the net by slightly tightening the chain that was attached to the central vertical tape and hooked to a bar in a hole in the ground. He then slapped the netcord three times with his racquet. There was no handle, Bond noticed, to raise or lower the net from the post. The netcord itself ran down the post and disappeared beneath a small metal plate into the ground—presumably on to a wheel where it was pre-tensioned by the staff. This left the central tape and chain for fine-tuning purposes.

"Good," said Gorner. "Will you spin?"

Bond twirled the racquet in his hand. "Rough or smooth?" he said.

"Skin," said Gorner. He leaned over and inspected Bond's racquet. "Skin it is. I'll serve."

Bond walked back to the receiving position, wondering what a "skin" was, unable to suppress the thought that the slang term might apply equally to rough or smooth.

Although they had taken a few practice serves, this was the first chance Bond had had to see Gorner's action properly. "Watch the ball," he muttered to himself.

This was easier said than done. Gorner bounced the tennis ball in front of him with his racquet once, twice, three times, then started to turn round, like a dog when it makes its bed. When he'd completed a 360-degree circle, he threw the ball high with his left hand and kept the arm, with its large white glove, extended until the last second—when the racquet smashed through and sent the ball thudding down the centre line. So put out was Bond by the whole procedure that he had barely moved.

"Fifteen," said Gorner, and moved swiftly to the advantage court.

Forcing himself to concentrate and not to watch the circling rigmarole, Bond dug his toes into the beaten earth. His backhand return was cut off by Gorner, who had moved swiftly to the net and slammed his volley into the far corner. "Thirty."

Bond won only one point in the first game. Gorner opened a bottle of Evian from the fridge and poured some into a glass, from which he took a single sip. He made a gesture with his left hand towards the fridge, as though inviting Bond to do likewise. As he did so, the buttoned cuff of his shirt separated for a moment from the white glove. When he moved off again, Gorner playfully smacked the net twice more, as though for good luck.

Trying to put out of his mind what he had seen of Gorner's hair-covered wrist, Bond walked back to serve. One's first service game is always important in setting the tone for a match. Bond, who had a strong first service, decided to throttle back a little and concentrate on accuracy. He pushed Gorner wide on both sides, but whenever he came in for the volley found himself adroitly lobbed. At 30–40 down, he twice served into the top of the net and saw the ball rebound on to his own side. Double fault: a craven way to lose one's service.

It was difficult for Bond to find a way to break up Gorner's rhythm. He remembered with Wayland in Barbados that he could sometimes slow the game down, mix it up and make the young man overhit in his desire to attack. Gorner made no such mistakes. His slashed forehand was hard for Bond to volley: he had to get his racquet right out ahead and punch through it to nullify the spin—not that Gorner gave him much chance to volley, since as soon as he saw Bond advance, he unleashed another lob that fell, with irritating regularity, just inside the baseline, leaving a clear mark in the reddish surface.

When Bond served, Gorner would swiftly call "Out" and make no attempt to play the ball, which would hit the back netting and rebound. Just as Bond was about to hit his second serve, Gorner would shout "Hold on" and trot back to push the rogue ball out of the way. "Can't be too careful," he explained. "I saw a man break his ankle by standing on a ball only last week. Carry on." By then, Bond's rhythm was disrupted and he was glad just to get his second serve in play.

Tenaciously, Bond clung on to his service games until he found himself facing Gorner at 4–5 down.

It was his last chance of breaking back before the set was over. He decided to stay back, work Gorner from side to side and hope to elicit a mistake. For the first time, Gorner began to look fallible. He twice hit his fizzing forehand long, and for the first time in the match Bond had a break point, at 30–40. Gorner served wide to the backhand, but Bond hit a solid cross-court return and got himself into the rally. He then hit deep to the baseline and Gorner spooned up a half-court ball off the backhand. This was Bond's chance. He closed in, kept his eye on the ball, and whipped a forehand topspin winner down the line. "Out," called Gorner. "Deuce."

Gorner was into his service procedure again before Bond had time to protest. Gorner won the game and the set: 6–4. As they changed ends and Bond went back to serve for the first game of the second set, he went over to where he thought his forehand drive had bounced. There was a clear scuff mark three inches inside the sideline.

Bond gathered himself. As he went into his service action, Gorner was jumping around, twirling his racquet, feinting to come in, then rapidly retreating. It was an old tactic, Bond knew, but not an easy one to counter. He forced himself to watch the ball and smacked a hard first service down the centre. "Out," called Gorner.

"I think not," said Bond. "I can show you the mark where it landed." He walked up to the net and pointed.

"An old mark," said Gorner.

"No. I saw my service land there. I deliberately left a margin for error. It's at least six inches inside."

"My dear Mr. Bond, if your idea of English fair play is to question a man at his own club, then please be my guest and play the point again." Gorner smacked the sole of his shoe with his racquet to remove any loose particles of dirt. "Go on."

Bond's first re-taken serve was long. He hit the second crisply, with slice, and was disappointed to see it hit the netcord and skew off into the tramlines.

"Double fault," said Gorner. "Poetic justice, don't you think?"

Bond was beginning to feel enraged. From the advantage court, he fired his best angled serve wide to his opponent's backhand. "Out," came the prompt and confident call.

As he wound up for his second, Gorner called, "Careful! Behind you."

"What?"

"I thought I saw a ball just behind you."

"I'd prefer it if you left me to look out for these things."

"I understand, Mr. Bond. But I could never for-give myself if my guest were to come to some harm. Please do carry on. Second service."

Tennis, more than most games, is played in the mind. Anger is useless unless it can be channelled and kept under control—as a key to concentration.

Bond knew he had to change his game against Gorner. For a start, he seemed to be having no luck at all. He had hit an inordinate number of netcords on his service, few of which had rebounded into play, whereas Gorner, even with his rather flat ser-vice, had not once touched the net. Furthermore, there was no point in Bond's hitting the ball close to the line. Every shot he played from now on had to bounce at least two feet inside the court. With this in mind, he began to play more and more drop-shots, since no one can dispute that a ball which lands only a few feet over the net is in play. The drop-shot itself seldom wins the point in club tennis, however, and the player who produces it must at once go on to a high state of alert. Bond had learned this lesson at a heavy price from the speedy Wayland. Gorner was not so quick, and Bond was ready for all his attempted lob and flick replies, even punching sev-eral successful volleys past the man he had finally dragged out of position.

Gorner now circled not once but twice before

serving. At the top of the ball toss, he held his white-gloved hand for as long as he dared in front of the white tennis ball before hitting it. He became a jack-in-the-box while waiting to receive. He interrupted almost every service point of Bond's with a move to swat away a ball that had conveniently rebounded from the back netting, or "fallen" from his pocket. But the distractions only succeeded in making Bond concentrate harder until, in the eighth game of the set, he finally and for the first time in the match, with a sliced forehand volley, hit straight down the middle of the court—far from any line—and broke Gorner's service.

Bond hit two unreturnable first serves to go 30–love up, then netted an easy backhand volley. On the fourth point he was lobbed. 30–all. Serving into the forehand court, he had the choice of swinging it out wide or hitting flat down the middle. He chose neither. He punched an 80-per-center straight at Gorner's ribs, so as to give him no width. Gorner, surprised by the change of line, spooned up his return and Bond collected the winning volley with relish.

It was 40–30: set point to Bond. As he began to serve for the set, Gorner called out, "Excuse me, Mr. Bond. Will you forgive me? A call of nature. I shan't be one minute."

He jogged off the court to the clubhouse.

Bond pushed his hand back through his damp hair in irritation. The man was shameless. And the trouble with people who are shameless is that they are curiously invulnerable.

At the umpire's chair, Bond pulled a bottle of Pschitt from the fridge and took a couple of sips. He was playing as well as he knew how, but he was wary that Gorner might have yet further means to avoid the possibility of losing. He was clearly a man who would rule nothing out.

Gorner returned swiftly from the clubhouse. "Do forgive me, Mr. Bond. Now where were we? Was I serving?"

"No. I was. It's forty–thirty. Five–four."

"How could I have forgotten? So this is set point?" There was a guileless yet patronizing note in his voice, implying that such matters as the score were generally beneath his notice.

Bond said nothing. He had worked over Gorner's backhand so much that it must be time for something new. Taking careful aim, he served hard down the centre. Gorner anticipated well, but Bond's serve hit the line—a tape that stood a fraction proud—and bounced up awkwardly towards Gorner's chest, where he mis-hit it into the base of the net. It was the first bit of luck Bond had had all morning, and there was no point in Gorner calling the service "out" as only the line-tape itself could have caused the difficult bounce.

As they sat on their chairs, Gorner said, "You're quite a fighter, aren't you, Mr. Bond?"

"Does that bother you?"

"On the contrary." Gorner stood to one side and did some stretching exercises. "I would like to propose that we raise the stakes a little."

He didn't look at Bond as he spoke, but busied himself with the strings on his racquet.

"All right," said Bond. "It's a hundred pounds, isn't it?"

"I believe so. So . . . Shall we say a hundred thousand?"

Gorner was still not looking at Bond. He was bending over his bag to extract a new racquet and was testing the tension by banging the frame of another racquet against the strings. He said, "I mean francs, of course, Mr. Bond."

"Old, presumably," said Bond.

"Oh, no. New. As new as we can find them."

Bond calculated rapidly. It was more than seven thousand pounds, silly money, far more than he could afford, but in the strange tussle to which he now appeared committed, he felt he could show no weakness. "All right, Dr. Gorner," he said. "Your serve."

"Ah, the good old English 'fair play,' " said Gorner, heavily, in his oddly accented voice. "I suppose to turn down my bet would be 'not cricket.' " He spat out the words with such bitterness that it took a moment for him to register the joke. "Not cricket," he repeated, laughing mirthlessly as he walked back to serve. "Not cricket at all. Ha ha. Just tennis."

The sum of money that had been bet and all the antics with racquet and bag and stretching added up to just one thing, thought Bond: a threat. You can't beat me, Gorner was saying, and it's foolish to try. Be sensible, be realistic, let me win and it'll be better for you in the long run.

The means by which he'd made himself clear were subtle, Bond had to admit. Unfortunately for Gorner, however, the threat only made Bond more determined.

For the first six games, the set went with service. With the score at 3–3, Gorner served again and went 15–40 down. Bond knew it was a crucial moment. He sliced a backhand return deep—but not deep enough to risk being called out—then retreated to the baseline. Gorner slashed a fizzing forehand slice down the centre of the court. Most of these shots stopped and stood up as the backspin told, though occasionally they didn't grip, but merely hurried through. This was a hurrier, and Bond was almost cut in two as he tried to slice it back. Gorner was on to his weak return, pushing him deep into the corner, but Bond lobbed diagonally, and drove his man back. He didn't charge the net, but stayed back, and the rally ground on for sixteen strokes, from side to side. Bond felt his lungs burning and eyes aching with concentration. He kept pounding Gorner's backhand, pushing his forehands as close to the line as he dared. When he could hear Gorner panting and gasping with the effort, he suddenly dropped the ball short. Gorner ran in, but failed to make it. Game to Bond.

"Bad luck," said Bond, unnecessarily.

Gorner said nothing. He raised his racquet and smashed it down on the net post, so the wooden frame collapsed. He chucked the racquet to the side of the court and pulled another from his bag.

The show of rage seemed to galvanize him, and he ripped into Bond's service with no sign of the nerves that had threatened both players in the cautious exchanges of the previous games. With his combination of slice, lob and competitive line-call, he broke back at once. Four–all. Bond cursed himself silently as he prepared to receive.

For the first time that Bond could remember, Gorner hit the netcord with his first service. The ball ballooned out, and Bond successfully attacked the second with a cross-court forehand. Emboldened, he unleashed an aggressive backhand to the incoming Gorner's feet to go love–30 ahead. Suddenly the tightness in Bond's chest and the heaviness in his legs seemed to have gone. He felt confident, and hit another low, flat return of serve that skimmed an inch above the net to give him three break points.

Gorner circled three times in the advantage court, finally tossed the ball high with a flash of white glove and served with a grunt. The ball hit the top of the net and dropped back. He gathered himself and hit a flat second serve, which hit the netcord, ran along three feet and fell back harmlessly on his side.

"That is unbelievable!" he exploded. He ran to the net and hammered it with his racquet.

"Steady on. You'll have the secretary out here," said Bond. "Five–four. My serve, I think."

Bond drank a full glass of Evian at the change. The match was almost over and he wasn't bothered about having too much fluid in his stomach.

While he waited for Gorner to complete his changeover rituals, Bond bounced the ball and planned his service game. Three-quarter speed down the middle to the deuce court, out wide to the backhand on the advantage court. Then, if 30–love up, hit the variants: slice wide to the forehand, then straight down the middle in the advantage court.

Gorner finished towelling himself and went slowly back to receive. As Bond prepared to serve, Gorner advanced almost to the service line, then doubled back. He managed a decent backhand return, but Bond put the volley away a safe two feet inside the sideline.

Gorner advanced to the net. "I wonder if you'd like to raise our bet, Mr. Bond. I was thinking of a double."

Bond didn't have the money and he didn't have the authority of the Service to presume on theirs. But he felt that in the last two games the odds had turned inexplicably in his favour.

"If you insist," he said. "Fifteen–love."

He netted his first serve, but hit a deep second with topspin. Gorner's return was short and Bond was able to pressure him into a backhand mistake.

Following his plan, he swung the next serve out wide and stunned Gorner's return with a drop volley, giving himself three match points.

Now for the middle line, he thought. He threw the ball a little lower than usual, and slightly further in front of him, then hit with all his power, flat down the centre. It bounced in the corner of the service box and curved away from Gorner's flailing racquet to hit the back netting half-way up. It lodged there, whitish grey, smudged with red.

Bond went to the net and held out his hand. Gorner came to meet him and, for the first time since they had met, looked him in the eye.

The relief and elation of victory evaporated as Bond felt the intense and violent hatred of the eyes that bored into him.

"I look forward to a rematch," said Gorner. "In the very near future. I do not think you will be so fortunate a second time."

He went to gather his belongings without another word.

6. QUITE A GIRL

When he emerged from the shower, Bond found no trace of Gorner in the changing room, though on top of his racquet was a white envelope, stiff with banknotes. On it was written: *"À bientôt."*

Bond tracked down Scarlett to one of the upstairs bars, where she sat on a stool in the window, innocently sipping a drink.

"Did you enjoy your game, James?"

"Good exercise. I think I lost a few pounds. Not as many as Gorner."

"But you did win?"

"Yes."

"And are you going to take me out to lunch to celebrate?"

Bond pushed back his hair, which was still damp from the shower, and smiled at the girl's earnest expression. "Let's have a drink first," he said.

Bond joined Scarlett in the window, bringing a fresh *citron pressé* for her, a litre of Vittel and a bottled beer for himself.

Scarlett crossed her legs and turned to Bond. "It all seemed to come right for you just at the end."

"You were watching?"

"From a safe distance. I didn't want Gorner or Chagrin to see me."

Bond nodded.

"The thing is," said Scarlett, with an enigmatic smile, "that you seemed to have no luck at all until the last three games."

"That can happen in any sport," said Bond. "Golf, tennis . . ."

"Well, it seemed more than a coincidence to me," said Scarlett, "so I did some investigation."

"You did what?"

"Every time you hit the ball into the netcord, it seemed to rebound out of play. Gorner's shots never seemed to touch the net. I became suspicious."

Bond leaned forward, intrigued despite himself. "And?"

"I noticed that your court was the only one without a handle on the net post to tighten the net—that the cord just ran down out of sight."

"Yes, I presume there's a wheel let into the ground there."

Scarlett laughed. "Not so fast, James. I worked out whereabouts indoors would be directly under the net post and went to have a look. I reckoned it would be a small storeroom to one side of the indoor courts. I found my way to the room and looked through the glass in the door. And there was Mr. Chagrin, watching television."

"Television?"

"Yes, on closed circuit, like the ones in the entry hall. But in this room there's a monitor with a console which allows you to follow any of the games going on outside. You know, like the director's room in a television studio. And Chagrin was watching your game."

"And?"

"There was a brass handle attached to a wheel in the concrete wall. It seemed to have something that looked very like a netcord running down to it. Depending on who was serving, Chagrin could turn the handle one way or the other to raise or lower it. Very simple—just an extra-long netcord."

"So that's why Gorner insisted on playing on Court Two."

"Chagrin waited till he could see on the screen that your back was turned," said Scarlett. "He'd got the cord wound so tight when you were serving that any shot of yours that touched it just flew out."

"And Gorner kept hitting it with his racquet between games. Presumably that was some sort of signal. So what did you do?"

"I ran upstairs and looked around till I found someone I knew. A young man called Max, who works for Rothschild's. He's asked me out a few times and I knew he'd want to help. Obviously the staff are all in on Gorner's little game, so I couldn't go to the secretary or anything. Anyway, I got Max to go into the storeroom and tell Chagrin he knew what he was up to and if he didn't stop fixing the net that he, Max, would go on court and tell you in front of Gorner."

"At what point in the game was this?" said Bond.

"I'm not sure exactly. By the time Max had got Chagrin out of there and reported the all-clear to me, it must have been well into the third set."

"Then what did you do?"

Scarlett looked slightly ashamed. "I took Chagrin's place and made things a bit fairer."

Bond smiled. "That must have been when he smashed his racquet. He thought it was impossible for him to serve a double fault."

"I'm afraid so. But I only raised it a fraction. Nothing like as much as Chagrin had been doing."

"And for me?"

"I let it go back to the correct height. So all those lovely winners you hit were legitimate."

Bond smiled. "You're quite a girl, aren't you, Scarlett?"

"So now am I invited to lunch?"

"I think it's . . . destiny," said Bond.

"Good," said Scarlett, jumping down from her stool. "First I shall show you the Sainte Chapelle. Culture before gluttony. I don't suppose you've ever been there, have you?"

"I've always been too busy for rubbernecking," said Bond.

"I'll go and get the car," said Scarlett. "See you on the steps."

There was a short queue of weekend sightseers outside the Sainte Chapelle, but after ten minutes Bond and Scarlett were inside. The ground floor was bare and unremarkable, largely taken up by an extensive souvenir stall.

"Not impressed, are you?" said Scarlett.

"It's like a bazaar."

"My father told me that outside the Church of the

Holy Sepulchre in Jerusalem he was offered an egg
from the cock that crew."

"The cock that—"

"When Peter denied Christ for the third time."

"Improbable."

"For a number of reasons."

"And what's special about this place?" said Bond.

"This is," said Scarlett. "Follow me."

She went to a stone staircase and began to climb.
Bond followed, watching the muscles of her slim calves
and thighs in the shadow of the short linen dress.

The upper chapel was a blaze of stained glass.

"It was a miracle of engineering," said Scarlett.
"They managed to build it without flying buttresses
to support it, otherwise you'd see them and they'd
spoil the pictures in the glass."

Scarlett spent some minutes walking round the
chapel, and Bond watched the reflections of the
coloured glass as they played across the stone floor
and over the slim figure of the girl who so admired
them. Her enthusiasm seemed quite guileless. Either
she was the most accomplished actress he had ever
met, or she was what she claimed to be.

She came back and lightly took his arm. "That's
your culture for today, James. Now you can take me
to La Cigale Verte. It's only five minutes away. We
can leave the car here and walk along the river."

The restaurant she'd chosen on the Île St. Louis had a long terrace overlooking the Seine with only a footpath between the tables and the river.

"I was rather presumptuous, I'm afraid," said Scarlett as the maître d' greeted them. "When I saw which way the game was going I telephoned to book a table. It's very popular at the weekend."

The maître d', who seemed unable to take his eyes off Scarlett, ushered them to a table directly overlooking the river and the Left Bank beyond.

"Do you like shellfish?" said Scarlett. "They do a spectacular selection. Langoustines, crab, little flat-faced spiky things that look like Chagrin . . . And they make this wonderful mayonnaise. It's the best in Paris. Shall I order for you, too? Will you trust me?"

"Trust you? Why ever not? Then we'll talk business," said Bond.

"But of course."

Bond felt elated by the tennis, and hungry too. The waiter brought a bottle of Dom Pérignon and some olives. The cold bubbles fizzed on Bond's dry throat.

"Now, Scarlett, I want to hear all about Dr. Julius Gorner."

"I first heard of him through my father, Alexandr," said Scarlett, pulling the tail of a langoustine from its shell. "My grandfather came to England during the Revolution. He had estates near St. Petersburg and a house in Moscow. My grandfather was an engineer by training, but he managed to get some of the family money out of Russia and he bought a house near Cambridge. My father was only about seven years old when they fled and he hardly remembers Russia. He became bilingual in English and went to very good schools and eventually became a fellow of a college in Cambridge, where he taught economics. During the war he worked for British Army Intelligence, and afterwards he was offered a senior post at Oxford, where he encountered Gorner, who'd gone there as a mature student."

"So your father taught Gorner?"

"Yes, though he said he was an unreceptive student and loath to admit there was anything he didn't already know."

"But he was clever?"

"My father said that with more humility he could have been the best economist in Oxford. But the trouble was, he blamed my father when things started to go wrong."

"What happened?"

"According to my father, his manner alienated people."

"So he was like that even then."

"He had this Baltic or Lithuanian accent and of course . . . the hand. But that was all right. I think people felt sorry for him. But he was crooked. He cheated in exams—though according to my father he didn't need to. He was contemptuous of the undergraduates, because he was a bit older and had fought in the war."

"For both sides, I gather," said Bond.

"Perhaps he wanted to be on the winning side," said Scarlett. "And he had undoubtedly seen things at Stalingrad—or Volgograd as they're trying to call it again now—that made him feel older, or more worldly . . . But quite a few of the British students had broken off their studies to go and fight."

Scarlett was interrupted by the waiter, who had come to clear the remains of the shellfish.

"You're going to have fried sole now," said Scarlett. "Can I order some wine?"

"Be my guest. Or Gorner's," said Bond, tapping the thick envelope in his breast pocket.

Scarlett lit a cigarette, pulled her feet up under her on the red-cushioned seat and wrapped her arms round her ankles. As the sun disappeared behind a tall building, she pushed her dark glasses on to the top of her head and, Bond thought, looked suddenly younger. Her dark brown eyes engaged his.

"Gorner became obsessed by the fact that people

didn't like him and he put it all down to xenophobia. He viewed Oxford as an elite English club that wouldn't let him join. I imagine one or two of the rowing types probably did tease him, but my father reassured me that most of them were perfectly polite and kind. I think it was this experience that somehow put the iron in his soul and he determined to take his revenge on what he saw as the stuck-up English. He became obsessed by English culture and all that rather dreary stuff about cricket and fair play and tea-time. He thought it was all a gigantic fraud. He took it far more seriously than any English person. He made a fetish of British foreign policy and the Empire and thought he could show how brutal and unfair it had all been. I suppose the whole process must have taken some years to come to fruition but, to cut a long story short, he hated England because he felt it had laughed at him, and he decided to devote his life to destroying it."

"Perhaps he'd already had feelings like that," said Bond.

"What do you mean?"

"When he changed sides in the war. Perhaps, when it became clear that the Nazis couldn't beat the British, he thought the Russians were the next best bet."

"That's clever of you, James. I didn't know you were such a psychologist."

"The waiter wants you to try the wine."

Scarlett gave the Bâtard Montrachet a quick sniff. "*Très bien*. Where was I?"

"Being flattering."

"Ah, yes. Well, my father got wind of the fact that Gorner was unhappy and he tried to sympathize. He was only a tutor that Gorner went to see occasionally, he had no responsibility for his welfare, but my father's a kind man. He asked him to dinner at our house. Poppy and I must have been there, as little girls, but I don't remember. He sympathized with him about being an outsider and told him his own father had found it hard, coming from Russia, but that England had a good reputation with immigrants. Half the science faculty at Cambridge were Jewish *émigrés*, for heaven's sake. Then my father made his big mistake. He asked him about his hand."

Bond put down his knife and fork. "What did he say?"

"My father said he'd known someone in Cambridge before the war—in Sidney Sussex College, I don't know why I remember that—who had the same thing. He was trying to be reassuring, to let Gorner know he wasn't the only one with this peculiarity, but I suppose it was something Gorner'd never spoken about before. I suppose he was very ashamed of it. As though he or his family hadn't properly evolved."

Bond nodded and filled their glasses.

"Anyway," said Scarlett, "as a result, far from being his friend, a fellow exile, Gorner viewed my father as even worse than the English—as a kind of successful traitor, a turncoat who'd become one of the enemy. From that day onwards he wore a glove over his hand. And he had a new burning hatred to add to his list. At joint number one with England and its culture were Alexandr Papav and his family."

"A list I feel I've joined this morning," said Bond.

Scarlett clinked her glass against his. "To the enemies of Julius Gorner. Anyway, many years later, he came across Poppy. And that was when he saw his chance."

As the waiter brought a cheeseboard and fresh bread, Bond looked down the Seine to where the pleasure boats stopped to deposit their passengers. The most popular tourist boat, he noticed, was a Mississippi paddle steamer—the *Huckleberry Finn*—with a banner on the hull that said she was on loan to the city of Paris for one month only.

Bond brought his eyes back to the table. "You'd better tell me about Poppy."

"Poppy . . ." Scarlett cut a slice of Camembert and put it on Bond's plate. "Try that. Poppy . . . Well, Poppy's not that much like me . . . She's a bit younger and . . . She never took her studies very seriously."

"Unlike you," said Bond.

"That's right."

"And where did you go to school?"

"Roedean. Don't laugh. It's not funny. Then I went to Oxford, to Somerville."

"Where you were doubtless awarded a first-class degree, like Gorner."

Scarlett coloured a little. "My father said that boasting of exam results was the height of vulgarity. Poppy didn't go to university. She went to live in London and moved with rather a fast set of people. She went to a lot of parties. For some reason I don't understand, she decided she wanted to be an air hostess. I suppose it just seemed glamorous to her. Jet travel was still quite a novelty. And I suppose she was rebelling against her academic family. My mother was a consultant at the Radcliffe hospital and she also had high expectations of us. Anyway, Poppy worked for BOAC for three years. She fell in love with one of the pilots. He was married and he kept saying he'd leave his wife, but he didn't. Poppy was very unhappy. In the course of a layover in Morocco, she tried taking drugs. Just a little. But soon she was taking more. Partly for fun, I suppose, but also because she was miserable. Then, at some point, her lover went to see Gorner in Paris because he was fed up with the BOAC routes and he'd seen an advertisement Gorner had placed. He needed a pilot for his private planes. In the course of following up his references, Gorner got to hear about Poppy and, of course, recognized the name. He pounced. He told the pilot he wasn't interested in him, but offered Poppy a huge amount of money to go and work for him. And a lot of flying and perks and holidays. Clothes. Shoes."

"Anything else?" said Bond.

"Yes. One other thing." Scarlett bit her lip. "He offered her drugs."

"And that was a lure for her?"

"Undoubtedly." There were tears on the lower lids of Scarlett's eyes. "He was able to promise her an unlimited supply of anything she wanted, and it would be good quality, not mixed with poison or anything, as it can be if you buy on the street. And I suppose it looked like a way in which she could control her habit and always have the money for it. Although, in fact, the drugs were free." Scarlett wiped her eyes with a handkerchief. "She was such a gentle girl. She always was."

The waiter brought fresh pineapple and cream.

With the dark espresso that followed, Bond lit a cigarette and offered one to Scarlett. "So, Scarlett, if I find her, will she come? Or is she a willing slave?"

"I haven't seen her for two years, so I don't really

know. I've occasionally managed to speak to her on the telephone. The last time was just the other day. She was in Tehran and had managed to get to the post office."

"Tehran?"

"Yes, Gorner has a big business interest there. It may be a front. I don't know. But Poppy told me she was making efforts to come off the drugs. It's very difficult. But I think she would come if you were able to find her. Then we could get her into a clinic. The trouble is, Gorner won't let her go. He's slowly killing her, and he's loving every moment of it."

Bond swore succinctly. Then he said, "Don't cry, Scarlett. I'll find her."

After one more coffee, Scarlett drove Bond back to his hotel, keeping the Sunbeam rather closer to the speed limit than she had on the way to the Bois.

"You'll call me with any news, won't you?"

"Of course," said Bond. "If I'm near a telephone."

She leaned over from her seat and kissed his cheek. She had put on her sunglasses to conceal her swollen eyes. Bond's hand lingered for a second on the red linen dress. Something about this girl had got right under his defences, and he felt profoundly uneasy.

He was tempted to turn and wave from the door of the hotel, as Mrs. Larissa Rossi had waved from the lift in Rome, but forced himself to push straight through and into the gloom of the lobby.

"Monsieur Bond," said the receptionist. "A cable for you."

Up in his room Bond ripped the cable open. It was marked PROBOND at the beginning and PRISM at the end, to show that M had cleared it.

URGENT YOU GO PISTACHIO SOONEST STICK CLOSEST TO SUPPLIER STOP US OFFICE REPORTS CAVIAR SALES LINK IMMINENT STOP LOCAL REP EXPECTS YOU STOP

He began to pack at once and asked Reception to call the airport. "Pistachio," in the latest codes, was Persia, and "Caviar" the Soviet Union. The US office was the CIA, and if they were feeling edgy about Gorner it could be that the Russian connection M had spoken of in London was further advanced than had been thought.

Gorner and the Russians, thought Bond. It was a marriage made in hell.

7. "TRUST ME, JAMES"

The start of a journey in Persia resembles an algebraical equation: it may or it may not come out.

ROBERT BYRON, *The Road to Oxiana*

As the plane began its descent, Bond looked out of the window and lit a cigarette. Away to his left, he could see the tops of the Elburz mountains and, beyond them, a faint blue smudge that must be the southern waters of the Caspian Sea. Work had never previously taken him to the Middle East, and for this he was thankful. He regarded the lands between Cyprus and India as the thieving centre of the world. He'd visited Egypt as a child, when he was too young to remember, and had once spent a few days' leave in

Beirut, but had found it little more than a smugglers' den—of diamonds from Sierra Leone, arms from Arabia and gold from Aleppo. It was true that the Lebanese women had been far more modern in their attitudes than he'd expected, but he'd been pleased to get back to London.

He drained the last of the bourbon from his glass as the plane banked for its final approach. There'd been no time for any briefing on Persia and he would be relying on the local head of station, Darius Alizadeh, for guidance. He heard the thump as the landing gear was dropped from the belly of the plane, and the hydraulic whine as the brake flaps slid out of the leading edge of the wings. Then, beneath them, Bond could see what he'd seen a hundred times before in different continents, the telephone wires, the small cars on the airport ring road, the low terminal buildings, then the sudden rushing strip of concrete with its black skidmarks as the plane thumped twice in a perfect landing and the pilot switched the engines to reverse.

As soon as he stepped from the plane, Bond felt the intense heat of the desert country. There was no air-conditioning inside the arrivals building, and he was already sweating by the time the customs official had chalked his bags. When going through US Customs, he used a British diplomatic passport, number 0094567, but always hated the thought of his name being flashed to and from CIA headquarters in Langley for clearance. Any wisp of evidence that he was present—even that he existed—diminished his security. In Tehran, the passport he showed to the earnest, moustachioed official in the glass booth identified him as David Somerset, company director. It was an alias Darko Kerim had given him in Istanbul, and he used it in memory of Darko, the loyal friend who'd died in helping him escape from SMERSH.

Outside the building, after he had swapped some currency, Bond stepped into a taxi and gave the driver the address of his uptown hotel. The entrance to Tehran was drab. There were factories pouring black smoke, featureless rectangular skyscrapers, cuboid houses, broad tarmacked roads with trees along the edge—little to distinguish it from any modern city if you discounted the odd piles of lemons on the roadside.

They went past Tehran University on Shah Reza Avenue, into Ferdowsi Square where the famous poet, cast in bronze, pointed upwards to the sky as he declaimed his verses, then turned left and started to head north towards the more affluent end of town. From this point there were fewer livestock lorries, painted garishly in lime or sapphire, and not so many cars with family possessions strapped to the roof. It was as though at this latitude the city had taken a grip on itself in its desire to be more Western.

Bond offered the driver a cigarette, which, after two or three refusals that Bond could tell were half-hearted, was gratefully accepted. The man tried to engage him in conversation about football—"Bobby Moore, Bobby Charlton" seemed to be the only English words he knew—but Bond was thinking of one name only: Julius Gorner.

He handed a fistful of Persian rials to the driver and went into the hotel, which was mercifully air-conditioned. His room was on the twelfth floor, with a picture window on either side, one looking south over the seething, smog-covered city and one looking north towards the mountains, of which one ("the mighty Mount Demavend, who measure 5,800 metre," the translated city guide on the table told him) stood apart, towering above the rest. There were patches of snow at its summit and in the high wooded ravines on the south face.

When he had done his usual security checks on the room, Bond stood under the powerful hot shower, keeping his eyes open beneath the needling spray until they smarted. Then he turned the water to cold until he felt he had washed all traces of the journey from him. Wrapped in a towel, he called room service and asked for scrambled eggs, coffee, and a bottle each of mineral water and their best Scotch whisky.

No sooner had he replaced the receiver than the phone emitted an urgent bleep.

"Yes?"

"It's Darius Alizadeh. Did you have a good journey?"

"Uneventful," said Bond.

Alizadeh gave a deep laugh. "I like things to be uneventful," he said, "but only on aeroplanes. I'm sorry I didn't meet you at the airport. It's the one place I try not to be seen in public. I'm sending a car for you in half an hour, if that suits you. Then I'm going to give you the best dinner in Tehran. I hope you're not too tired? First you can come to my house for some caviar, fresh from the Caspian this morning. Does that suit you?"

He had a warm, bass voice with hardly a trace of accent.

"Half an hour," said Bond. "I'll be ready."

He called down to countermand the eggs, but told them to hurry with the whisky. He dressed in a short-sleeved white shirt, loose cotton trousers and black moccasins with reinforced-steel toecaps. He checked that his tropical-weight jacket, bought in a hurry that morning at the airport in Paris, showed no sign of the Walther PPK he'd strapped on beneath it.

Outside the hotel, a blue Mercedes was waiting for him. "I am Farshad, Mr. Alizadeh's driver," said a small man with a large white smile, holding the back door open for Bond. "My name, it means 'happy' in Farsi."

"Good for you, Happy," said Bond. "Where are we going?" The car shot off the hotel forecourt on to the road.

"We go to Shemiran, best part of Tehran. Very nice. You like it."

"I'm sure I shall," said Bond, as Farshad swerved between two oncoming trucks. "If we make it alive."

"Oh, yes!" Farshad laughed. "We go up Pahlavi Avenue. Is twelve miles long, is longest avenue in Middle East!"

"It certainly looks like the busiest," said Bond, as the car wove through a furiously contested junction where the traffic-lights seemed to offer no more than suggestions. After twenty minutes and what seemed a similar number of escapes from death, the Mercedes swung left and climbed a quiet road flanked by judas trees before turning into an asphalt driveway that snaked up through green lawns to a house with a white-pillared portico.

Bond walked up the steps to the front door, which opened as he approached.

"It's a pleasure to meet you. In my darkest hours I

feared that destiny would never bring James Bond to my home town. I am aware of the danger you have placed yourself in, but I rejoice in my own good fortune. Come inside."

Darius Alizadeh held out his hand and clasped Bond's. It was a firm dry shake that spoke of frankness and friendship—not the half-hearted, slippery recoil that Bond had encountered in Beirut and Cairo. Darius was over six feet tall, with a large head and dark features in which the deep-set brown eyes sparkled with conspiratorial camaraderie. His thick black hair was swept back from his forehead, and unashamedly shot through with grey at the temples and the sides. He wore a white suit with a raised collar in the Indian style and an open-necked blue shirt that had a look of the shop windows on Rome's via Condotti.

He led Bond through a long, wood-floored hall, past a wide staircase, then out through french windows and into the back garden. They crossed the terrace and went down into the green shade. Next to a pond was a table set with candles and numerous bottles. Darius gestured Bond to a low, padded chair.

"Relax," he said. "Enjoy the garden. It's good to be cool at last, isn't it? I normally take a beer before cocktails, just to wash away the city dust. The beer's pretty filthy, imported American, but it'll give you something to do while I mix you a proper drink. And it's very, very cold."

He rang a small brass bell on the table, and a young man in traditional Persian dress emerged from the dusk of the terrace. "Babak," said Darius. He clapped his hands. "We have a guest. Let's move."

The young man gave a short salaam and a wide smile as he scurried off.

A few seconds later Bond held an icy beer in his left hand. Behind him, a row of tall cypress trees gave privacy to Darius's garden, and in front of them were innumerable roses, mostly black and yellow, so far as Bond could make out by the light of the torches in the lawn. Round the rectangular pond were mosaic tiles in intricate patterns.

"Gardens mean a lot to us here," said Darius, following Bond's eyes. "Water is almost like a god to us in such a dry country. Listen. You can hear our little waterfall at the end of the lawn. I designed it myself and had it made by a craftsman from Isfahan whose grandfather worked on one of the mosques. Would you like a dry martini, vodka and tonic, or Scotch whisky and soda?"

Bond opted for the martini and watched as Darius shook the ingredients in the silver shaker. He nodded his approval over the rim of the glass:

the ice had fiercely chilled the liquor without dilut-
ing it.

"Now," said Darius, "you'd better tell me how I
can help you."

As Babak returned with a silver dish of caviar,
Bond told Darius what he knew of Julius Gorner. He
had trusted Darius from the first moment and his
instinct in such things was seldom wrong. He also
knew that Darius had been head of the Tehran station for twenty years and was well regarded by M.

Darius spooned a large dollop of caviar—equivalent in size to a small plum—on to one of the delicate
plates and squeezed lime juice over it. With a quick
movement of his hands, using a small piece of flatbread, he transferred the whole plateful to his mouth,
following it with a long pull of iced neat vodka.

"Terribly Russian of me, I know," he smiled, "but
it's how I like it best. It's not bad, this Beluga, is it?"
He bent his nose to the plate. "It should smell of the
sea but never of fish."

He lit a cigarette and settled back in his chair.
"Well, I've heard of this man Gorner, James. Of
course I have. But perhaps you should know a thing
or two about me first. My mother was from the
Qashqai tribe, widely regarded as the most treach-
erous, bloodthirsty and ruthless people in Persia.
When the Shah was plotting his return with the

Americans, he never even considered trying to win them to his side." Darius threw back his head and laughed. "The Kurds, the Arabs, the Reformers, the Baluchistanis, even the mullahs, yes, but never the terrible Qashqai. My father, on the other hand, came from a diplomatic family in Tehran which had long ties of allegiance to the West. He himself was educated at Harvard and I studied at Oxford, which, in case you're wondering, is why I sound like an English gentleman. I know this country from all sides. I can lose myself with the tribesmen in the desert or I can make small-talk in French at their embassy down the road—though frankly I prefer the former. I've seen many nationalities come and go in Persia—or Iran, as Reza Shah, the current Shah's father, wanted us to call it. Turks, Russians, French, German, American, British. Here we are at the hinge of East and West. The only country between Russia and a warm-water port. Of course, they have the Black Sea, but they can't get past the Turks, who are the gatekeepers at the Bosphorus and the Dardanelles. Good God, can you imagine more cantankerous guardians?"

Darius leaned forward and helped himself to more caviar, which he dispatched in the same way as before. "My point is this, James. We are used to being interfered with. Sometimes we feel ourselves like a poor old hooker in the rue St. Denis. Anyone can have us for a price. During the war, the Allies thought we were too chummy with the Germans, so they invaded us and the Shah was booted out. Then they thought Mr. Mossadegh, our fine independent prime minister, was too open to the Russians. They also distrusted him because he was often photographed in public wearing what looked like pyjamas. So the Americans sent a gentleman called Kermit Roosevelt to help mount a coup and bring the Shah home from exile and back on to the throne. I confess I was of some minor assistance to Mr. Roosevelt. We don't mind any of this too much, so long as we are left to get on with our own lives. Tehran is a nest of spies. It always has been and it always will be. One witty British visitor suggested that the Russians and the Americans should simply share apartments to cut down on the cost of mutual bugging. But there's one thing that always sets alarm bells ringing— and that's when a foreigner comes in and wants too much. People are welcome to try and make money here, though it's difficult to do it legally. Apart from oil. We also accept a degree of political interference if there's something in it for us: protection, influence, arms, dollars. But not both at the same time. And everything I've heard about this Gorner has made me extremely uneasy. And, as I hope I may have suggested, I'm not easily frightened."

Darius made another jug of martinis. "Have some more caviar, James. In ten minutes I'll get Farshad to drive us down to the best restaurant in Tehran. It's in the south of the city, near the bazaar. No one'll recognize me there. Pretty well everyone in Tehran knows I work for your employer. Your boss has a theory that more people with useful information can come to me if they know who I am, and he may be right. The drawback is that I can't be seen in public with you. It would be dangerous for you. But down there, no one knows who I am. Also, the food, James . . ." He spread his arms wide. "Better than your mother made it. As good as a poem by Hafez."

"I never imagined you were so poetic, Darius," said Bond, with a smile. "My colleagues are normally cold-eyed men with guns."

"I don't believe you for a minute, James. But gardens and poetry are close to the Persian soul. And poems *about* gardens, even better. 'I saw a garden pure as paradise,' as Nezami put it. 'A myriad different hues were mingled there / A myriad scents drenched miles of perfumed air / The rose lay in the hyacinth's embrace / The jasmine—' "

"The car is waiting, sir." Babak had materialized from the darkness.

"Damn you, Babak! You have no soul. I've told you before not to interrupt when I'm reciting poetry.

Are you ready, James? Shall we go and do battle with the madmen of the highway? Are you hungry?"

"Certainly." Bond had declined the airline food and, apart from the caviar, had eaten nothing since a limp croissant at the airport in Paris.

Farshad was waiting at the front with the Mercedes, and within a few moments they were heading south on the cacophony of Pahlavi Avenue, weaving through the traffic as though Farshad believed this was their last ever chance of eating.

After they crossed Molavi Avenue, Bond gave up trying to orientate himself and surrendered himself to Darius's narrative.

"Kermit Roosevelt," Darius was saying, "was rather an absurd man, to be honest. I used to play tennis with him sometimes and when he hit a bad shot he would chastise himself by saying, 'Ooh, Roosevelt!' This was unfortunate since he was meant to be called 'Mr. Green' or some such thing. I've never seen a man drink so much liquor on the job. You'd think he was nervous or something. Cases of whisky and vodka used to go into the little place where he and his friends were hiding out. When the big day came to put the Shah back on the throne Roosevelt discovered that it was the Muslim weekend, a Friday. Then, of course, it was the Christian weekend. So they all had another drink and waited for Monday. When they'd finally got the tanks out and the thick-necks from the bazaar had been paid to get the demonstrators on to the street, they found the Shah hadn't signed the *firmans*, which were the binding documents dismissing Mossadegh and empowering himself. So the Shahanshah, the King of Kings, was lurking on the Caspian coast, the tanks and the mob were on the street and the paperwork was in an office in Tehran!" Darius gave his huge, throaty laugh. "We got there in the end."

He leaned forward and gave a brief order in Farsi to Farshad, who swerved with a tearing-tyre screech into a side road and accelerated.

"Apologies, James. I have talked too much. I have so much to tell you about this wonderful country. I think it's important that you know as much as possible before you confront this Gorner and his people. Forewarned, as the English proverb has it, is forearmed."

"There's no need to apologize. But why the Grand Prix tactics?"

"In my verbosity I'd failed to notice a black American car—an Oldsmobile, I believe—that was behind us. Just as I was telling you about the Shah I realized we were being followed. I asked Farshad to lose him."

"And he was certainly happy to oblige."

"Happy by name, happy by nature. He loves a chase. We're off the map now, James. Foreigners don't come this far south. Over there is what they call the New Town. It's full of brothels, bars and gambling dens. That way, down there, is a shanty town, the really poor arrivals from the country. Arabs and refugees from Afghanistan. They live in squalor."

"You don't think much of the Arabs, do you?" said Bond.

"One doesn't disparage foreigners in one's own country, even refugees," said Darius. "The Persians, as you know, are an Aryan people, not Semitic like the Arabs. As for the Arabs themselves, well . . . They lack culture, James. All they have in their countries—the Iraqis, the Saudis, the Arabs of the Gulf—are a few things they stole or copied from us. But that's enough. Here we are."

Darius insisted that Bond precede him through the doorway of what looked like a carpet shop with a red bulb over the lintel. Just inside, an old man was sitting on a low bench, smoking a water-pipe.

Bond hesitated, but Persian etiquette apparently obliged him to go ahead of his host.

"Trust me, James," said Darius, putting his hand on Bond's shoulder.

Just as Bond ducked to go beneath the low lintel, he noticed from the corner of his eye that a black Oldsmobile had pulled up opposite and immediately doused its lights.

8. WELCOME TO THE PARADISE CLUB

Bond found himself in a large underground room lit by candles held in iron sconces. They were shown to a table on which were already set out bowls of pistachios, mulberries and walnuts, a bottle of Chivas Regal and two jugs of iced water. There were no menus. A group of four musicians was quietly playing stringed instruments on a low, carpeted platform and the other dozen or so tables were all occupied.

Darius let out a sigh of contentment as he poured the whisky. A waitress arrived with a tray full of small dishes that included various flatbreads, yoghurts, salads and fresh herbs. Next, a steaming tureen was placed between Bond and Darius.

"Lamb's head and feet soup." Darius translated the words spoken by the waitress as she ladled some into Bond's bowl.

It had a surprisingly clean and delicate flavour.

"James, you must put in some *torshi*," said Darius, handing him a small bowl of pickles. "That's right. Good, isn't it?"

"Extremely," said Bond, trying not to sound surprised.

"And the waitress. Isn't she lovely?"

"She's ravishing," said Bond, appreciatively. It was no exaggeration.

"Some visitors still expect Persian women to be veiled from head to foot. Thank God Reza Shah put an end to all that. He wanted a modern country run on Western lines, and you couldn't have half the population creeping around like nuns in mourning. You'd be amazed, but some of the women in the most traditional families were reluctant to give up the symbol of their slavery. Policemen were told to rip the veils off them in the street. It was a farce. Of course, the *chador* was only ever a city phenomenon. Country women had their own clothes and didn't cover their faces anyway. Persian women today are

127

very . . . What's the word I read in all the London papers nowadays? 'Liberated'! After dinner, I'll show you what I mean. Your good health."

Darius raised his glass and Bond lifted his in return. He thought back to his lengthy sabbatical and the doubts about his future that had troubled him in Rome. It seemed a long time ago. Darius Alizadeh's company was enough to extinguish any sense of uncertainty. Merely sitting next to him was like being plugged into a high-voltage power source. Darius would be paid modestly by the Service for his work in Tehran, Bond thought—though his house suggested family wealth, or at least happy dealings on the stock exchange, which had perhaps made the salary unimportant. In any case, Bond saw in Darius a kindred spirit, someone who was prepared to risk his life not for money but for the thrill of the game.

Thinking of Rome brought to mind Mrs. Larissa Rossi, as he had first known her. Bond never allowed personal sentiment to influence his work, but it would be foolish to deny that the urgency of his mission for M, and for his country, was made more intense by his recollection of the tears he had seen Scarlett shed when she spoke of Gorner's treatment of her sister.

The black-haired waitress bent over the table once more. This time she put down an iron pan still spitting from the flame, containing sautéed shrimps with herbs and tamarind. Then came a flat earthenware dish piled up with concentric layers—orange, green, white and scarlet—like a multi-coloured volcano on the point of erupting. It seemed amazing that something so exotic and bright could have been conjured from the darkness at the back of this subterranean room.

"Javaher polow," said Darius. "Jewelled rice. The layers are orange peel, saffron, barberries and—I forget what else. Anyway, it tastes almost as good as it looks. *Nush-e Jan!"*

"Same to you," said Bond. "Now, Darius, is there anything more I need to know about Gorner? For instance, where to find him."

Darius looked serious for a moment. "You won't need to look, James. He'll find you. He has more spies out there than Savak. It wouldn't surprise me if the car on our tail was one of his. He has an office in Tehran, which is connected with his pharmaceutical business. It's near Ferdowsi Square. I'm pretty certain he's got something going on in the Caspian as well. But it's very hard to get near him there. It looks like a boat-building yard, nothing more than that. It's in Noshahr, which is a smart resort. It's a Shemiran-sur-Mer, where the richer people from Tehran go in the summer to escape the heat and fumes. The Shah has a summer palace there. But it's got commercial docks as well and that's where we think Gorner has some secret activity. As for his main base, that's somewhere in the desert."

"Do we know where?" said Bond.

Darius shook his head. "Nobody knows. He's a hard man to track down. He has at least two small planes and a helicopter as well, I think. Savak, if you know who I mean—"

"I know them by reputation," said Bond. "Your very own secret police, trained by Mossad and the CIA, with Israeli ruthlessness and American guile."

"Indeed. They're not something we're always proud of, James, but . . . Anyway, Mossad dispatched a four-man squad to Bam, on the southern edge of the desert, with a brief merely to search from there and send back photographs or details of any desert hideout or unusual activity."

"And?"

"Nothing came back."

"Nothing? Not even the men?"

"Nothing. Well, to be strictly accurate, a parcel came back, addressed to Savak headquarters in Tehran, postmarked Bam. It contained two tongues and a hand."

"Delightful," said Bond.

"Characteristic," said Darius.

The waitress leaned over the low table to take away the plates. She was barefoot, with a long blue linen dress whose bodice was inlaid with small golden sequins and mother-of-pearl decorations. It was cut modestly across the top, though low enough to give Bond a close-up of her golden skin as she bent over him. She smiled in a natural, unembarrassed way as she drew herself up.

A few minutes later she brought a bottle of French wine with bowls of stuffed peppers, aubergine and tomatoes. Then came an oval salver on which lay six sweet-and-sour stuffed quail with rose petals.

"I hope you like it, James," said Darius. "The way they cook it is one of the best-kept secrets in Tehran. The birds have no bones, you can cut them with your fork. The only thing to match it is their whole baby lamb stuffed with pistachios. But even between the two of us . . ." He spread his arms wide.

"What do you know about his sidekick?" said Bond, as the taste of the hot roast quail exploded in his mouth. "The man in the legionnaire's hat."

"Not much," said Darius. "Chagrin, they call him, though I doubt that's his real name. I believe he's North Vietnamese. A veteran of jungle warfare. God knows where Gorner found him. Tehran, probably. We do attract some unusual people. Misfits, vagabonds. I used to know a couple of Americans called

Red and Jake. I'd meet them in the bars and cabarets and it would be like talking to a Brooklyn taxi driver. Then I heard them speak a Persian dialect, say Kermanshah or Khorramshahr, and they were perfect in it. They'd got it from their parents who'd been *émigrés* to New York. They'd spend a week or so in town, working their way through whisky and women, then vanish back into the desert. I never knew if they were CIA or what. It's one of the things I love about Tehran. It's a bit like Casablanca in 'forty-two. The country itself is not at war, but you still have partisans, *francs-tireurs*, stool-pigeons, agents, secret police. You have to watch your back, but in the meantime you meet some pretty interesting types."

"Do you know the CIA people?" said Bond.

"I know one," said Darius. "Guy by the name of J. D. Silver. 'Carmen,' they call him. 'Carmen' Silver. Don't ask me why."

"Do you work with him?" said Bond.

Darius shook his head swiftly. "No, no, no. There are two types of CIA man in my experience. Those who came out of the OSS and before that the Marines or similar. Men like you and me, James. Or Big Will George, Jimmy Ruscoe, Arthur Henry. Soldiers, patriots, adventurers."

"Or Felix Leiter," said Bond.

"Yes," said Darius. "I've never met him, but I've

heard he was one of the good guys. Then there's the new kind."

"Who are they?"

"Technocrats. Thin, pale men in button-down collars. Carmen Silver's one of those. I'm not sure he has a mind of his own."

"Isn't he just doing what his bosses at Langley tell him?"

"Probably. But you know as well as I do, James, that even a secret agent has a choice. In fact, a secret agent especially has a choice. Follow the line of short-term profit in a bank and the worst is that you're a small cog in a dull machine. But if you fail to exercise your judgement as a licensed agent with a gun on foreign soil . . ."

Bond smiled. "You're quite a sentimentalist, Darius."

"No, James. I don't believe in sentiment, I believe in class. It's easy for a children's doctor, say, to have what they call 'soul.' Save the kid's life, well done, you're a good guy. But put a man like you, James, in a place like this with just that Walther under your armpit and—"

"You—"

"I saw the shape, I guessed the make." Darius shrugged. "What I mean is, the more your life is in the shadow, off the record, the more you need to have a compass. With guns pointed at your head, in one split second, you must make decisions far more complicated than that children's doctor. For him, it's operate or not. He's got time to work it out. You've got no time in which to choose between ten shades of grey. And you, James, I can tell you have the class, the sense of truth in you. My father had a phrase for it. The man who has what it takes, he used to say, is a 'citizen of eternity.'"

"Whatever you say, the Americans have been with us since Pearl Harbor," said Bond. "I operate alone, but it's good to know they're there."

"Sure," said Darius. "Like a big, dependable puppy."

After the waitress had returned once more to the table and gone back to the kitchen with their plates, Darius said, "You like her, don't you, James? I can ask her to join us at the cabaret, if you like."

"I'm in your hands tonight, Darius. Do what comes naturally."

Bond was thinking how, for all his talk and geniality, Darius had never stopped observing, either in the car or in the restaurant.

The girl returned with a bottle of *araq*, a harsh aniseed liqueur to go with a bowl of cantaloupe and peach, served with honey and pistachio cakes. Coffee followed, sweet and thick, then Darius spoke quietly to the waitress.

"Zohreh is happy to come with us, James," he said. "I told her we'd bring her back in two hours' time."

"Zohreh?"

"Yes, it's a pretty name, isn't it? It means Venus."

"The goddess of love?"

"No, the planet, I suspect. But you never know your luck. Let's go."

Farshad was standing by the car, finishing a plate of rice and kebabs that had been sent out to him. He put it down quickly and ran round to open the back door for Zohreh.

When Farshad had started the car engine, Zohreh spoke to him in Farsi. He chuckled happily and slotted the gear lever into first.

"She's telling him where to go," said Darius. "Some special place she knows. It's just opened. A kind of East meets West, I gather."

"In the New Town?"

"Certainly not, James. South Tehran, maybe, but a classy place, I promise you. It's just opened. It has a lot of gimmicks and a lot of Western money behind it."

As they moved off, Bond saw the lights of the black Oldsmobile come on behind them. He gestured with his thumb and Darius nodded.

Farshad drove rapidly down narrow, tree-lined streets. There were fewer cars in this part of town and it was nearly midnight, so the roads had started to empty.

"Hold tight, James," said Darius, then barked an order to Farshad, who swung the wheel and took them down a side alley. The wing of the big Mercedes clipped a dustbin and sent it clanging over the cobbles. Farshad stamped on the accelerator, took them blind through a junction, right with a tearing of rubber into an unlit back-street, then three more lurching turns until they emerged on to a wide boulevard, where he dropped his speed and sat back with an evil-sounding laugh.

"Thank you, Farshad," said Darius, drily, in English. He put his hand on Zohreh's to reassure her, but she seemed unperturbed. From what he'd seen in Tehran, Bond thought, it was possible that the girl thought this was normal driving.

Eventually, they stopped beside what looked like a warehouse, set back in a fenced yard a short way from the street. There were no signs or coloured lights. It reminded Bond of some of the dingier back lots of Los Angeles.

"It's called the Paradise Club," said Darius.

For Bond, the name stirred the faint memory of an exciting juvenile visit to the gaming tables. They went past the bouncer on the front door, into whose hand Darius pressed some notes, then down a concrete-lined corridor to double wooden doors with iron studs. A young woman in traditional costume welcomed them and pressed a pedal with her foot. The doors parted silently, letting Bond, Darius and Zohreh into an enormous room, the size of an aircraft hangar, whose furthest wall contained a waterfall cascading over crimson-illuminated rocks into a pool of turquoise water in which a dozen naked women were swimming. Around the pool, arranged as though in a garden, the guests lay on imitation-grass carpets or reclined on loungers and padded chairs, where the chastely clad waitresses brought them drinks and sweetmeats. To one side of the huge area was a raised platform where people danced to Western pop records, but in the "garden" there was a string quintet of traditional Persian musicians.

Zohreh turned to Bond and smiled, her lips parting over dazzling white teeth. "You like it?"

A young woman approached them and spoke to Darius in Farsi. She wore the same uniform as the doorkeeper—a cream-coloured robe held with a scarlet sash. Although it was quite demure, Bond could see from where the two halves of the material met between her breasts that she wore nothing beneath it. The candlelight and the coloured bulbs in the wall brackets gave a glow to her skin, the colour of rose under gold.

"This is Salma," Darius explained. "She is here to make sure we enjoy ourselves. There are a number of options open to us. I suggest we look into the opium room first, then the famous hammam."

"I'm not sure I feel like a Turkish bath," said Bond.

"You will," said Darius, "when you see this one. It's a rather special kind, I understand."

They followed Salma to a raised platform on one side of the huge open area.

"The name Salma, by the way," said Darius, into Bond's ear, "means 'sweetheart.' "

"Her parents must have been clairvoyant."

"Enough English charm, James—though I shall tell her what you said. Have you ever smoked opium?"

They found themselves in a square room with tapestry-covered couches round the walls. On the floor lay outsize cushions, on a few of which men reclined as they sucked at opium pipes prepared for them by one of Salma's colleagues at a low central table with a glowing brazier in the middle. Soft Persian music was playing, although no musicians were visible.

Zohreh sat down cross-legged near the table and gestured to Bond and Darius to do likewise. The girl took a stick of opium, shaped as a tube, and cut a piece from it. She placed it in the china bowl of a pipe, then, with silver pincers, took an ember from the brazier and held it over the opium. She gave the mouthpiece of the pipe to Darius, who took it with a wink at Bond. Then the girl blew on the ember until it glowed red and the opium beneath it sizzled. Smoke rose through a small hole above the china bowl and Darius sucked it in. Eventually, he passed the pipe to Bond, who took it with some hesitation. He didn't want his capacities impaired by drugs, but was reluctant to offend his host. He took some smoke into his mouth, nodded his approval, and passed the pipe back to Darius. When he thought no one was watching, he allowed the smoke to escape through his nostrils.

Around them, half a dozen men lay back among the cushions, their eyes closed, with expressions of dreamy pleasure.

"It's a problem for some of these men," Darius said. "Opium used in moderation is all right. Say once a week. But in this country too many people are its slave, not its master. At least it's a pure drug, the untreated juice of poppy. Its compounds and derivatives, like heroin, are far more dangerous."

The pipe was offered to Zohreh, who laughed and shook her head. Darius smiled. "Our women are 'liberated,' but not quite that liberated yet, James."

"Who are the girls swimming in the pool beneath the waterfall?"

"Celestial virgins," said Darius, and began to cough. Bond couldn't tell if he was laughing or whether it was the opium smoke.

Wiping his eyes with the back of his hand, Darius said, "They are paid by the management to disport themselves in the water. I expect when they have their clothes on they are hostesses, like Salma. I think the setting is meant to represent heaven. If you have been a very good boy on earth, the Prophet promises that you will be welcomed in heaven by numerous virgins. I forget whether they merely serve you drinks or perform more intimate functions. It's a long time since I read the Koran."

"But you used to believe it?" said Bond.

"Of course," said Darius. "I was a well-brought-up little boy in a proper Muslim household. My father had spent a good deal of time in America but that doesn't mean he'd lost his roots. Anyway, once upon a time I dare say you believed in Father Christmas."

"Yes," said Bond. "The evidence was more immediate. Coloured packages. Half-eaten carrots left by his reindeer on the hearth."

Darius shook his head. "And to think that all we had was faith." He got to his feet, a little unsteadily. "I believe Salma would like to show us the hammam now."

They went first to a bar in the main room, where

Zohreh ordered gin and tonic and the men had whisky. Salma invited them to bring their drinks and follow her. They went down an open internal staircase until they were alongside the turquoise waters where the "virgins" splashed. Bond found himself being taken by the arm. "Come along, Mr. Bond," Zohreh whispered. "There are more good things to see." She gave a tinkling laugh.

Through another iron-studded wooden door, they came to a tiled area where a young woman in a white robe welcomed them and handed Darius, Bond and Zohreh two large white towels each.

Zohreh pointed to a door with a figure of a man, then went through the women's entrance.

"This is where we take our clothes off, James," said Darius.

"Are we joining the virgins?"

"I should explain," said Darius, removing his shirt to reveal a deep chest covered with black and grey hair. "The hammam plays an important part in Persian life. We are a clean people. Everyone must wash their hands and face before praying, but in certain circumstances—for instance, after sexual activity—a Grand Ablution is necessary. Even the meanest village will have a bath-house where such things take place. Men and women go at different times. For the women it's generally during the day,

141

when the men are meant to be at work. Of course, it's a very easy way for women to keep tabs on one another. A young bride generally goes every day until she's pregnant. Then—sadly—rather less often. If a woman in her forties still goes regularly you can be sure the others will be gossiping like mad."

"So we'll be going to the men's section?" said Bond.

"Not exactly," said Darius. "Wrap your towel round your waist and take the spare one with you. As I understand from Zohreh, the idea of the Paradise Club is that you find heaven already on earth. And this is it: a mixed hammam. Shall we see?"

They went through a door and found themselves on a balcony that overlooked two large baths. Around the walls there were open steam rooms of differing temperatures and between them private cubicles with doors.

Although the whole area was clouded by steam and the lights were low, there was no mistaking the fact that in the main baths men and women bathed naked together, laughing and occasionally drinking from the long glasses set down on the edge of the baths by girl attendants in white tunics.

Traditional music was playing, and the scent of roses and geraniums was carried on the steam. The tiled walls were painted with scenes from a heavenly garden. Bond saw Zohreh drop her towel and go down the steps into the smaller of the two baths.

"Do you have clubs like this in London?" said Darius, innocently.

"Oh, yes," said Bond. "Pall Mall is full of them. But you don't have to choose between the opium and the hammam. Just remember to pot the blue before the pink at snooker."

A few moments later, Bond found himself face to face with Salma in the heated water. An attendant threw some fresh rose petals on to the surface. In this light Salma's skin was an even more beguiling colour.

"I've asked Zohreh to join us," said Darius.

Shortly afterwards, the foursome was complete. Bond leaned back against the side and sipped the cold mint drink that had been offered him.

"Is this . . . heaven?" said Salma, in faltering English.

"If so," said Bond, "I shall convert to Islam on my return home. What happens in those cubicles?"

"Whatever you negotiate," said Darius.

"For money?"

"No. For love of your fellow heaven-seeker. But not, alas," he added, looking at Salma, "with the staff. Otherwise it would not be a club but—"

"I know what it would be," said Bond.

Too quickly, their time was up. Zohreh indicated to Darius, with a regretful glance at her watchless wrist, that she needed to return. Bond allowed his eyes to linger on the naked girls as they preceded them from the water and took up their towels.

"You look sad to see them go, James."

"It breaks my heart," said Bond.

"We'll see what we can do to mend it while you're with us in Tehran. Now let's go and rescue poor old Farshad."

Dried, dressed and reassembled, the three said goodbye to Salma, whom Bond and Darius tipped handsomely, then walked back through the main area, past the waterfall and up to the entrance.

Outside, the air, by comparison with the fragrance of the Paradise Club, seemed unbearably hot, and heavy with exhaust fumes. They began to walk across the lot to where the blue Mercedes was parked.

As they approached it, Bond grabbed Darius's arm. "Wait here," he said.

He took his gun from its holster and went forward carefully. Something about the angle of Farshad's body, visible through the driver's window, was wrong. Holding his gun ahead of him, Bond circled the car with his back to the bodywork.

Without looking round, he opened the driver's door. Farshad's body tumbled out on to the ground. The footwell was awash with blood. Farshad was dead, but his hand was clamped tight round something that had recently been ripped from his mouth.

9. THE STRAWBERRY MARK

Breakfast was brought to Bond's room at eight the next morning, although he had placed no order. It consisted of tea without milk, a rectangle of sheep's cheese with herbs and a slab of flatbread that looked like the bathmat in the next room. He told the waiter to take it away and try again. After two tense telephone calls, he eventually managed to extract some black coffee and an omelette from the kitchen, which he consumed while he glanced through the *Herald Tribune*, sitting at his window overlooked by Mount Demavend.

Darius had to go to Farshad's funeral, which,

by Islamic law, had to take place within twenty-four hours. Bond felt uneasy at the thought that his own presence in Tehran had led to the man's death, which he presumed was a warning from Gorner's people. But Farshad must have known the risks his job entailed, and doubtless Darius would compensate his family well. "Happy" in his life, but not in its ending, thought Bond, as he headed for the shower.

He decided to drive to Noshahr to investigate the docks and see if he could find out what Gorner was up to there. He would need an interpreter and thought that whoever he found might as well double as a driver. It was unlikely that Tehran would come up with a car that he would want to drive, and in any case a local man would be more at home with the rules of the road—if there were any—on the hairpin bends of the Elburz mountains.

First, Bond took one of the orange taxis from the rank outside the hotel and ordered it to the main post office. It was another intensely hot day and, as the cab engaged with the traffic of Pahlavi Avenue, he thought wistfully of the cooler air he might find at the Caspian. The taxi eventually swung on to Sepah Avenue, with ministerial offices on one side, the old Palace of the Kingdom and the Senate on the other.

They pulled up outside the yellow brick façade of the post office, and Bond told the driver to wait. In his hotel room he had already composed a hundred-group cable addressed to the Chairman, Universal Export, London. He used a simple transposition code based on the fact that it was the third day of the week and that the date was the fourth of the seventh month. He knew little about cryptography and, for security's sake, in case he was ever captured, had preferred to keep it that way.

He lit one of his remaining Morland's cigarettes with the three gold rings and stood beneath the idly turning ceiling fan while he waited for the cable boy to tell him he had transmitted successfully.

As he did so, he noticed that he was being watched by a thin man with reddish-brown hair and white skin. He was sitting at a table where other Tehranis were filling in forms and stamping letters. He held a paper cup of water to his mouth, but didn't seem to drink from it. Although his head was steady, his eyes were swivelling constantly round the room, while the unmoving cup seemed only to be a cover for his mouth.

The cable boy called out the all-clear and Bond collected his papers from the counter.

As he went down the steps of the post office, he heard a voice behind him.

"Mr. Bond?"

He turned, without speaking.

It was the man from inside. He held out his hand. "My name is Silver. J. D. Silver. I work for General Motors."

"But of course you do," said Bond. The handshake was wet, and Bond discreetly wiped his fingers on the back of his trousers.

"I wondered if I could buy you a cup of tea. Or a soda."

Silver had a reedy voice. Up close, his long nose and fair eyelashes gave his face the look, Bond thought, of a watchful fox terrier.

Bond glanced at his watch. "I have a few minutes," he said.

"There's a café on Elizabeth Boulevard," said Silver. "It's quiet. This your cab?"

Bond nodded and Silver gave the driver instructions. Sitting alongside him, Bond had time to note the Brooks Brothers suit, the button-down striped shirt and college tie. The accent was educated East Coast— Boston, perhaps—and his manner was relaxed.

"Where you staying?"

"Uptown," said Bond, noncommittally. "How's business? I see a lot of American cars, but not many new ones."

"We get along," said Silver, unembarrassed. "We'll maybe talk more when we get there." He looked meaningfully at the driver.

Bond was happy to keep silent. The phrase of Darius's—"a citizen of eternity"—went through his mind.

"Tell you what," said Silver, "maybe we'll just stay on the sidewalk. Elizabeth Boulevard. It's named for your queen of England. It has trees, benches, ice-creams . . . I like it there."

"I notice there's a Roosevelt Avenue, too," said Bond. "Would that be Franklin D. or Kermit?"

Silver smiled. "Well, I guess it wasn't Eleanor at any rate," he said.

Bond paid the fare and followed Silver to a bench beneath a tree. Further up the street, he could see the entrance to a park, and on the other side the campus of Tehran University. It was, Bond thought, typical spy country: brush contacts, dead drops, all the rudiments of "tradecraft" could be unobtrusively carried out in this busy, recreational area. In the middle of the road a channel, with swiftly running water, was flanked by plane trees. At intervals there were long sticks with metal drinking cups wired to the end, which thirsty passers-by dipped into the water.

"Cute, isn't it?" said Silver. "The water starts in the Elburz. It's pretty clean up in Shemiran, but by the time it gets south of the bazaar . . . Oh, boy. But they're proud of it. These little channels are called

jubs. They come from underground waterways—
qanats—their big irrigation scheme. They've managed to get water down into half the desert. You can
tell where they are in the countryside when you see a
kind of molehill on the surface."

"Is that the access point?" said Bond.

"Yeah. It's their major contribution to modern
technology." Silver sat down on the bench. "You
wanna get an ice-cream?"

Bond shook his head. He lit the very last of his
Morland's while Silver went to a vendor a few yards
behind them.

When he returned, Silver took out a clean handkerchief and opened it on his lap while he licked the
pistachio ice-cream.

"What is it you want to tell me?"

Silver smiled. "Ah, just shooting the breeze. People come into town, they're new, maybe they don't
get straight away what a delicate situation we have
here. You look around, you see these desert guys, like
Bedouins, in their run-down automobiles . . . And,
hey, look at that."

A red double-decker bus—a London Routemas-
ter—went slowly past, leaving a cloud of black diesel
exhaust.

"You sometimes think it's kind of like Africa
someplace," said Silver. "And all the kebabs and rice."

He laughed. "God, I'd die happy if I never looked another piece of skewered meat between the eyes. And your people. The English."

"British," said Bond.

"Right. We're sitting on your Queen Elizabeth Boulevard. It all looks hunky-dory, doesn't it? The Shah's your pal. The Allies pushed him out in the Second World War because he looked a little too open to the Germans. We were happy enough with the guy who took his place—this Mossadegh in his pyjamas. But you got the wind up when he nationalized the oil and kicked out all the BP men. Boy, did you not like that. You came to us and said, 'Let's get Mossy out, let's get the old Shah back and BP running the oil wells again.'"

"And you did," said Bond.

Silver wiped his lips carefully with the handkerchief, then reopened it on his lap. "Well, by chance, things started to go wrong. Mossy starts to look too pally with the Soviets. They have a border, you know. This country is the one we watch most carefully, along with Afghanistan. And so we decided to make a move."

Bond nodded. "I'm grateful for the history lesson."

Silver's tongue came out and licked neatly round the edges of the ice-cream. "What I'm trying to say is that this is a place where everything is on the move. There's not just two sides—us and them. The Persians know that better than anyone. That's why they put up with us. More than that, they use us to protect them. They have American arms and thousands of our personnel. And do you know what? Three years ago they passed a law making all Americans stationed in Persia immune from prosecution."

"All of you?" said Bond.

"You got it. If the Shah runs over my pet dog, he gets called to account. If I run over the Shah, they can't lay a finger on me."

"I'd still take cabs if I were you," said Bond.

Silver wiped his mouth one more time and, having finished his ice-cream, folded the handkerchief and replaced it in his coat pocket.

He looked across the street, through the plane trees and the column of orange taxis.

He turned to Bond and smiled. "It's not easy, Mr. Bond. We need to work together. Things are balanced on a knife edge here. America is fighting a lonely war for freedom in Vietnam and, despite all we did back there in the Second World War, you haven't sent a single soldier in to help. Sometimes the people back in Washington—not me, but those guys—they get to thinking that you people aren't serious about the war on Communism."

"Oh, we're serious about the Cold War," said Bond. His own body bore the scars of just how serious he himself had been.

"I'm glad to hear that. But don't rock the boat, will you?"

"I'll do what I came here to do," said Bond. "But I've never had any problems with your countrymen." He was thinking of Felix Leiter, his great shark-maimed Texan friend. The first time he had met Felix, Bond saw that he held the interests of his own organization, the CIA, far above the common concerns of the North Atlantic allies. Bond sympathized. The Service was his own first loyalty. He also agreed with Felix in distrusting the French, whom he regarded as riddled with Communist sympathizers at every level.

"That's good." Silver stood up and began to move off. He hailed a taxi from the rapidly moving orange stream.

"One last thing," he said. "This Julius Gorner character. He's part of a much bigger plan than you can imagine."

Silver got into the taxi and wound down the rear window. "Don't go near him, Mr. Bond. Please take my advice. Don't get yourself within a hundred miles of him."

The cab pulled off into the main stream without

signalling, to be met by a cacophony of horns. Bond stuck out an arm to hail a taxi for himself.

With Darius unavailable at Farshad's funeral, Bond was forced to rely on the hotel's front desk to find him a car and driver for his visit to the Caspian. The concierge said the car firm's best man, who spoke fluent English, would be available from eight the next morning, and Bond decided it was worth waiting.

He ordered lunch of caviar and a grilled chicken kebab to be sent to his room with a jug of iced vodka martinis and two fresh limes. After he had eaten, he spread out some maps he had bought from the hotel shop on the bed and made a study of the Noshahr waterfront, its bazaar at Azadi Square, its commercial docks, marinas and pleasure beaches.

Then he looked at the map of Persia. The country was between Turkey to the west, and Afghanistan to the east. Its southern frontier was the Persian Gulf, its northern limit the Caspian Sea. While it also bordered Soviet Russia in the north-west corner, through Azerbaijan, the roads looked poor. But from the northern shore of the Caspian, through Astrakhan, it was only a short way to Stalingrad.

Bond tried to think through the implications of the geography. If Gorner had a drug connection with the Soviet Union, it was difficult to see how he could get the drugs out by air from a remote airstrip in the southern desert. Small planes wouldn't have enough fuel, while larger ones would appear on Soviet radar.

There was something about the Caspian that kept drawing his eye back to it. The problem was that the Soviet town of Astrakhan in the north was about six hundred miles, he calculated, from the Persian littoral in the south. What kind of sea-going vessel could make that distance feasible?

Meanwhile, the Persian interior was largely taken up by two deserts. To the north, and closer to Tehran, was the salt desert, Dasht-e Kavir. To the south-east, much more remote, was the sand desert, Dasht-e Lut. It appeared to support no human settlement at all, yet it was to its southern edge, at Bam, that Savak had sent its patrol in search of Gorner.

Presumably Savak knew something. Although it was less convenient for Tehran and the Caspian, this desert, the Dasht-e Lut, had a railway on its southern rim through the sizeable cities of Kerman and Yazd, both of which also had airstrips, though it was hard to tell from the map how big they were. There were also major-looking roads on this southern side of the Dasht-e Lut desert via Zahedan right up to the Afghan border just beyond Zabol.

Zabol. It sounded like the end of the world. What kind of frontier town might that be? thought Bond. He found his curiosity aroused.

The telephone on the bedside table let out its strange electronic peal.

"Mr. Bond? Is Reception. Is a lady to see you. She no say her name."

"Tell her I'll be right down."

There was certainly no chance of his being lonely in Tehran, Bond thought grimly, as he went towards the lift. He could only presume this was someone Darius had sent, since no one else, except maybe three people in Regent's Park, knew his whereabouts.

Across the white marble floor of the lobby, with her back to him as she looked into the window of the gift shop, was a woman with dark hair tied back in a half-ponytail, wearing a white sleeveless blouse and a navy blue skirt to the knee, with elegant bare legs and silver-thonged sandals.

Bond felt his pulse quicken a fraction as he approached. At the sound of his footsteps, the woman turned. When he saw her face, Bond could not keep the exhilaration from his voice. "Scarlett," he said. "What on earth are you—"

She smiled and placed her finger on his lips. "Not here. Perhaps your room."

Bond was not so disorientated by seeing Scarlett again that he was likely to forget elementary precautions. "We'd better go for a walk."

"I have five minutes."

"There's a small park down that way."

When they were outside, with the noise of the traffic pressing their ears, Bond said, "Tell me, Scarlett—"

"I'm not Scarlett."

"What?"

"I'm Poppy."

"She told me—"

"She told you I was younger? She always says that." Poppy smiled briefly. "And so I am. By twenty-five minutes. We're twins. Though we're dizygotic."

"You're what?"

"We're not in fact identical, we just—"

"You could have fooled me. Come on, let's move."

A hundred yards or so up the road, there was a green area between the houses, with wooden seats and some children's swings. They sat on a bench and put their heads together. To outside observers, Bond hoped, they would look like lovers in negotiation.

"I'm here with Gorner," said Poppy. "He knows you're in Tehran. He let me out of the office to post a letter. Chagrin will kill me if they know I've seen you. I've got something for you."

After looking round, she handed him a folded piece of paper.

Bond felt the desperate pressure of her eyes on him.

"Are you going to Noshahr?" she said.

Bond nodded.

"Good. That paper will help."

"Where's Gorner's desert headquarters?"

"I don't know."

"But you've been there."

"I live there. We go in by helicopter. But he puts me to sleep so I don't know. Only the pilot knows."

"Is it near Bam?" said Bond.

"Maybe, but my guess is that it's nearer Kerman. We drive to Yazd first. That's where he dopes me."

Bond looked steadily into Poppy's wide, pleading eyes. She was so like her sister that it was almost frightening. Was she an ounce or two skinnier? Was there a slight flush of drug-fever high in the cheeks? Was her accent slightly more Chelsea and less French cosmopolitan? The full mouth was the same. The only real difference he could see was that where Scarlett had deep brown eyes, Poppy's were a lighter hazel, flecked with green.

"Poppy," he said gently, placing a hand on hers. He felt it twitch beneath his grasp. "What do you want me to do?"

The girl looked deep into his eyes. "Kill Gorner," she said. "That's the only thing you can do. Kill him."

"Just walk up and—"

"Kill him. It's too late for anything else. And, Mr. Bond, it's—"

"James."

"James. It's not just for me. I do need your help, it's true, I desperately need your help . . ." She faltered for a moment, then regained control. "But it's more than that. Gorner's going to do something terrible. He's been planning it for months. He's ready to do it any day and there's nothing I or anyone else can do to stop him. If I had access to a gun I'd kill him myself."

"I'm not an assassin, Poppy," said Bond. "I'm here first of all to find out what the man is doing, then report to my people in London."

Poppy swore—a single pungent word that Bond had never heard a woman use before. Then she said, "Forget it. Forget reports. There isn't time. Don't you understand, James?"

"Everyone I meet keeps telling me to be careful or to stay away from Gorner altogether. Now you're saying I need to get in close to him. Kill without question."

"I know more than anyone else," said Poppy. "I know him better than anyone else does."

Bond felt a clutch of unease, the same feeling he had had when he had found Scarlett in his hotel room in Paris. "How do I know you're who you say you are?"

"You mean, how do you know I'm not Scarlett?"

"Among other things," said Bond. He said nothing about the eye colour.

"Have you seen Scarlett with no clothes on?" said Poppy.

"Do bankers usually strip for business acquaintances at first or second meeting?"

Poppy stood up and pointed to the top of her thigh. "Well. I have a small birthmark here. She doesn't. She's flawless. Come."

She took Bond by the hand into a small clump of trees by the wall of the playground. With her back to the wall, she loosened the waistband and zip of her skirt, looked both ways, then lowered it a few inches. Just below the line of her white cotton pants there was a mark of about the size and colour of a strawberry.

"There." She quickly refastened the skirt.

"Charming," said Bond, "but until I've seen Sca—"

"Of course. But it's the best I can do for now."

Bond nodded.

Poppy took his hands between her own. "Please

don't let me down, James. I beg you. It's not just my life, it's much more than that."

"I know," said Bond.

"I've got to go. I pray God I'll see you soon."

Bond watched the frail girl as she ran across the playground, then dodged through six lanes of speeding traffic till she reached the other side of the road. Unlike Scarlett, she didn't turn to wave, but dived into the first taxi she could stop.

Back in his hotel room, Bond went out on to the balcony that looked south, over the city, and unfolded the piece of paper. It was a plan of the waterfront at Noshahr, drawn in pencil, presumably by Poppy herself. She had marked a hotel called Jalal's Five Star "better than the rest."

In the margin was written "Isfahani Brothers Boat Building." A line ran from the words to a spot in the middle of a dockside street. Poppy had also written down the name and address in Farsi script.

10. A SHIP WITH WINGS

It was with a sense of relief and excitement that Bond climbed into the back seat of the grey Cadillac outside his hotel the next morning.

"I am Hamid," said the driver, a solemn-looking man with grey hair and a huge black bootbrush moustache. "I take you to Caspian Sea. You bring bathing trousers?" Hamid was eyeing the small attaché case which was all Bond had brought with him.

"Yes," said Bond. "I bring bathing trousers. Among other things."

The case held a sponge bag, maps, a spare shirt and a change of underwear. He expected to spend no more than a day in Noshahr. In a concealed compartment at the back, beneath the hinges, were a silencer for the Walther, spare ammunition and what the armourer, Major Boothroyd, looking at Bond with his peculiar, unflickering grey eyes, had called "a little something extra in case things get hot."

Bond, who didn't like gadgets, hadn't bothered to familiarize himself with it. It was only with considerable reluctance that he had been persuaded to carry a Ronson Varaflame lighter, whose apparently regular side-action in fact triggered a small dart with a poison that could immobilize a man of average build for six hours. For the rest, he preferred to travel light, trusting to his reflexes and, if necessary, the stopping power of the Walther PPK. Even the silencer he viewed as an encumbrance likely to cost him precious moments to fit or, if already in place, liable to snag on his clothing as he drew.

As he sat back, watching the northern suburbs of Tehran recede, he broke the seal on a packet of Chesterfields, the best American cigarette he could find in the hotel shop. A fresh, toasted smell filled the car and he offered one to Hamid. After refusing three times—which, Bond had come to learn, was par for the course in Tehran—Hamid accepted with enthusiasm.

Bond could feel the sea-island cotton of his shirt

sticking to his chest in the furious heat of the morning. In the absence of air-conditioning, he wound down his window on to the fuggy atmosphere of the streets. Once, before the city had sprawled north, Shemiran itself had been considered a retreat from the worst of the summer. Then, according to Darius, when Shemiran became urbanized, wealthy families would find themselves a *bagh*—a rustic orchard or garden with a peasant hut—in the lower green valleys of Mount Demavend where they would spend an idyllic two months next to a stream, living the simple life of their ancestors, eating food from the village allotments, going on walking trips into the mountains and reciting poetry late into the night.

Finally, in order to find tolerable weather and to escape the ever-increasing crowds, they had been forced to decamp across the Elburz mountains. The damp, cooler air of their destination was abundantly desirable, but Persian driving made it an eventful journey.

"The Way of a Thousand Abysses," said Hamid, gesturing to the right.

As they began to climb, the road was obliged to snake and double back on itself. Hamid kept his foot in the same position on the accelerator, whatever the terrain. He steered with his left hand only, leaving the right free to gesticulate. "The Valley of Fate," he said. "Hill of the Virgins . . . Lions' Den . . . Crossing of Great Peril."

Sometimes in the gullies and ravines below them Bond could see the rusting wrecks of upturned cars and coaches. When Hamid approached a particularly fierce hairpin, he cried out piously, *"Allahu Akbar,"* preferring to trust in the greatness of God than in any change of speed he might have achieved by raising his right foot.

Slowly, the air began to clear. After two hours, Hamid pulled in at a hillside tea-room and gestured to Bond to follow him. They sat on a veranda and drank sweetened black tea, looking back towards the great southward sprawl of Tehran, barely visible in the haze of heat and fumes, a gigantic symbol of human endeavour in the surrounding desert.

Hamid retired inside to do some business with the tea-room owner, who appeared to be a relation, then summoned Bond back to the car. After another hour or so, they crossed the high point of the mountains, and from the moment they began to descend towards the Caspian plain, there was moisture and a blessed coolness to the air. On the horizon, shimmering like a mirage, lay the turquoise waters of the world's largest inland sea.

Far beneath them, Bond could see the valley road, snaking through the lush vegetation, and could make out donkeys and camels on its dusty surface as well as coaches bound for the coast, their roofs piled high with luggage. The animals moved slowly among numerous Volkswagens, both camper vans and the distinctive Beetle saloons, as well as boxy rectangular cars of, he guessed, local manufacture.

Bond breathed in deeply as they went through the orange groves—partly for the citrus scent in the tropical air and partly to gather himself for what lay ahead. Something told him that his holiday was over. After barely thirty-six hours in which to acclimatize himself, he was now approaching what Felix Leiter would have called the "sharp end" of his trip.

It was siesta time when they arrived in Noshahr, and Bond told Hamid to drive him round for a while so he could get a feeling of the place. The best houses, including the Shah's summer residence, were some way back from the sea, in palm-lined streets, but there were also good hotels along the front, including Jalal's Five Star, the one Poppy had recommended, and it was here that they stopped to eat.

"Hamid," said Bond, as the driver tucked into a pile of lamb kebab and rice in the empty dining room, "we need to have a system. Do you understand? You drive me to the place I'm going in the dock area, then you leave me. If I'm not back right here in this hotel by eight o'clock this evening, you telephone Mr. Darius Alizadeh. This is his number. He'll know what to do."

Bond handed the driver some rials. "This should cover anything," he said. "You all right?"

"Allah will provide," said Hamid, without much conviction. "I can pass any message you like, Mr. James. I understand dead-letterbox."

Bond laughed. "You what?"

"I drive once for American man. Mr. Silver. He need translating too. One thing, Mr. James. I like to eat caviar. Here is very good."

"Well, I suppose it would be. Right from the sea. You know why caviar's so rare?"

Hamid nodded. "Is sturgeon egg. But not fertilized by man sturgeon."

"That's right. 'And the virgin sturgeon needs no urgin'. / That's why . . .' Never mind, Hamid. Not really a Persian poem, I suppose." Bond put his hand into his back pocket. "Take this. That should cover it. In return, you be on your toes."

"On my toes," said Hamid, pocketing the extra notes and walking heavily towards the door of the hotel dining room.

"Give me one moment to change," said Bond, heading for the cloakroom.

A minute later, they got back into the car and

drove slowly into the main dock area with Bond navigating from Poppy's map and Hamid barking out the names of the streets. There were two or three large merchantmen at anchor, as well as fleets of commercial fishing-boats. The size of the docks was impressive, Bond thought. Though it was only a short distance from the beaches where the tourists bathed, they could have berthed a couple of destroyers in this forlorn area with its endless walkways, warehouses and construction yards.

"This is it," he said. "Down here. Now read out the names on the front of the buildings."

Hamid went through a long list as they drove past, reciting from the Farsi script, till he came to "Isfahani Brothers Boat Building."

"Good girl, Poppy," said Bond, as he got out of the car. "Remember what we said, Hamid?"

"Eight o'clock, Mr. James."

"Before you call Mr. Alizadeh, just check down this hollow stanchion here." Bond pointed to a rusting metal tube that had once presumably held a traffic signal. "Look in it and see if there's a note."

For the first time that day, the light of animation came into Hamid's solemn face. His eyes sparkled and the great moustache lifted as he smiled. "Dead letter," he said.

"More or less," said Bond, surprised by his

own precautions. Some instinct was telling him to beware.

He watched Hamid turn the car and disappear, then approached the building.

An external staircase ran up one side and seemed to be the only pedestrian entrance. Bond walked along the road, looking for a less obvious way into the plant. As he did so, he noticed that the main building was not all it seemed from the front of the dock. Attached to it, at a lower level, was a sort of annexe, about a third of an acre in extent, and this was not covered, like the rest, in shabby, creosoted wood but in what looked to Bond like new stainless steel. It extended about fifty yards into the sea, presumably offering a deeper dock than was available elsewhere.

His curiosity aroused, Bond went to the side of the building to see if he could find a way in. The shell appeared to have no break in it—no door, window or opening of any kind. The only entrance was via a closed gangway from the old wooden building.

After walking up and down the dockside twice to make sure he was not being watched, Bond went behind a Fiat lorry and stripped down to his swimming trunks. He folded his clothes and—with some reluctance—the Walther PPK into a bundle then hid it behind a rubbish skip. While changing in the hotel, he had attached a commando knife to his left leg, strapped just below the knee. Checking both ways, he hurried across to the edge of the dock and lowered himself feet first into the water. The surface was slick with rainbows of spilt fuel and gave off the sweet, choking smell of diesel. Bond emptied his lungs, duck-dived and powered himself downward.

Opening his eyes, he could see the great metal legs that held the shell. There were about a dozen on each side, anchored in concrete blocks on the sea floor. What he had not anticipated was that the sides of the building had been continued right down to the same level. Someone had been very thorough, and very cautious. He swam along the edges of the wall base, looking for a way in. The natural undulations of the sea floor, particularly so close to the shore, must surely mean that there would be a gap. It was likely, he thought, that the building was open at the sea end, but it would take him too long to swim there without having to surface.

He had been underwater for nearly a minute, and although he was an experienced diver with outstanding lung function, he knew he couldn't last much longer. Above him, the metal sides rose vertically, disappearing in the mist of seaweed and cloudy water. With his hands, he could feel the rivets and joins, but they made a single, adamantine wall.

Whoever had built this thing had money, expertise and industrial power.

Bond could feel his legs weaken as the oxygen in his blood began to run short. It was the construction of the thing that made him sure he was on to something of importance. Determination gave one more thrust to his aching legs as he opened his eyes wide in the murky water. Beside a rock, the steel had been cut to make a fit. Between the rock and the jagged edge there was a space just wide enough, Bond calculated, to wriggle through. He approached on his front, preferring to take steel cuts on his back and to use the handhold of the rock to keep himself down, against natural buoyancy. His lungs were hot and constricted. It was as though his ribs and sternum were being driven outward by a steam-hammer in his chest. He kicked forward and felt the shredding teeth of the cut steel on his spine and the slimy hardness of the rock on his abdomen. With one last, desperate kick, he was through. He swam three or four powerful breast-strokes forward into clear water, then allowed himself to rise, with his head tilted back and his hands ahead of him in self-defence. After a few seconds, his fingers encountered metal. He flipped on to his back and could see the outline of a huge, slightly rounded hull. His brain, deprived as it was of oxygen, still told him that a hull must lead upward and that he should follow its contour.

As he rose rapidly up the side, his hands met something else that extended at right angles to the hull, like a wing from the fuselage of a plane.

A ship, with a wing... It wasn't possible, Bond thought, flailing along the underside of the "wing" with his last vestige of strength. Perhaps this was no ship or plane at all, but simply a floor beneath which he was trapped and would at any second expire. He clawed his way frantically along the underside of the metal, and as numbness crept through his limbs and into his brain, the water cleared and he broke the surface with a tearing gasp.

For a minute he needed all the replenishment of air just to give him strength to tread water. When at last his pulse rate and breathing started to return to normal, he looked about him.

The sight that met his eyes was one of the strangest he had ever seen. The giant steel enclosure was like a hangar, but contained one craft only. What that craft was exactly, he had not the smallest idea.

Gingerly, feeling the salt water in the cuts on his back, and quietly, so as to attract no attention, Bond eased himself away from the monstrous thing so he could get a better picture of it. Taking a handhold on the side of the hangar, he let his eyes absorb the astonishing sight.

It was, he calculated, from its tail, which was at the land end, to its nose, which stuck out beneath camouflage nets into the Caspian Sea, more than a hundred yards long. It had a raised tail with two large fins and it had wings, but they were cut off— amputated almost before they had begun to taper. The nose was like that of a large passenger plane, but behind it, mounted on top of the fuselage, were what looked like eight jet engines.

The craft was clearly at home in the water, yet it had no propellers beneath the surface and must therefore travel through the air. On the other hand, the abbreviated wings could surely not give it enough lift to fly at any altitude. But then, Bond suddenly thought, perhaps that was the point of it: a fast, low-flying amphibious vehicle that could cover large distances under radar.

If it worked on the principle of a hovercraft, or something like it, then perhaps it could even operate over dry land as well—provided the surface was flat. Bond's mind went back to the maps he had laid out on the bed in his hotel room. He remembered the Soviet lowlands north of Astrakhan on the far north-western shore of the Caspian. Was it possible that this monstrous machine could go in a straight, unstopping line from the docks of Persian Noshahr right through to Stalingrad?

There was a loading door on the starboard side, which was attached by a temporary steel walkway to the surrounding gallery. At the back of the hangar, piles of cargo in crates were lashed to wooden battens. Bond could see two or three forklift trucks standing idle.

When he was sure that he had fully recovered from his dive, he slid below the surface of the water and set off to explore. He wanted to establish that no one else was in the hangar and to find a way up on to the gallery, since it would clearly be impossible to scale the sides of the convex fuselage. He surfaced quietly from the cloudy water towards the tail of the big amphibian and, in front of him, saw a metal ladder attached to the side of the dock. With silent strokes, he made his way towards it.

Taking a minute to collect himself after he had climbed up, Bond made a swift visual inspection of the hangar. What he needed was a camera. He would have to return, he thought, with the specially waterproofed Minox B that had been made for him in London. It was normally used for close work, but he had a custom-built Zeiss lens for distance.

Meanwhile, having run up the connecting steps to the upper level, he went to the nearest cargo crate and levered the top off with a tyre iron he found on one of the forklift trucks. The crate was not much bigger than a tea chest but was packed to the brim with bags made from heavy-duty polythene of the kind used by builders for damp-proof courses. Bond picked one up. It weighed about four pounds. The covering was so thick that it was hard to say what was inside. The packages were all of the same size and had clearly been produced and loaded not by hand but from an industrial assembly line.

As Bond was considering his next move, he heard grinding metal, as of a door being pushed open on to the gallery, and flung himself to the ground behind the stacked cargo crates. There was the sound of a man's voice, then of another answering it. As he pressed himself against the ground, Bond noticed what looked like a lump of brownish earth.

He cursed silently. No wonder he'd been heard. The lump was an SID—a Seismic Intruder Detection device—one of the most discreet telltale gadgets of the last decade. It could detect movement of people, animals or objects up to three hundred yards away. It was powered by three mercury cells and had a built-in dipole antenna with a 150 MHz transmitter, which relayed its findings through coded impulses—and all this in what looked like a small cowpat or clod of earth.

Bond heard the noise of running feet and shouting. If he went back into the water, he would have to surface for breath before he reached the relative safety of the open sea. Even if he kept beneath the fuselage he would have to come up for air at some point and could then be picked off. There was no chance he could find again the fissure in the steel wall through which he'd entered. He would have to make his exit by land.

The sooner he could get on to the guard and relieve him of his weapon, the better chance he had. There was no point in waiting while the SID alerted other guards to his presence.

Cautiously, aware of his vulnerable near-nakedness, Bond edged out from behind the crates. The guard had gone down on to the lower gantry, presumably to make sure the craft had not been damaged. It was fifteen feet below the gallery level where Bond stood and he judged the drop too far for him to be sure of landing uninjured on the man's shoulders.

Unsheathing his knife, he took the tyre iron to the rail that edged the gallery and threw it as far as he could. As the guard ran towards the clanging noise, Bond dropped to the lower gantry and sprinted along it to the tail section of the plane. He leaped up and was just in time to conceal himself behind the vertical as the guard turned and started to retrace his steps.

With his face a few feet from the tail section, Bond noticed a strange thing: it was painted with the British flag.

He heard the guard come heavily back, and when he was level with him, Bond jumped down the five feet or so from the tail. The man let out a startled grunt as he fell face down beneath Bond's weight.

"The gun," said Bond, now pressing the tip of his commando knife against the man's artery. "Drop the gun."

The man twitched and struggled, so Bond jabbed the tip of the knife into his flesh, where it drew blood. Reluctantly, the guard released his grip on the gun, and Bond pushed it away with his knee, a few feet across the metal walkway.

Rather than cut the man's throat, Bond used the carotid takedown. Only eleven pounds of pressure to the carotid arteries is necessary to stop blood-flow to the brain and, once the flow has stopped, the average person loses consciousness within ten seconds. As Bond squeezed hard on the man's perspiring neck, he knew that if he left it at that, the thug would regain consciousness within fifteen seconds, but he would be weakened and disorientated—and fifteen seconds was long enough for the hasty exit he was planning.

When he felt the heavy body go limp beneath him, Bond grabbed the gun and ran up the stairway to the upper level, where he scooped up the polythene-wrapped package. As he made it to the door, he heard the recovering man call out from the gantry below.

Bond had no time to think what might lie beyond the door as he ran to the opening and leaped through it.

11. GOOD TROUSER

It took a moment for his eyes to become accustomed to his new surroundings. It was a boat-building yard with a single vessel under construction. There was a high screech of sheet metal cutting over the sawing and hammering. Bond stood still for a moment. Then he began to make his way slowly along the gallery, at the end of which he could see wooden steps down to a platform where a door stood open, leading to the outdoor stairs—and freedom. He had got as far as the top of the steps when he heard the guard running back from the hangar and shouting from the connecting doorway. Bond turned and fired once, then ran down the steps and along the platform towards the door. He heard shots ring out and the whine of a bullet as it passed through the wooden wall above his head. He ran a zigzag pattern to the door, side-stepping three low shots that ricocheted off the platform.

In front of him, in the doorway, was a second guard with his feet spread, preparing to shoot. Bond emptied two shots from the first guard's gun into the man's midriff and jumped over the slumped body to emerge into the evening sunlight.

There was a time in life to go forward—to attack—but there was also a time, in Bond's opinion, to get the hell out. Survival lay in knowing which was which. Even the Prophet's famous journey, his *hejira* to the Holy City, Darius had told him, had been in truth a tactical withdrawal. So it was the Arabic word that Bond muttered to himself—"*Hejira*"—as, without looking back, he ran as fast as he could towards the road. He had gone only a hundred yards towards the town when he heard a clangorous hooting from a side-street.

It was coming from a grey Cadillac, through whose driver's window Bond could make out only an outsize moustache.

"Get in, Mr. James. You don't go nowhere in your bathing trousers." Hamid flipped open the back door and Bond dived across the seat.

"Go, Hamid! Go!" he shouted.

Hamid needed no encouragement as he left black streaks of rubber down the dockside road, screeched back beside the neat little bazaar off Azadi Square, then whisked the car away up into the palm-lined millionaires' rows behind the town.

When he was sure they were not being followed, Bond said, "All right. Slow down."

Hamid looked disappointed, but did as he was told. Then he turned round, and his moustache twitched in amusement. "What you have?" he said, pointing to the package.

"I don't know," said Bond. "I'm going to find out back in the hotel. You drop me off, then you're going to buy me some new trousers and a shirt."

"You like American clothes?"

"Yes," said Bond, cautiously. "Something plain, no checks or stripes. And tell me, Hamid, why were you waiting?"

Hamid shrugged. "I nothing else to do. I pull in, have a look round. It looks . . . not so good. I have bad feeling. I think you need Hamid."

"You think right, my friend."

Back at the hotel, Bond explained that he wanted the best room they had. The desk clerk handed him a key, looking up and down suspiciously at Bond's semi-naked, bleeding figure.

"My luggage is on its way," Bond explained. "Tell the man—Hamid—which number I'm in."

The room was on the second floor and had a balcony with a good view over a tropical garden to the sea. It was a simple arrangement with no radio, fridge or other frills, but a large, clean bathroom. Bond didn't bother with any security checks. No one could have got in before him, since he himself had only just decided to take a room. He went to the shower and for once turned it only to half-power as he stood with his back beneath the water and winced.

As he dried himself, he heard a knock at the door. He opened it to see the desk clerk, holding a small silver tray.

"Lady send up this card," said the man. "She like to see you. She wait down there."

"Thank you."

Bond took the business card and flipped it over. "Miss Scarlett Papava. Investment Manager. Diamond and Standard Bank. 14 *bis* rue du Faubourg St. Honoré."

He swore once, coarsely, but more in disbelief than anger.

"What I say to lady?"

Bond smiled. "You say to lady, Mr. Bond can't come downstairs because he has no trousers. But if she would like to come up here and bring a bottle of cold champagne and two glasses with her, I would be pleased to entertain her."

As the puzzled clerk disappeared, Bond let out a low, incredulous laugh. It was one thing for Scarlett to have found him and attempted to commission him in Rome and Paris, but to turn up when he was in the thick of things . . . It was almost as though she had no trust in his abilities. Presumably she had been contacted by Poppy on the telephone from Tehran, and Poppy had given her the name of Jalal's Five Star. But even so . . .

There was a knock at the door. Bond checked himself in the bathroom mirror. The comma of black hair, dampened by the shower, hung over his forehead. The scar on his cheek was less distinct than usual, thanks to the tanning effect of the Persian sun. His eyes were bloodshot from the salt water but retained, despite the spidery red traces, their cold, slightly cruel, sense of purpose.

Bond shrugged. There was nothing he could do to make himself more presentable for Miss Scarlett Papava, so he went to open the door.

"James! My God, are you all right?"

"Yes, thank you, Scarlett. Bloodied but unbowed. And extremely surprised to see you."

"Surprised," said Scarlett, entering the room with a tray on which stood a bottle of champagne and two glasses. "I can understand that. But not pleased as well? Not even just the smallest bit pleased?"

"A scintilla," Bond conceded.

"I've come almost direct from Paris."

"So I see," said Bond.

Scarlett wore a charcoal grey business suit and a white blouse.

She followed Bond's amused gaze. "Yes. I . . . I haven't had time to buy proper clothes yet. Thank heavens it's a bit cooler here than it is in Tehran. I shall have to go shopping tomorrow."

"Wait and see what Hamid brings me first. You might not like the local fashion."

"Hamid?"

"Yes. My driver. And now my tailor. Champagne?"

"Thank you. What a heavenly view."

Bond turned towards the window to open the champagne.

"Oh, my goodness, your back!" said Scarlett. "It's terrible. We must get some iodine. How did you do that?"

"I have a lot to tell you," said Bond. "For one thing, I've met your sister."

"Really? Where?" Scarlett's expression, which had been both playful and embarrassed, suddenly became serious.

"In Tehran. She called at my hotel. I must say I've

never met anyone quite like you Papava girls for just materializing out of thin air. I'm beginning to think that when I get home to my flat in Chelsea there'll be a message waiting for me from a third sister."

Scarlett looked down, a little shamefaced again. "So you know she's my twin."

"Yes."

"I'm sorry, James. Perhaps I should have told you before. It doesn't really make a difference, does it? To you, I mean. To me it makes it all the more painful than it would be if she was a normal sister."

"Perhaps."

"But how was she, James? Did she seem all right?"

"I don't know how she usually seems. I spent most of the time thinking it was you, but somehow not quite. It was . . ."

"I know, I know. Did she say which one of us was older?"

"Yes. And she showed me a way of telling you apart."

"What—she actually showed you?" Scarlett looked amazed. "Here?" She pointed to the top of her left thigh.

"Yes. We were in a park. She's a wild child."

"And do you want me to show you, too? To prove I'm not her?"

Bond smiled. "No. I don't think that'll be necessary.

There's something very Scarlett about you. You're Mrs. Larissa Rossi from Rome, all right." He said nothing of the distinctive darkness of her eyes.

"Good. Now I'm going to get some iodine and bathe those cuts."

Scarlett made for the door.

"And when you come back," said Bond, "perhaps you'd like to tell me exactly what a Parisian banker is doing in a Caspian resort in the middle of July."

"It's a deal," said Scarlett, closing the door behind her.

Bond finished his glass of champagne and poured another. He couldn't deny that he was pleased to see Scarlett, but he would have to be firm with her. He couldn't be distracted at this stage of the proceedings by concern for a woman's safety.

Some ten minutes later, Scarlett returned with a brown medicine bottle and some cotton wool. "I think this is the right stuff," she said. "My Farsi isn't up to much."

"Unlike Poppy's. At least she can do the script."

"Well, she's had a chance to learn, poor girl. Now, keep still."

Bond looked out over the sea while Scarlett gently dabbed the cuts on his back.

"You're supposed to yelp in pain," she said. "That's what they do in westerns."

"It doesn't hurt that much," said Bond.

"Perhaps it's not an antiseptic at all. Perhaps it's a placebo. And I noticed you had some cuts on your chest as well."

Scarlett came round and stood in front of Bond, and as she leaned over him, he saw her shining clean hair up close and smelled a discreet lily-of-the-valley scent. Despite what must have been a rigorous journey, she seemed as fresh as though she had just stepped from the bathroom.

She stopped, and her hesitation suggested she felt his eyes on her skin. She turned his face to hers. She was only a few inches away.

"Just here," said Bond, pointing to the scar on his cheek.

"You poor boy," said Scarlett, and now, in her narrowing eyes, Bond saw for the first time since Rome a different, more feline expression.

She dabbed the cotton wool on the scar, then lightly kissed it.

"Is that better?"

"Yes," said Bond through gritted teeth.

"And here," she said, touching a mark on his neck with her other hand. She kissed the place, lightly.

"And here," said Bond, pointing to his lower lip.

"Yes, my poor darling, of course. Just here."

As Scarlett's lips lightly touched his, Bond held

her hips firmly and forced her mouth open with his tongue. As she drew her head back, he moved one hand up to the back of her neck and pulled her mouth, roughly, on to his. This time, her tongue did not hesitate but went eagerly to meet his while he ran his hands up and down over her hips. He felt her arms lock behind his neck as she kissed him hungrily.

Eventually, Bond moved back his head. "And now, Scarlett," he said, "I think I should like to see the proof that you are who you say you are."

Flushed and breathless, Scarlett lifted the hem of her black skirt over the honey-coloured stocking so he could see the skin between the top of the stretched nylon and the pink cotton pants. There was no mark.

Bond smiled. "Flawless," he said. He gripped her hand where it was, kissed her hair and whispered into her ear, "But who would have thought a banker would have pink underwear?" He was also smiling at the memory of how Poppy, the supposed Bohemian, had demurely lowered the waistband of her skirt with a practical sense of the quickest way to show him, while the elder sister, the purportedly sensible one, had lifted her skirt in her passionate hurry.

He touched the blemish-free skin of her thigh with his fingertips, then leaned forward and kissed it.

"Soft," he said. "As well as flawless."

He felt Scarlett's hands running through his still-damp hair as he kissed her thigh again.

Then he stood up and wrapped his arms round her. "You can take that skirt off now, if you like," he said.

Scarlett did as he suggested, then removed her jacket and blouse as well. As she sat on the edge of the bed in her underwear, Bond stepped towards her and loosened the knotted towel at his waist. As he did so, there came a knock at the door.

"Hello, hello. Mr. James. Is Hamid. I have good trouser for you."

"Exactly what I need at the moment," said Bond, grabbing the towel.

He looked at Scarlett's flushed, expectant face. "I'm sorry," he said.

She inhaled tightly, as though she found it hard to breathe. Then she nodded briefly and picked up her clothes from the floor.

"It's work," said Bond.

"Or destiny," said Scarlett, with a sigh.

They ate in the hotel dining room, and Bond invited Hamid to join them.

"I presume you didn't have time for the caviar this afternoon," said Bond.

"No, Mr. James. I wait for you."

"All right, let's see what they can do."

Bond was wearing a casual white shirt and some navy cotton trousers. They were a little loose at the waist, but the outfit was surprisingly tasteful, he thought, by comparison with what most men in Noshahr appeared to be wearing.

Scarlett had had time to go out and buy herself a light dress from a tourist shop. Although she complained that it was cut for a Persian grandmother, the pale blue went oddly well with her dark brown eyes. She had reserved herself a room along the corridor from Bond's.

The caviar was brought in a casket, whose lid was taken off to reveal an inner glass bowl set on ice. Hamid's eyes were bulging as he scooped out a large helping on to his plate and started to lever it into his mouth, using a piece of flatbread as a trowel. To Bond's dismay, he drank Coca-Cola with it. Bond had switched to whisky, and Scarlett, since the hotel had no other wine, drank champagne.

Over the course of dinner, Bond explained to Scarlett what he'd done in Tehran and described the ship-plane he had discovered in the hangar. "If I can get some pictures of it," he said, "we'll wire them back to London."

"It sounds most peculiar," said Scarlett. "Like something from science fiction."

"It's real enough," said Bond. "I suspect it's of Soviet manufacture. But what intrigues me is precisely what it does. And why it has a British flag on it."

"That points to Gorner," said Scarlett. "I told you about his British obsession."

"Sound like Caspian Sea Monster," said Hamid.

Bond had almost forgotten that the driver was still with them, so quiet had he been with his head down in the food.

Now Hamid looked up from his plate, and brushed some rice and fava beans from his moustache. "Caspian Sea Monster. This last year have been two seeings."

"Sightings?"

"Yes. Has been seen from aeroplane over sea. People very frightened. Is bigger than any ship or plane. And goes faster than any car. They think it is an animal. Alive, like your famous monster."

"Loch Ness?"

"Yes."

"Well, I can assure you it's very much more solid than Nessie," said Bond. "But what I'd like to know is whether it only carries cargo or whether it has some sort of weapons payload."

The waiter brought roast duck with pomegranate seeds and served it to them with a herb salad that looked past its best.

"Do you think it would be safer to go back at night?" said Scarlett. "We'd be less visible."

"We?" said Bond incredulously.

"I could be an extra pair of eyes."

"Me too," said Hamid. "I come."

Bond considered, as he drained the glass of whisky and sat back. "Well. I need to get my gun. That heavy American thing I left in your car, Hamid, it's too cumbersome. Let Scarlett have it. Do you know how to fire a gun?"

"I'm a banker, James. As you keep reminding me."

"Stand with your feet planted firmly about this far apart. Hold the gun with both hands in front of you, so your arms make an equilateral triangle with the gun at its apex. Squeeze, don't pull, the trigger. Try not to rush. This is the target area," he said, running a finger round his torso. "Anywhere below is no good. Anywhere higher and you risk missing. Got that?"

"I think so," said Scarlett. "It's easier than mergers and acquisitions."

"Good. We'll have to try to find a way in through the main building. I'm not going swimming again."

Upstairs in his room, Bond reattached the commando knife to his leg and slipped on his loafers with the steel toecaps. Into his pocket he put some spare ammunition for the Walther and the Minox B camera with its distance lens. He wound in an ultra-high-speed film and calculated that, with the moon shining in from the open end of the hangar, there would be just enough light. He wasn't going to win any photography prizes with the results, but the boffins in Q section would at least have something to go on.

He then handed the polythene-wrapped package to Hamid and told him to deliver it to Darius Alizadeh for analysis in Tehran if there was a problem at the docks.

Outside in the car, Bond found there were only two rounds of ammunition left in the guard's Colt. "Better than nothing," he said, handing the gun to Scarlett.

"Where do I . . . er, keep it?" she said.

"I wish I still had my old Beretta," said Bond. "The armourer told me it was a lady's gun. You could have hidden it in your underwear. Can you find room for this thing in your bag?"

Scarlett rummaged for a moment as Hamid started the engine. "I'll have to leave my makeup behind," she said.

"We all have to make sacrifices for our country," said Bond. "Let's go, Hamid."

The grey Cadillac crept quietly forward through the semi-tropical night, with Hamid, on Bond's instruction, keeping to a sedate pace. The windows were open to the mingled sound of the waves on the seashore to their left and the cicadas in the palm trees on the right. The perfume of the orange groves was powerful in the stillness of the air.

"Damn it. I've just had a thought," said Bond. "There'll be dogs."

"Dogs?" said Hamid.

"Yes. At night there are bound to be guard dogs."

Hamid shook his head. "Persian people do not keep dogs. Is habit of Europeans. Dirty. We leave dogs to walk outside, like cats."

As they left the residential part of town, the streetlights grew less frequent until they were gliding quietly into the murky world of the docks. There were no other cars in sight, no headlights and no sound. It was as though the darkness had smothered all sign of life, here at the edge of the inland sea.

The three in the car found nothing to say. Bond treasured such moments before action. They allowed him to collect himself and to run a check over all the reflexes that time and experience had wired into his system.

He liked the silence of this foreign land, and felt the familiar tightening in his gut that preceded danger. He breathed in deeply, and for a moment had a picture of the trainer, Julian Burton, back at the headquarters in London. Was this the kind of breathing exercise he'd had in mind?

"Pull over here." The time for reflection was past. "You stay right back here, Hamid. Don't come any closer. Whatever happens, you need to be able to get away cleanly. We'll see you in half an hour, with any luck. Scarlett, you come with me."

The two made their way forward on foot along the main road, then turned off into the yard that held Isfahani Brothers Boat Building. There were a few security lights, but nothing that worried Bond.

"Wait here. Stay behind this truck. Cover me while I go over there."

Bond kept to the shadows at the side of the building until he had to break cover. He ran towards the metal hangar and ducked down behind the rubbish skip. His searching hand found the bundled clothes, and within a second he felt the reassuring weight of the Walther against his palm.

He glanced back across the open area towards the street and the lorry behind which Scarlett was stationed. She had positioned herself so as to cast no shadow. Good girl, thought Bond.

He made his way round the side of the building to the door he'd run through earlier that day. It was padlocked. With his pocket knife, he set about probing the small levers inside. The lock gave way, and he pushed open the wooden door. Scarlett followed him into the old building and Bond led her swiftly to the stairs. He was surprised by the lack of security—and worried by it. Even the most innocent enterprise should have a nightwatchman, he thought. They went along the gangway to the entrance into the metal hangar.

Bond put his hand on Scarlett's wrist. "It's too easy," he said. "Looks like a trap. I think you should stay here. Have you got the gun? Now cover me. There should be enough moonlight from the sea end for you to see me. Take the safety catch off. Right. There's a second safety here—this metal strip down the back of the grip. It releases automatically if you squeeze it hard enough. Good girl."

Bond unlatched the door and went into the main hangar. The outline of the Caspian Sea Monster filled his view. It was an awe-inspiring piece of work. It could only have been made in the Soviet Union, he thought, and it was a frightening reminder of recent days when the West had been falling behind—the period of Sputnik, Yuri Gagarin and the feats of Soviet weapons engineering. Now it seemed the Soviets once again had the ingenuity and the power.

Bond began to take pictures of the beast. The shutter noise of the Minox was barely audible after the photographic boys had been to work on it. Bond didn't bother to look through the viewfinder, but just pointed and fired.

He went down on to the lower gantry to get closer to it. As he raised the Minox once more, he heard a loud voice in the echoing, moonlit hangar.

"More light, Mr. Bond!" It was a Persian accent and a voice unfamiliar to him.

Suddenly the hangar was drenched in dazzling light. Bond threw his arm across his eyes to shield them. All around him he could hear the thunder of booted feet on the clanging metal walkways.

The voice came again. It was amplified through a megaphone. "Put down your gun, Mr. Bond. Put your hands on your head. The party's over."

Bond looked along the length of the illuminated fuselage. As he did so, he saw the top part of the cockpit slide back hydraulically. From the open space appeared a Foreign Legion kepi, followed swiftly by a pair of shoulders and the body of Chagrin. He hauled himself out, then walked along the top of the fuselage towards Bond, a semi-automatic rifle in his hand.

He lifted the barrel and pointed it at Bond's head. He was now close enough for Bond to see the expressionless features in the dead-seeming flesh.

There was the sound of a single shot and the hangar went suddenly dark. Bond flung himself on to his front. He had no time to work out what had happened, but knew he must put the darkness to good use. He went as quietly as he could along the gantry towards the ladder, but had gone up one step only before a crushing blow behind his ear caused a thick darkness—far deeper than that of the Persian night—to flood his brain.

12. THE BELLY OF
THE BEAST

When Bond regained consciousness, it was to find himself being pushed and dragged over tarmac towards a helicopter, whose blades were whirring in the night. The air on his skin told him he'd been stripped to his underpants. His hands were tied behind his back and the commando knife had been removed. The pain in his skull was such that it was all he could do to keep from vomiting as he was pushed up into the helicopter. Inside, it was like a military aircraft with primitive seating for six at right angles to the pilots. Bond was thrust to the floor, where his ankles were tightly bound with nylon cord. A woman's body—Scarlett's, he presumed—was pressed up against his, and lashed to him, back to back. He could feel her bare skin on his.

As the nausea rose inside him, Bond fought to recover any sense of what had happened. He recalled bright lights . . . Then nothing. The noise of the helicopter's angry rotors pressed his ears, then it surged upwards and immediately banked violently, causing his weight to roll on to Scarlett, who let out a cry. Even in the wordless sound, Bond recognized her voice.

"Scarlett?" he said.

A boot exploded against his mouth and a tooth broke from his jaw.

"No talk."

Looking up, Bond saw that all six seats were occupied by armed guards. Six guns with their safety catches off pointed at him and Scarlett, while six pairs of unsmiling eyes bored into them. While the pain in his head increased with the passing of the minutes, his memory of events slowly started to return. The appearance of Chagrin was evidence that he had found Gorner's Caspian secret, and he had little doubt that he was now on his way to the desert headquarters.

Bond spat blood. He could see one positive aspect of his situation. He would never have found

Gorner's headquarters without help. The mountain had not come to Mohammed, but Mohammed, it seemed, was being airlifted to the mountain. Good.

After about an hour, they lost height, and Bond sensed growing anxiety in the men. They landed without incident and he heard abrupt orders being given. The six guards made no move, but pointed their guns a little closer at their captives. Bond heard the sound of a diesel engine outside and presumed it was a fuel lorry. Sand blew in through the open loading bay.

Finally, the doors were closed and they were on their way again. It was pointless to try to work out in which direction they were heading, so Bond allowed himself to drift in and out of consciousness. He sought a way of reassuring Scarlett, but could communicate nothing through their touching skin.

After what seemed a night-long journey, Bond felt the helicopter lower itself again. This time, as it hovered on the cushion of air above the sand, the six men stood up and, using rough hands and boots, got Bond and Scarlett to the open door. As the rotors died, they lowered the steps and pushed their captives on to the ground. Scarlett screamed as her naked ribs grazed the metal steps. The pair were moved over the sand till they came to a prepared track, about ten feet wide, on which stood an electrically driven cart, like a forklift truck. With guns held against their heads, they were manhandled on to a low platform at the back.

The cart drove towards a dark hill of sand, perhaps sixty feet tall, like the wall of a desert fortress. As they approached, huge sliding doors parted to allow them entry. The belly of the beast, thought Bond, as the doors closed silently behind them.

The cart moved forward on to a circular platform and stopped. There was a hiss of hydraulics and they began to sink. The platform descended within a larger tube, into which it was telescoped, and came to a halt some thirty feet below ground level. The cart was driven off the unrailed platform along a dark corridor and stopped outside a heavy door. The guards pulled Bond and Scarlett, still clamped together, off the back and pushed them through the door into a cell.

Chagrin appeared in the doorway. "You wait here," he said. "There no way out. You move, we kill. We see you," he added, pointing to the ceiling.

The door clanged shut and was bolted. The room was a cell about six feet by six. The walls were rock and the floor was sand.

"Are you all right?" said Bond.

"Yes. Are you?" Scarlett's voice sounded weak and close to tears.

"A headache. Nothing worse than I woke up with after a night playing cards at my boss's club once. Benzedrine and champagne. God. What are you wearing?"

"Just these." Scarlett moved her hips.

"The pink ones."

"They're white since you ask. I changed before dinner."

"What happened in the hangar? I remember when the lights came on. Then . . ."

"Chagrin came down the top of the fuselage. I thought he was going to kill you. So I fired."

"At him?"

"No. I shot through the main light cable. It was only a few feet away."

"Still. A hell of a good shot."

"The gun kicked like mad. But I did what you told me. Squeeze not pull. I thought maybe you could escape in the darkness."

"There were too many of them."

"Now what, James?"

Bond thought for a moment. "Well, I don't suppose Gorner has had us brought to the middle of the desert for no reason. If they wanted to kill me—or you—they would have done it by now."

"So?"

"So he must have a use for us. A purpose."

"Or just information."

"Perhaps," said Bond. "Until we find out, I think we should try to rest. And by the way, Scarlett, you never did tell me what on earth you're doing in Persia."

"It sounds a bit silly now," said Scarlett, and Bond felt her wriggle slightly. "Do you promise you won't laugh?"

"I don't feel that mirthful."

"I'm on holiday."

"You're what?"

"Even bankers take a rest sometimes. I have three weeks' annual leave and I took ten days. I wanted to be on hand when Poppy came out of Gorner's clutches. I couldn't concentrate at work while you were here. And I wanted to see Persia."

Despite what he had said, Bond found himself laughing drily, then wished he hadn't, as the cuts on his back rubbed against Scarlett.

"Now you've seen Persia," he said, looking at the sand and rock. "Right up close."

Light from the corridor was filtering into the cell when the bolt was drawn. Bond groaned as he shifted his weight on the sand.

Two armed guards came in. One bent down with a knife and cut the ropes that joined them, but kept their wrists bound. The second guard gave them water, which they drank with their shackled hands.

"Go," he ordered.

They were marched at gunpoint down the passageway and into a primitive washroom, where, under close supervision, they were allowed to clean up and use a lavatory in a cubicle.

"Can I have a shirt?" Scarlett looked down at her bare torso.

The guard shook his head. He ordered them out, down another corridor to a stainless-steel door.

"Wait."

The man entered a code and offered himself to a concealed camera to be recognized. The door slid open. Bond and Scarlett went forward into a spacious air-conditioned room that was painted crimson: floor, ceiling, walls—there was almost nothing in the room that wasn't poppy-red. Behind a desk stood an old-fashioned swivel chair with a maroon leather seat, and in it sat a man with an outsize gloved left hand.

"For God's sake, give the woman a shirt," said Dr. Julius Gorner. There was such disgust in his voice that Bond wondered for a second whether he found all women's flesh repulsive.

Gorner stood up and walked round the desk. He wore a cream linen suit, blue shirt and red tie. His corn-coloured hair, driven back from the high fore-head, hung over his collar at the neck. He put his face close to Bond, who noted the high Slavic cheekbones and the look of intensely arrogant impatience he had first seen on the dock at Marseille.

More chilling still was the aloofness—the way that Gorner wouldn't quite engage with his eyes, as though he knew that being exposed to the demands of others might dilute the purity of his own driving purpose. This slight reserve made him almost invulnerable, Bond thought—with no Achilles' heel of pride or lust or pity.

"So, you are my guest again, Commander Bond," Gorner said. "Don't make a habit of trespassing on my hospitality. Not cricket."

Bond said nothing. A man came in with a grey army shirt for Scarlett. Bond noticed that even after washing, her breasts were smeared with blood—his or hers, he didn't know. The man handed a similar shirt and trousers to Bond, who quickly put them on.

"Now. Sit down." Gorner gestured to a pair of wooden chairs. "Listen to me carefully and don't speak. I am not a sporting person. We won't be playing any more tennis. No more 'Have it again, old chap.' You are here to work. I'm going to show you my factory and then I will give you your operating instructions, Bond. You are going to help me pull off one of the most audacious military interventions of the century. One that I am confident will change the course of history. Do you follow?"

Bond nodded.

"By the way, you don't mind if I call you 'Bond,' not 'Mr. Bond' or Commander Bond, do you? That's what English gentlemen do, isn't it? Just the surnames for their 'chums.' We need to play by the rules, don't we?"

"What about Scarlett?" said Bond.

"The girl? I've no interest in her. Though I imagine my workforce might."

"What have you done to my sister?" said Scarlett. "Where's Poppy?"

Gorner walked across his office and put his face against Scarlett's. With his gloved monkey's hand he cupped her chin and twisted her face one way, then the other. Bond saw the hair-covered wrist between the glove and cuff.

"I don't know what you're talking about. I think you've perhaps been listening to rumours. We have a way of dealing with people who listen to rumours."

"Where is my sister? What have you—"

The back of the monkey's hand whipped across her mouth with a crack.

Gorner raised the forefinger of his human hand

to his lips. "Ssh," he said, as a trickle of blood ran out of Scarlett's mouth. "No more talk."

Turning to a guard, Gorner said, "Lock the girl in the cell till tonight when she can entertain the early shift."

The man took Scarlett away, blood still running from her lip, and Gorner turned to Bond. "You come with me."

He touched a spot on the crimson-draped walls, and a panel slid aside. Bond followed him on to a walkway whose sides and floor were made of glass. Below them was what looked like a chemical factory.

"Analgesia," said Gorner, walking forwards. "I learned about it on the Eastern Front. How to take away pain. People talk a lot of nonsense about the horrors of chemical warfare. No one who fought at Stalingrad can be in any doubt that 'conventional' warfare is far worse."

The size of the works was astonishing. Bond calculated that there were almost five hundred men on the assembly lines or transporting raw materials to the stills and centrifuges.

"When you have seen men with their faces missing," said Gorner, "literally sliced off by bullets that have spun and turned on the bones of the skull . . . When you've seen men trying to hold their liver and intestines in their hands... Then you understand the need for the rapid relief of pain."

They came to a junction in the walkway.

"On that side, those large steel vats are processing poppy extracts into what will become painkillers and anaesthetics. Codeine, dihydrocodeine, pethidine, morphine and so on. Some products are transported through the Persian Gulf to Bombay for the Far East and Australasia. Some go overland to my plant in Paris, then to America and the West. And some, believe it or not, go through the Soviet Union and on to Estonia. In Paris and Bombay, some of the chemicals are further refined, turned into powders, liquids, tablets, whatever local markets want. The brand names and the packaging in which they are sold are different in Paris and Bombay. The client health services and the private clinics pay into offshore accounts and no one is able to connect all the operations. Otherwise I would be accused of running a cartel. In fact, the man in the emergency field hospital in Nigeria is receiving the same drug as the woman in the private clinic in Los Angeles. Only the box and trade name are different. Both come from here."

"What about the competition?" said Bond.

"I'm able to compete with the older companies because I have very low labour costs. In fact, they work for nothing."

"Nothing?"

"No money. They're all addicts. We find them in Tehran, Isfahan and Kabul. Some in Baghdad and further afield. Turkey. They work twelve hours a day in return for water, rice and heroin. They sleep on the sand. They never run away."

"You give them heroin?" said Bond.

"It's cheaper and stronger than opium. They may come as opium addicts but we quickly change them over. Then we can just shoot them up once a day. They queue up like children for their injection. You should see their little faces."

Gorner turned and walked a few paces. "On this side of the plant, we make heroin. Doesn't look much different, does it? That's because I am the only manufacturer in the world who has brought a truly industrial technique to the manufacture of this drug. Putting it alongside my conventional works has allowed me to make huge economies of scale. The powder that comes out of here is produced with the same efficiency as the tablets and liquids that emerge from the other part of the factory. One lot ends up in the emergency rooms of Chicago and Madrid, the other in the back alleys of the Paris *banlieue* or the Watts ghetto in Los Angeles. And increasingly, Bond—it makes me very happy to say this—in the jolly old British streets of Soho and Manchester.

Once I've sold it, I dare say it may get cut with amphetamine or rat poison or weedkiller. But that's not my responsibility, is it? Once Chagrin has signed it off, I lose interest in the product—though not in what effects it has."

The workers were only a few feet below them. They wore grey shirts and loose trousers of the kind issued to Bond. Each man bent to his task with terrified intensity, particularly when he sensed the approach of one of the supervisors with his bullwhip and his Alsatian dog straining at its flimsy chain.

"Do you know what heroin is?" said Gorner. "A short chemistry lesson for you, Bond. We start with a pretty flower: the poppy or *Papaver somniferum*. A beautiful name for a beautiful plant—'the sleep-bringing poppy.' The juice from its seedpods gives you opium—the prince of drugs, extolled by poets from Homer to the present day. You've encountered it, I dare say."

"Briefly."

"Opium is expensive," said Gorner, "but highly desirable. The greatest drug cartel the world has ever seen—before my own modest enterprise—was run, of course, by your British Empire. They fought two opium wars with China to retain their trafficking monopoly—and twice they defeated them. By the treaty of Nanjing in 1842, they stole Hong Kong and opened five new ports to the opium trade, turning millions of Chinese into gibbering addicts. It's not unreasonable that someone should attempt to repay them in their own coin, is it? I'm doing nothing that the British haven't done themselves."

Bond said nothing.

"It takes time, though," said Gorner, remorsefully. "God, it takes time."

As he spoke, Bond was looking down at the row upon row of slave workers in their sweat-drenched uniforms. One seemed to have fainted or died and was being dragged away by the guards. The others alongside him were too scared to stop working.

"Between opium and heroin came morphine," said Gorner. "It was first isolated by a German in 1805—the year of your famous Trafalgar. Then, in 1874, an Englishman called Wright produced diacetylmorphine, a white, odourless, bitter, crystalline powder, made by the acetylation of morphine. Heroin."

Gorner coughed. "That's what they're doing there. Acetylation. That's the smell. I think you must know my reputation, Bond. I have a number of degrees from universities around the world. Perhaps these long words are confusing to you, but they are like love poetry to me. 'My love is like a red, red rose,' your Scotsman wrote, did he not? But my love is a red, red poppy. So various, so glorious. It gives me great pleasure that the poppy is the sentimental emblem of your pointless imperial sacrifice against the Germans in the Great War. I make sure that everyone in my narcotics supply chain repeats the words of your vacuous little poem: 'In Flanders fields the poppies blow . . .' It's their code. The code for death."

Gorner coughed again and brought himself back as though from a reverie. "Anyway, your English chemist, this Wright—most unusually for an Englishman—failed to exploit his discovery for personal gain. It was a German, Heinrich Dreser, the head of Bayer's pharmacological laboratory, who was the first to see the commercial uses of heroin. He tested it on his workers and they chose the name 'heroin' because it made them feel heroic! Pharmacologically, heroin had the same effect as morphine, but you needed only about a quarter as much. It was also cheaper, quicker and easier to use. It was a wonder drug. Soon every American chemist was lacing his own preparations with imported heroin. 'Bliss was it in that dawn to be alive,' as another of your poets put it . . ."

Bond found it hard to look at this man with his yellow hair and demonic sense of purpose. He seemed to be beyond reach, locked in a world where ordinary human concerns couldn't touch or weaken him.

"We have two shifts of twelve hours each," said Gorner, "so we're never idle. That's a further economy that none of my competitors can make."

"Don't they have a break?" said Bond.

"They have a two-minute water break every three hours. There is a degree of . . . natural wastage. They die at their post. They are carried out. You probably saw one go just now. We have no shortage of replacements. Even the Shah's government admits there are two million addicts in Iran, and each day more young people become addicted. Chagrin has a recruitment team that brings in roughly twenty men a day through Yazd and Kerman. It's a revolving door."

"That's despicable," said Bond.

"It's good business," said Gorner. "Everything I know about slavery I learned from the British Empire and its colonies. Africa, India, the West Indies. I was a most willing student of British techniques, Bond. And these men . . . They're trash. They'd die anyway. We prolong their lives. And at the end of each shift I even give them an entertainment. You'll see. We'll go back to my office now."

Back in the red-walled room, Gorner sat at his desk. He pressed a button beneath the top, and a panel slid back behind him, giving him a window on to the factory floor. "Sometimes I like to look at them," he said, "and sometimes I grow tired of their struggles. Anomie, Bond. I feel it sometimes. It is the weariness that eats the soul—the enemy of great achievement."

He caused the panel to close and swung round in his chair. "One day, Bond, I will make as many heroin addicts in Britain as Britain made in China. One day soon. Then you'll lose your precious status at the United Nations. You'll lose the Cold War, too. You'll become the third-world country you deserve to be."

"Tell me one thing," said Bond. "How did you manage to fight for both the Red Army and the Nazis with your disability? Your hand."

It was a risk he had calculated.

For a moment, the hard blue eyes were hidden as the cheekbones rose and the teeth met in an audible grinding. Then Gorner breathed out with a snort.

"You can know nothing of the Eastern Front, you idiot. These were not jolly Tommies with a cup of tea at five and stab you in the back at six. These were animals, freezing to death, killing with their bare hands, raping, torturing and murdering. They welcomed any recruit—the maimed, the mad, the deaf, the syphilitic. If you could pull a trigger—if you could find a rifle—you were in. It was what you would call 'all hands to the pump.' "

Gorner had regained control. He almost smiled. "There. I think I have made a joke. All hands . . . Even this one."

Then he lifted the white glove and stared hard at Bond, challenging him to meet his eye.

"Would you like to see it?"

"No."

"Go on, Bond. I know you're curious. You don't become a secret agent without curiosity. Let me show you."

Gorner peeled off the glove and held his hand close to Bond's face. The palm was long and flat, whitish-pink on the underside, black and wrinkled on the back. The first joint of the fingers was exceptionally long, and the blackened nails were triangular. All the skin was dry, and deep with simian lines. The thumb was short and set so far down towards the wrist as to be of no use working with the other digits. From the knuckle upward, the thing was covered in thick blackish-brown hair, like a chimpanzee's. Midway between the wrist and the elbow, the forearm became a man's.

Gorner replaced the glove. Bond showed no reaction.

The two men stood about a foot apart, staring into one another's eyes. Neither blinked.

"Why did you change sides in the war?" said Bond.

"Because the Nazis could no longer win. Their war was over. By 1944 the Cold War had already begun in Eastern Europe. I wanted to be on the side that would eventually beat the British. So I switched to the Soviet Army."

Bond said nothing. Most of what Gorner had said confirmed what M had told him. What Bond had learned was that the question of his hand could still unbalance him, even if only for a moment.

"Now to business," said Gorner. "My opium—my raw material—has to come from somewhere. I can't get enough from Turkey. I am using Chagrin's connections to open up the Far East. Laos is a good source, and the Americans have been most surprisingly helpful there. Did you know that the CIA has its own airline, Air America, that actually flies out cargoes of opium?"

"That's absurd," said Bond.

"That's politics," said Gorner. "Air America takes weapons to the anti-Communist warlords and returns with consignments of opium poppies. What do you expect from an airline whose motto is 'Anything, Anytime, Anywhere'? Thousands of GIs are addicts now. The CIA headquarters in northern Laos has a plant where they refine heroin. That part of Asia is the source of seventy per cent of the world's illicit opium and the major supplier for America's insatiable market."

"And are you getting your hands on that too?"

"Yes. Chagrin is working on it. I'm paying over the odds there at the moment. It's an investment. I don't really like it because my money goes directly to funding the American war effort. But there's one major advantage. It means the CIA is unofficially inclined to look on my global activities with a rather forgiving eye. I'm sure you understand why that might be helpful."

"Russia, America... You've covered all the angles, haven't you?" said Bond.

"That's certainly my intention," said Gorner. "It makes sound business sense. One day I'll buy at better prices in the Far East. For the moment, the bulk of my supply is coming from Afghanistan, in Helmand province. And this is where you come in, Bond. The border is causing us some problems at the moment. There are bandits everywhere, some with rocket launchers and grenades as well as hand-guns. There's a run my men have to make near Zabol, when they're loaded up with opium. They call it Hellfire Pass. Do you know why?"

Bond shook his head.

"It's named after a section of the Burma railway built by Anzac prisoners-of-war under the Japanese. They say one man lost his life for every yard of track laid down. They were very brave men, those Anzacs, fighting your war for you."

"I know they were," said Bond. "They were among the finest."

"Anyway, that's what we've been losing. Not quite a man a yard, but too many. And I can't send addicts, so I'm having to waste real men. I want you to go to Zabol with Chagrin. You leave tomorrow morning."

"Why?"

"I think it would be an education for you."

Gorner stood up, and the panel behind him opened. "And now," he said, "it's time for the evening entertainment. Come over here, Bond."

A guard pushed an automatic rifle into the base of Bond's spine.

In the glass walkway on the far side of the heroin plant, a door opened. A woman was pushed out by a guard and left alone as the door closed. She had no clothes on.

"We call it the Lambeth Walk," said Gorner. "A good old Cockney entertainment."

Three more women, also naked, were propelled on to the walkway.

"They have to make a complete circuit," said Gorner. "The men like to stand underneath and watch."

"Who are these women?"

"They're no one. They're prostitutes. Most are addicts. They get scooped up along with the men. When they're losing their allure, say after two or three days, I let the men have their way with them."

"You what?"

"The guards lead them down on to the factory floor and the men take them outside. It's free entertainment and it's good for morale."

"And what do you do with the girls afterwards?"

Gorner looked at Bond curiously. "Why, bury them, of course."

Then he turned back towards the entry where the girls were coming in and came as close to smiling as he could. "Oh, do look, Bond. There's one just coming out that you're sure to recognize. I think the men are going to go crazy for her."

13. SMALL WORLD

In Paris, though it might have been a world away, René Mathis was glancing through *Le Figaro* as he finished lunch in a café near the offices of the Deuxième. A new Vickers VC10 airliner, he read, flying from Britain to be commissioned by Gulf Air in Bahrain, had vanished somewhere over the Iran–Iraq border. It had simply disappeared from the radar screens.

Mathis shrugged. These things happened. The British Comet had been particularly crash-prone, he seemed to remember. He had had a typical working lunch: steak tartare with *frites* and a small pitcher of

Côtes du Rhône, then a double café express. It was a quiet day in Paris, and on such days Mathis often had his best ideas.

The police investigation into the murder of Yusuf Hashim had been inconclusive. There were areas of Paris that the police couldn't really penetrate, either because it was too dangerous for the officers or because the denizens of the high-rises, even if they spoke French, would not co-operate. La Courneuve, a district of St. Denis with its infamous Cité des 4000, was one. Sarcelles was another: a ghetto with its own violent rules of dog-eat-dog that had little or nothing to do with the laws of the Republic. These places were viewed by most people as the price that France had been made to pay for her imperial misadventures.

The French abandonment of Indo-China had been humiliating, but had had few repercussions at home beyond the appearance of a vast number of indistinguishable Vietnamese restaurants. The Algerian war, on the other hand, had saddled the large cities of France, and Paris in particular, with thousands of disgruntled Muslim immigrants. While they were effectively fenced out of the city centres into the high-rise suburbs, Mathis viewed such places as a breeding ground for crime and subversion that would sooner or later explode.

Yusuf Hashim had been one of many runners in

a long supply chain of heroin. The police had found the narcotic on the estate and it was notable for both quality and quantity. This was not the fashionable dabbling of the cocktail set at Le Boeuf sur le Toit and other nightclubs of Mathis's youth. This was death-by-drugs, peddled on a national scale, and the supply line was expertly run with so many cut-outs that it was impossible to find the source.

Colleagues in Marseille, working with American detectives, had had some success in closing down shipments to America through what the FBI called the French Connection. What they had further discovered was that, although France was buying more heroin than ever before, the bulk of what came in was being shipped on to London.

It was almost, the French police told him, as though someone with limitless resources was waging a crusade against Britain.

Mathis looked at his watch. He had a few minutes to spare so he ordered another coffee and a small cognac. For several days something had been nagging at the edge of his memory, begging to be let in. And now, as he looked through the glass enclosure of his pavement café beneath its scarlet awning, it finally came to him.

The tongue removed with pliers . . . He had heard of this punishment before, and now he remembered where. His brother, an infantry major, had fought with the French forces in Indo-China and had told him of a particular Viet Minh war criminal they had tried to capture and bring to justice. He had supervised the torture of captured French troops, but had also been an enforcer of Communist doctrine against Catholic missionary schools. His speciality had been the punishment—or torture—of children, many of whom had ended up maimed for life after his attentions.

When Mathis returned to his office, he asked his secretary to search the files for photographs relating to war criminals from the Indo-China war.

After he had seen Bond at lunch, Mathis had commissioned one of his subordinates to find Julius Gorner's Paris factory and photograph its proprietor. Several prints came in of a tall, handsome Slavic man with a large, white-gloved hand and an intensely dismissive, arrogant expression. In two pictures he was accompanied by a man in a kepi with Oriental, possibly Vietnamese, features.

When the secretary returned with a brown cardboard file, it took Mathis only a few minutes to find a match. Side by side he placed the shiny new monochrome print of a man in a kepi standing next to a black Mercedes 300D Cabriolet and a faded eleven-year-old newspaper cutting showing Pham

Sinh Quoc, whose Wanted picture had once been on every wall in French Saigon. They were one and the same man.

Mathis, however, did not immediately lift the telephone or order a car to take him to Gorner's chemical plant. He tried instead to work out whether the Far East connection might mean more to Gorner than having provided him with a psychopathic aide-de-camp.

Lighting a Gauloise *filtre*, he put his feet up on the desk and considered what commercial gain there might be for Gorner in having an *entrée* to the dangerous triangle of Laos, Vietnam and Cambodia.

Nine hours behind Paris, it was nine o'clock on a bright morning in Santa Monica, and Felix Leiter was making a house call to a Spanish-style home on Georgina Avenue. He limped over the grass and up to the front door.

The grizzled Texan, who had been a partner in some of the most testing cases in James Bond's career, was working for Pinkerton's detective agency, and made no secret of his boredom. He had been hired by a producer at one of the Hollywood studios to make inquiries about a missing person. She was called Trixie Rocket, had appeared in two

B-pictures, then disappeared from sight, leaving no forwarding address, no number, nothing. The girl's parents, who came from Idaho, had been making threatening noises towards the studio. Suspicion had fallen on the producer who had cast Trixie and who was now anxious to find her so that he could clear his name before his wife got to hear anything.

It was tame work for a man of Leiter's abilities, but since he'd lost his right leg and arm to a hammerhead shark while helping out Bond in Miami, he was limited in what he could do.

There was a furious barking from behind the front door of 1614 Georgina, then an attractive, dark-haired woman poked her head out. She was on the telephone and gestured to Felix to wait. He went to sit on the grass verge and opened his copy of the *Los Angeles Times*.

After about twenty minutes on the telephone, the woman, whose name was Louisa Shirer, finally called him in and showed him through to a small backyard, where she brought coffee. Mrs. Shirer turned out to be a charming, voluble woman. Trixie Rocket had been her lodger and she remembered her well, but Trixie hadn't lived there for three months now. She hadn't left a forwarding address but . . . At that moment the telephone rang again, and Felix had to stare into his coffee for another fifteen minutes.

The visit had been pleasant but pointless. When he eventually got back to his cheap hotel in West Hollywood, he felt worn out. A slovenly ceiling fan rotated above the potted palms in the lobby and the elevator was stuck on the tenth floor. But there was a message for him at the desk, asking him to ring a number in Washington. Felix recognized the prefix and felt a sudden surge of excitement.

The last real action he had seen was on a train with Bond in Jamaica. Before that, he'd been redrafted by the CIA in the Bahamas when they ran short of manpower. Once you'd been on the books, you were a lifelong reserve.

When the revived elevator had finally taken him up to his room, Felix called the number on the piece of paper. After a barrage of security checks he was eventually put through. A voice spoke to him in a flat, serious tone for almost two minutes.

Leiter stood by the bed, smoking a cigarette, nodding at intervals. "Yup . . . yup . . . I see."

Eventually the voice stopped and Leiter said, "And just where the hell is Tehran?"

Meanwhile, it was early evening in that city, and Darius Alizadeh was on his way to the top of the *andaroon*—the women's section—of his traditional

house. He was too modern and secular to observe
the ritual distinction of the sexes in his household,
but used the separate buildings to keep his work
and domestic affairs apart. Darius had been married
three times for brief periods and had three sons by
his different wives. He had followed the Shia provi-
sion of the *mut'a*, which allows a couple to contract
a marriage for as short a period as they like and to
end it without divorce. He was fond of quoting the
helpful lines from the Koran: "If you fear that you
will not act justly towards the orphans, marry such
women as seem good to you, two, three or four;
but if you fear you will not be equitable, then only
one . . ."

Darius had had no such fears and had provided
handsomely for his sons and their mothers. He kept
a sharp eye open for the fourth wife the Prophet
permitted him, and allowed himself the occasional
trial run with likely candidates. He was seeing one
of them—Zohreh from the restaurant where he had
dined with Bond—later that evening.

The air-conditioned top floor of the *andaroon*,
Darius's office, was a single open-plan space with
wooden "American" shutters, a stripped wood floor
with a single antique rug from Isfahan and a gilded
cage in which he kept a white parakeet. At 1800
hours each day he transmitted his report to London.

If he failed to come on air at precisely this time there was a reprimand in the shape of a "blue call" from Regent's Park half an hour later, then a red call at 1900. If that went unanswered, London would set about trying to find out what had happened to him.

Darius had never received reminders of either colour, and this evening he was particularly keen to be on time. He put on the headphones and positioned himself in front of the transmitter. His practised fingers went to work on the keys, tapping out his call sign—"PXN calling WWW"—on 14 megacycles. He heard the sudden hollowness in the ether that meant London was coming in to acknowledge him.

He had a great deal to tell them, but it was important to keep calm as he did so. In the control room in Regent's Park, there was an entire wall of glass dials with quivering needles which, among other things, measured the weight of each pulse and the speed of each cipher group, and registered any characteristic stumbles Darius had with particular letters—the s, for instance, under the weak second finger of his left hand. If the machines didn't recognize his personal "fist," a buzzer would sound and he would immediately be disconnected.

He knew of an agent in the West Indies who, when overexcited, frequently transmitted too fast and found himself cut off by the electronic guardians. There were subtle ways in which agents who had been captured could let it be seen from the variations—either in their "fist" or by previously agreed groups of words in the message—that they were operating under duress. But Darius was distrustful of such measures. The whole of the British SOE group in Holland, having been captured in the war, had faithfully included the agreed telltale signs in their Nazi-supervised transmissions only for their bosses in Baker Street to come on the line and tell them to stop messing about.

Darius informed London in code that there was still no word from 007 and requested instructions as to whether he should himself proceed to Noshahr. He included the slender details of what he had so far discovered in Tehran—from Hamid among others—about the Caspian Sea Monster. At lunchtime he had gone downtown to the elegant French club and bought cocktails on the veranda for some old Indo-China hands who viewed themselves as having seen it all. Over *côtelettes d'agneau* and red Burgundy, he had learned that they were aware of sightings and that their photographs suggested the Monster had been modified to fire rockets. On his way back, Darius called in at the club known only as the CRC, one of the chicest venues in Tehran, where ten-pin bowling was played in a marble alley by the city's most fashion-conscious people to the background music of Frank Sinatra and Dave Brubeck.

Here, from an American who had drunk too much bourbon, Darius learned something even more interesting. A Vickers VC10, which was meant to be delivered to the BOAC-owned Gulf Air in Bahrain two weeks earlier, had mysteriously never arrived. The American had heard from a friend whose son worked on a USAF base that the VC10 had in fact entered western Persian airspace but had not emerged. The plane was thought either to have crashed or to have put down in the sand desert, the Dasht-e Lut, somewhere near Kerman. No trace had been found.

Darius's fingers relayed the news with measured urgency. He knew that M would understand the implications—and the danger—as completely as if he had transmitted the entire message *en clair*.

An hour later, in the middle of the London afternoon, the pulse high on M's right temple was showing, as it did when he was tense. He struck a match and held it to his pipe, inhaling noisily. On his desk were cables from Paris and Washington, as well as Darius's latest offering from Tehran. Between them they might make up an entire picture, but for the time being they were only fragments—urgent, frustrating, incomplete. On the roof, only a few feet above M's head, were the three squat masts of the most powerful radio transmitters in Britain. The ninth floor was almost entirely taken up by a hand-picked group of communications experts who spoke a private language about sunspots and the "Heaviside layer." But as they had patiently explained to M, in reply to his tetchy questions, there was not much more they could do to help without further incoming signal traffic.

M walked to the window and looked out towards Regent's Park. A couple of weeks ago he had spent a morning down the road at Lord's, watching England on their way to victory over the touring Indians by an innings and 124 runs. There was no time for such frivolities now.

He buzzed the intercom. "Moneypenny? Send in the chief of staff."

Down the softly carpeted corridor from the green baize door that separated M's private staff from the rest of the world came the chief of staff, a lean, relaxed man of about James Bond's age.

Miss Moneypenny raised an eyebrow as he approached. "Go straight in, Bill," she said, "but fasten your seat-belt."

As the door of M's office opened and closed, a green light came on above it.

"Take a seat," said M. "What do you make of Pistachio's cable?"

"I've just had a report from the aviation people," said the chief of staff. "It's difficult to be sure from the information we've got in the cable, but they think it could be an Ekranoplan."

"What the devil's that?" said M.

"It looks like a plane with cut-off wings, but it operates like a hovercraft on what's called 'ground effect.' It weighs double the heaviest conventional aircraft, it's over three hundred feet long and has a wingspan of a hundred and thirty feet. You know when birds come in to land—geese on a lake, for instance—and they prolong their glide without effort? That's ground effect. That upward pressure you feel when a plane comes in to land? That's ground effect, too. A cushion of air is trapped between the wing and the runway and causes an updraught. The Soviets have found a way of harnessing this power. It's called a 'wig'—or wing-in-ground-effect craft. It's light years ahead of anything we've got. The details are in this report." He handed a file across the desk.

"If that's what it is," said M, "we have a problem."

"Yes. They're still testing at the moment. We know of only four in existence, but the Russians plan to build more than a hundred in the Volga shipyard. There are some low-quality photographs taken by US satellites over the Caspian and one by a U2 spyplane. Word got round from Persian fishermen who'd seen one. They call it the Caspian Sea Monster."

"What kind of damage can it do?" said M.

"We think it's designed to be a troop transport and assault craft. But it can carry a payload of roughly twenty-five tons—and only a few feet above the sea."

"What speed?" said M.

"I think you'd better sit down for this bit, sir," said the chief of staff. "It can do four hundred kilometres an hour."

"What?"

"Yes. That's two hundred and fifty miles per—"

"I know exactly how fast it is," said M. "But what the hell is it doing in Persia?"

"Well, Pistachio is only relying on word of mouth from a driver who took 007 to the docks, so we can't really say. But it doesn't look good. Particularly if it's been modified."

M puffed heavily at his pipe. "Well, I trust Pistachio. Did you get that sample he sent back analysed? The bag of stuff from Noshahr that came in this morning?"

"Yes. It's pure heroin. If heroin can ever be 'pure.' Bound for . . . Well, God knows. It looks as though it was bound for Russia. In the Ekranoplan."

"That means Gorner has some deal with the Russians. They'll traffic the heroin on to the West through Eastern Europe. Maybe through the Baltic states. Estonia, probably."

"I'm rather afraid it looks that way, sir."

M went over to the window again. With his back to the chief of staff, he said, "I don't think that's the whole story, though. I don't believe it's only commercial, just a drug deal—however enormous. The Americans are pouring people into Persia at the moment."

"Don't they always?"

"Yes. But not like this. I haven't seen such panic in the Middle East since that man Philby surfaced in Beirut. The people in Langley know something big's going on."

"Are things any better between us and Langley?" said the chief of staff.

M shook his head. "Still cool, I'm afraid. It's Vietnam that's the problem. Until the politicians can see eye to eye on that or until we send some troops, there'll be this degree of . . . reserve."

"You mean that as far as Persia's concerned, we're both in crash dive but we're not talking to each other."

M sighed heavily. "That's about the size of it, Bill. That's why we so badly need to hear from 007."

"What about 004? Any word?"

"Not a squeak. What really worries me is what I'm getting from Washington. Pretty much every spare agent is being shipped off to Tehran. Even some in semi-retirement. It's all hands on deck."

"And we don't really know why. There's something they're not telling us."

M nodded silently.

Eventually, after a heavy silence, the chief of staff said, "If Gorner has some deal with the Russians so that he can use their Ekranoplan to transport his heroin, then he has to be repaying them in some way."

"Not just money," said M. "Are you thinking what I'm thinking?"

"I believe that's my job, sir," said the chief of staff.

M put down his pipe on the desk and pressed a switch on the intercom. "Moneypenny," he said. "Get me the prime minister."

14. THE END OF
THE WORLD

"It's as well for you my hands are tied, Gorner," said Bond. He spat the words.

"Tough talk, Bond, but I don't think my men would let me come to much harm." Gorner nodded towards the two armed guards at the door. "Don't you want to look at your little girlfriend? Everyone else is. And by the sound of it, they like her a lot."

Bond glanced through the window. Scarlett was running the gauntlet naked along the glass walkway, trying to preserve her modesty with her hands while an armed guard prodded her with a rifle butt and the slave workers roared their approval from below.

"Kill Gorner," Poppy had told him. "Just kill him." Bond would have to wait for his moment, he thought, but when it came, he would relish it.

"Don't worry about the girls," said Gorner. "They're just human flotsam. The kind of people your Empire found expendable."

Bond swore succinctly.

"And if you find it so distasteful," said Gorner, now fully back in control and obviously enjoying himself, "you can return to your cell."

Gorner beckoned to the guard and gave him a brief instruction in Farsi. "We'll send your little girlfriend in to join you later, Bond. We won't let the men have her tonight. I want to build up their appetite first."

In the solitude of the cell, Bond tried to form a plan of escape. It was possible that he could jump a guard and take his gun, but not until he had somehow loosened the nylon ropes that were biting into his wrists. Even then, he didn't want to do anything until he had the basis of a plan for getting himself, Scarlett and Poppy out of Gorner's lair.

In the meantime, he thought his interests were better served by doing as Gorner said. Sooner or later Gorner would have to disclose the details of his proposed "military intervention," and then Bond, given a chance, would at least be in a position to pass a worthwhile message back to London, or to Darius in Tehran. It was probable that he would die in the process, but if he could somehow get word back that enabled defences to be put in place, then at least he would have done his job.

Eight hours passed with no food, no water and no sign of Scarlett. Bond was dozing fitfully when he was summoned back to Gorner's office at gunpoint. This time, Chagrin was standing next to his master.

"You're going on an exercise, Bond," said Gorner. "You can view it as a kind of reconnaissance before the main action. Sometimes these preliminaries can be as dangerous as the real thing, however. You may not survive, but it will amuse me to see what you're made of. And I'm sure it'll be good for you. You'll learn a lot. I'm going to place you in the care of Chagrin, my most trusted lieutenant."

The man in the kepi stepped forward at the sound of his name. He then muttered something to the guard, who clicked his heels and left.

"I think it's time you knew a little more about Chagrin," said Gorner. "His real name is Pham Sinh Quoc. He fought for the Viet Minh. He was a dedicated Communist soldier against the French. When the French colonized Indo-China they sent many nuns and missionaries. Religion was not good enough for the great lay Republic of France at home, where church and state had been separate since 1789, but they always exported Catholicism to the little coloured people whose land they stole. I suppose it eased their conscience."

The guard, accompanied by three others, had returned with a gibbering workman in a grey uniform. The man fell to his knees, clearly terrified of what lay in wait.

"When Chagrin and his comrades came to a village in the north where the children had been listening to Bible classes, they used to tear out the tongue of the preacher with a pair of pliers. Then he couldn't preach any more. That's what we still do to people who talk too much."

Gorner nodded to Chagrin, who took a pair of chopsticks from his pocket. Two guards held the workman's arms rigid behind him while Chagrin inserted a chopstick into each of the man's ears.

"And this is what Chagrin used to do to the children who had listened to the Bible."

Bracing his feet at either side of the man, Chagrin banged the flat of his hands as hard as he could against the ends of the chopsticks, drilling them into the man's head. Blood spurted from his ears as he screamed and fell forward on the floor.

"He won't hear anything for a long while now," said Gorner. "Not till his eardrums grow back. Some of the children never heard again."

Two guards dragged the screaming man away while two remained in the room.

"And I expect you'd like to know how Chagrin came by his nickname. The word means both 'pain' and 'grief' in French. Remarkable that a language should use the same word for both, don't you think? But there was something else about Chagrin that made him a better, fiercer soldier than anyone else. When the Russians liberated the Nazi concentration camps they took the papers relating to the Nazi doctors' experiments. A highly secret section of the Soviet health ministry continued with experiments along the same lines for many years afterwards. Unlike the Nazis, they asked for volunteers. Travel costs and a financial reward were guaranteed. Word reached Chagrin's Communist cell in North Vietnam and he volunteered to go to a clinic in Omsk. Russian military doctors were interested in the neurological basis of psychopaths—by which we mean men who lack the ability to imagine the feelings of other people. They can't project. They have no concept at all of 'the other.' The doctors thought that such a capacity—or lack of it—might be useful to the army and particularly to the KGB. To cut a long story short, Chagrin was one of a dozen men who underwent brain surgery. Post-mortems of psychopaths had shown some abnormalities in the temporal lobe. Are you still with me, Bond?"

"Yes."

"In Chagrin's case the operation was a success. They cauterized an area of his temporal lobe the size of a fingernail. I don't imagine Chagrin was exactly a bleeding heart before, but afterwards his indifference to others has been total. It's really quite remarkable. Unfortunately, there was a small side-effect. The surgeons damaged a major cluster of pain-sensing neurons in his brain—quite close to the morphine receptors, as it happens. The brain registers pain in some of the same areas that govern emotion. If you try to stop someone feeling compassion, you may take away other feelings. As a result, Chagrin's ability to experience pain is uneven, sometimes barely existent. This means he has to be careful. He might jump down twenty feet and not even know that he's broken his ankle. At other times, of course, it can be an advantage. In combat, he is a formidable opponent."

"I see," said Bond. It explained the stroke-victim appearance of part of Chagrin's face. "But why the hat?"

"The surgeons raised what's called an osteoplastic

flap. They drill holes in the skull, then insert a thin saw between the bone and the membranes beneath and cut upwards through the bone. When they've got three-quarters of a circle, they lift and fold back the skull. But the gentlemen in Omsk were in a hurry and didn't finish the job properly. The flap doesn't really fit. Chagrin feels shy about it."

"Yes," said Bond. "But why the cap of the Foreign Legion, when he fought so bitterly against the French?"

Gorner shrugged. "I think perhaps the Russian neurosurgeons removed his sense of irony."

Bond struggled to contain his hatred of this man. Which unwise student, he thought, which unthinking joker at Oxford University had first teased him about his hand and so set his life's course on this perverted crusade?

"You must be hungry, Bond," said Gorner. "But today, as I said, is a day of education. The lack of food is to remind you of how the British systematically starved the Irish in the great potato famine. I think a few pangs of yours don't really compare to the pain of the millions who died. Do you?"

"When do I leave on this venture of yours?" asked Bond.

Gorner was looking through the window at the slave workers on his factory floor and seemed not to hear. "I did think of another way of bringing Britain to its knees," he said. "I considered investing the profits from my pharmaceutical company in the newspaper business. Suppose I had bought the most distinguished paper of your Establishment hypocrites, *The Times*. Then I could have put it in the hands of some malleable editor who shared my hatred of Britain and attacked the country from its own mouthpiece. I could have bought television channels, other papers . . . I could have piped in pornography and propaganda through every inlet until . . . But, no, Bond. It would have taken too long. And your 'fair play' laws that limit ownership might have stopped me. So I pipe death into the veins, with needles. It's the same, but quicker."

Gorner stood up. "Enough of this pleasant daydream. Chagrin, take Bond away. Make him work. Remember what the British did to the Kikuyu in the Mau-Mau rebellion. Go."

Chagrin walked in front of Bond while two armed guards followed. They took the open elevator up to the ground floor, then went by electric cart down a vaulted corridor to a barred iron door. Chagrin went to a keypad beside it and punched in a five-figure code.

Bond memorized the sequence of sounds, as each number Chagrin pressed emitted a slightly different note.

The door slid away and Bond was pushed into the open and forwards over the desert sand, towards what he recognized at once as a classic Soviet twin-engined Mi-8 Hip. It had a five-blade main rotor and was capable of carrying thirty-six armed men.

The sun was searingly hot during the short walk to the aircraft. The slowly moving blades were already whipping up the sand as they climbed the steps. There were ten more of Gorner's men inside, all armed and dressed in plain T-shirts with army combat trousers and heavy ammunition belts. The cargo door was pulled shut, the rotors accelerated and, with an effortless surge, the helicopter swept up into the air, banked left and roared away over the desert.

Bond could tell from the sun that they were flying east, towards Afghanistan. In his mind, he went over the sound of the electronic keypad Chagrin had used and fixed the sequence of noises in his memory as a primitive tune. He practised it again and again till it had lodged itself in his memory like the most annoying pop song on the radio.

When the helicopter eventually put down, it was next to a modest caravanserai, a rectangle of improvised buildings to which water had been fed from some distant mountain snowmelt by the system of underground *qanats* that J. D. Silver had described to him. Bond made out its path running to the building like that of a furiously burrowing desert mole. The men left the helicopter and were given water and food from a table in the open courtyard.

Bond could smell the kebab and rice and found himself salivating. He hadn't eaten since dinner with Hamid and Scarlett in Noshahr. But his hands were tied, and when the cook made to offer him some food, Chagrin shook his head.

"Irish men," he said. "No food."

"Water?" said Bond.

Chagrin poured some water into a bowl. "Like dog," he said. "Like English with slaves."

Bond knelt down and lapped at the warm water.

There were about a dozen tethered camels in the caravanserai. The local men placed ladders against their flanks, climbed up and thrust their hands through cauterized cuts into their humps. Their bloodied forearms were then withdrawn and in their hands were polythene-wrapped parcels, like the ones Bond had seen at Noshahr. Bond presumed the camels had been trained to follow a route across the desert by being heavily watered at each end.

"Go," said Chagrin, pushing Bond towards an all-terrain army vehicle that was waiting with its engine already running.

It was a six-hour drive over rough desert tracks,

then up through the mountains before the first sight of any human habitation. Bond remembered from his study of the maps that there were proper roads along the southern edge of the Dasht-e Lut, going from Bam to Zahedan, then up to Zabol at the border. But where there were roads there would be roadblocks and police searches, so the desert route was clearly better for Gorner's purpose.

The landscape became greener as they came down from the mountains and drove across the plain towards Zabol. About ten miles short, the all-terrain vehicle stopped, and the men transferred to ten waiting open-topped jeeps. With the jeep drivers, Bond and Chagrin, the party now totalled twenty-two. They left at three-minute intervals, not wanting, Bond presumed, to be seen as a group. The military lorry itself, though big enough to carry back several hundred-weight of opium, was obviously too conspicuous to be seen in town.

A few minutes later, Bond was in the city he'd imagined, in his hotel in Tehran, as the end of the world. It was a dusty, treeless place of grey-brown walls made of mud bricks. The streets were laid out on a closed grid, which gave it a tight, claustrophobic feeling. The dry heat was intense, and unmediated by any tall buildings. Although there were some Persians of the kind he'd seen in Tehran, in Western clothes, there were many more dark-skinned tribes-men with Afghan headdresses and unkempt black beards. Sizeable though it was, Zabol had the lawless feel of an old frontier town.

Bond was ordered out of his jeep, which then drove off to avoid being seen in the city. He was walked through the bazaar with the muzzle of Cha-grin's revolver against his lower vertebrae. It was a tawdry market. Instead of silk, the stalls sold ciga-rettes and imitation Western goods—records, per-fumes, plastics—made in China. In the food section there were displays of Sistani sugar melons, ruby grapes, boxes of Bami dates and orange-coloured spices, but over them all hung the sickly smell of opium, the *Papaver somniferum*.

"*Taliak*," hissed an old man at Bond, gesturing him to follow behind a curtain. His grey beard was yellow from years of smoking the *taliak* or opium he hoped to sell.

Chagrin pushed the old man in the chest, and he fell back through his curtain. What surprised Bond was how few police there seemed to be in Zabol. From this he concluded that the main trafficking was done far away from the bazaar and that the police were tolerant of small-scale dealing, no doubt because they were themselves implicated.

They walked through the town till they came to

an industrial area. Here, Bond saw the ten jeeps reassembled outside a low mud-brick warehouse which, to judge from the illustrated hoarding beside it, was supposed to deal in melons. The corrugated doors were reeled back, screeching on their runners, and the jeeps drove in.

In the gloom inside, a dozen Afghans, their tribal costumes criss-crossed with bandoleers of ammunition, pointed Soviet rifles at Chagrin's men as they loaded wooden tea chests into the back of the jeeps. There were twenty in all, two for each jeep. It was a colossal amount of raw opium, Bond thought, but nothing like enough to keep the wheels of Gorner's factory turning. Heaven knew how much he was flying in from Laos.

Under heavy cover from his men, Chagrin walked to the middle of the warehouse and placed a thick foolscap envelope on an empty crate. He stood his ground while one of the Afghans opened it and counted the fistfuls of US dollar bills it contained.

At the Afghan's silent nod of approval, Chagrin turned and gestured to the men. There was the sound of ten engines starting, and the convoy left at one-minute intervals. Bond and Chagrin were in the final jeep, which was driven rapidly round the edge of town by the youngest and most nervous-looking of the drivers. About ten minutes outside Zabol, they joined the nine other vehicles behind a hill of sand and rock.

The way ahead, back to the military transporter, which Bond could just make out on the flat horizon, was through a narrow defile with bare, pitted hills on both sides.

Chagrin took a pocket knife from his trousers and cut through the ropes at Bond's wrists. "Hellfire Pass," he said.

Then something resembling a smile crept over his half-inanimate flesh. Bond thought of the Vietnamese children in their Bible-study groups.

"You drive first jeep," said Chagrin. "Go."

All the other men were laughing.

Bond climbed into the driver's seat on the left-hand side. There was no time for *hejira*, or tactical retreat. This was the moment to go hard. He rammed the gear lever into first and dropped the clutch. The four drive-wheels screeched, then gripped the desert earth. The jeep went forward with such leaping eagerness that Bond was almost thrown from his seat. He battled with the steering-wheel and regained control as he put his right foot down and worked up through the gears. He felt the weight of the two tea chests in the back shifting from side to side on the ruts and potholes of the sanded track. He saw a flash of rifle fire from the hillside on his left, glanced up to where Afghan tribesmen were firing from behind rocks. He heard a bullet whine off the jeep's bonnet and wrenched the wheel from side to side to make himself a harder target. Then came the heavier wheeze of a hand-launched rocket, and the road in front of him exploded into a ball of spitting rock and sand, shattering the jeep's windshield and filling his eyes with dust. Bond dashed his sleeve across his eyes to clear his vision. A long shard of glass had cut through his cheek and impaled itself there, with the sharp end in his gum.

Gunfire started from the hill to his right, and he became aware that another vehicle was close behind, though he had no time to check if it was the next of Gorner's jeep convoy or an enemy bandit pursuing him. He knew only that he had to keep going. Automatic fire intensified from the hills to his right, and ripped through the flimsy passenger seat-back, ricocheting from the steel frame. It seemed the whole landscape had come alive in its insane hunger for the drugs he was carrying. Bond's knuckles stood white on the wheel and blood ran down his cheek on to his sweat-drenched workshirt. He thought of Gorner's face, of Scarlett on the walkway and Poppy held captive in the belly of the desert. He roared loud in anger and defiance, then rammed his right foot flat down against the floorboards while the dense gunfire hit the body of the jeep like mad sticks clattering on a snaredrum.

Suddenly Bond was in the air, catapulted from his seat by a grenade explosion beneath the axle. He landed on his left shoulder, agonizingly, rolled over and made for the cover of a rock. He glanced back to see his jeep upside down on the road, the wheels turning frantically under the command of the trapped accelerator. As a bullet embedded itself in a crevice of the rock behind him, Bond looked round and saw the raised molehill of an access point to a *qanat*, the underground water system that must run to Zabol. Sprinting zigzag across the stony ground, he ducked down behind the raised earth, and found a sheet of corrugated iron across an entrance. Hurling the sheet aside, he lowered himself in and dropped fifteen feet into cold water.

For a moment, he had time to think. It was possible that no one had seen him, though he doubted it, since Hellfire Pass seemed at that moment to be the most populated part of Persia. He guessed that he had been sent as a decoy while the other jeeps went through a safer route, north of the narrow defile, to regroup at the main transport lorry. The important thing was somehow to get back to Gorner's lair. Stranded in the desert, he was no use to Scarlett, or to Poppy, or to the Service. Somehow he had to find a way back to Chagrin's men.

The water was waist-high and cold. Bond lowered his face into it and carefully withdrew the piece of glass from his cheek. Then he snapped it into two jagged pieces of about two inches each and stowed them carefully in the buttoned breast pocket of his shirt.

A pistol shot disturbed the surface of the water. Someone was at the *qanat* access point, firing down. Bond began to make his way upstream, fording through the water from the distant mountains. The current was such that it was hard to make progress. He ducked beneath the surface and swam for as many strokes as his lungs permitted, but when he surfaced he could see that he had managed only a few yards. Another shot went past him. They were in the water with him. Bond pushed on with all his strength, but soon noticed something else was happening: the water was rising. This could only have happened by human intervention, he thought. There could not have been a sudden extra burst of snow-melt in a far-off mountain gully, so there had to be some sort of sluice that someone had closed downstream or a gate upstream that had been operated to divert more water. But he could see nothing in the darkness of the torrent.

He put his hand above his head and felt the roof of the narrow channel only a few inches above him.

If the flow increased much more, he would drown. He couldn't turn back, into the teeth of his armed pursuers, so he had no choice but to continue.

Forging onwards, with his hands ahead of him, Bond felt the water rising to the level of his mouth. He dipped his head beneath the flow and swam again, hoping to find a place where the uneven passage would be higher and so give him air above the surface. But when he came up, the headroom was so tight that he had to bend his neck sideways to breathe. Thrashing desperately now, Bond made one last push forward with his arms in the torrential darkness. His left hand encountered something different: air. There was a hole in the roof of the *qanat*, and against the rush of water he managed to grip its rocky side and get his head high enough up into it to breathe. A little further up, there was another handhold of rock, and as the rising water swirled round his waist, Bond knew that upwards was now the only way he could go.

He cursed the width of his shoulders as he pulled himself up the narrow funnel, the jutting desert rocks slicing through the skin of his palms. Eventually, his feet were clear of the water, and he was alone, wedged in the skintight tube of earth.

He made a fraction of an inch, and then another fraction. With bleeding feet and hands, he rose by almost imperceptible degrees through the narrow chimney. What, he thought, could be the point of this—when for all he knew there might be thirty feet of solid earth above him? He could hear the water below, and decided that when he was no longer able to move, he would try to drop down and die in its cold depths. His left shoulder, on which he'd landed when thrown from the jeep, allowed little movement from his left arm, so it was with one functioning hand only that he tried to fight his way up.

Half-inch by half-inch, with his lacerated and bleeding hands, he shoved himself up into the blind, tight funnel that held his shoulders. His hip was seizing with cramp, but he couldn't move it to free the muscle. Above him, the shaft seemed to grow narrower, the air less plentiful.

Bond had always known that death would come sooner or later in the service of his country and had remained indifferent to the thought. He was not, he thought, going to change his attitude now. Then his exhausted mind flashed back unaccountably to an evening in Rome and to the bar of a hotel where Mrs. Larissa Rossi had raised an eyebrow as she crossed her legs. He could see them now—and her mouth, whose upper lip occasionally stiffened into something like a pout. The light honey glow of her skin . . . the unrepentant wildness in her eyes.

Bond squeezed himself another inch through the constricting earth. He thought he must be hallucinating. He was dying, but he could think of nothing but Scarlett. The way she had glanced down a little nervously as she said, "My husband has had to go to Naples for the night . . . You could come up to our suite for a drink if you like."

Bond felt his breath failing in his lungs. Did he love this woman? Had he discovered too late? Stinging tears of frustration mingled with the sweat and blood on his face.

He gave no thought to his approaching death, only to Scarlett in the gilded armchair in his Paris hotel room, her long legs demurely crossed and her empty hands folded in front of her breasts . . .

Turning the last of his breath into a groan, Bond thrust himself upward with all his might in one final, dying effort. His hands went through packed sand and earth, then encountered air. He scrabbled frantically for a grip.

15. "DO YOU WANT ME?"

A ray of light broke the surface above him, then came a draught of dry, burning air. With a low growl Bond rammed his uninjured shoulder against the hard rim of earth above him till he was able to push himself up and his head at last was clear. With almost unendurable pain, he worked his shoulders, then his torso through the hole. Finally, he levered his waist and legs out and collapsed on to the sand, gasping and moaning as he fought the fog of unconsciousness.

When vision returned to him, he found he was looking at a pair of polished brown leather toecaps and the turn-ups of a cream linen suit. As he lifted

his head, the sole of the shoe came on to his cheek
and pushed his face into the dirt.

" 'The Cigar Tube,' " said Gorner's voice. "A test
of endurance invented by the public-school officers
of your finest regiments in the Malayan Emergency.
I thought you might enjoy it. And I thought I might,
too. So on a whim I made a special journey on my
own to watch you."

Gorner kept his foot on Bond's face. "It was
meant to weed out informers among the locals, but
your officers enjoyed it so much that they ended up
doing it just for fun." He turned to an unseen assistant. "Take the dirty English mole away."

The foot came off Bond's face and he rolled over
to see Gorner make the short walk to the small
helicopter that had brought him. Bond felt himself
being lifted under the arms and put into a jeep for
the drive back to the main lorry. He cried out at the
pressure under his left shoulder. Gorner's helicopter
was already airborne above them.

The crates of opium from the jeeps, less the two
from Bond's abandoned vehicle, had been loaded
into the all-terrain transport. As he lay on the floor
of the lorry, heading for the distant caravanserai
where they would rejoin the Mi-8 Hip transport
helicopter, Bond took advantage of the fact of his
presumed unconsciousness to work the two pieces

of glass from his shirt pocket and slide them beneath his tongue.

The journey back passed in a delirium of pain and fatigue, through some of which he slept. He was alert enough to take water when they transferred to the helicopter, where his hands were once more tied. He was aware of their descent and return to Gorner's fortress and of being stripped to his underwear and thoroughly searched. His torn clothes were returned to him.

When he next came to fully, he was back in the rock cell with Scarlett asleep next to him. He ached in the fibres of each muscle, and shifted on the sand to try to find a position that hurt less. He slid the pieces of glass from his mouth and used his tongue to cover them with sand, while his head remained motionless so no hidden camera could detect the movement.

The bolts on the door slid back and a guard entered. He delivered the usual reveille—a boot to the ribs—and told them both to stand up. Scarlett was wearing a grey workshirt and trousers. Her lower lip was swollen from where Gorner had hit her with the back of his hand. She looked pale and frightened, thought Bond, as he tried to reassure her with a smile and a nod. They were taken at gunpoint to the washroom, then given water and marched to Gorner's office.

Gorner, in a tropical suit with a carnation, looked, Bond thought, less like a global terrorist than a gambler come to break the bank at Cannes. He also seemed in dangerously high spirits. He made no reference to the events at Zabol or the "Cigar Tube." He seemed excited only by the future.

"Tomorrow," he said, when Bond and Scarlett were kneeling at gunpoint before him, hands behind their backs, "is a day I have waited for all my life. Tomorrow I shall launch an attack that will finally bring Britain to its knees. Like many of the best military plans, it will have two prongs—a diversion and a main thrust."

This was the man from the dock at Marseille, Bond thought, the supercilious impatience checked only by the unrelenting sense of purpose. For a moment, the arrogance had the upper hand. So delighted was Gorner by his own cleverness that any caution he might have had about divulging the detail of his plans had gone.

He went to sit at his desk and consulted a clipboard. "I had hoped to bring Britain down to its proper level by the use of narcotics alone. And I have high hopes of success in the long term. I think I can change most of your cities into drug slums by the end of the century. But I am an impatient man. I crave success. I need action. I need to see results now!"

Gorner smacked the desk with his gloved left hand. There was a dense silence in the room, in which only the low pulse of the air-conditioning could be heard.

"So," he said, "at ten o'clock precisely an Ekranoplan will leave its base in Noshahr and head north by north-west towards the Soviet Union. I think you are familiar with the craft, Bond, having spent a rather unwise amount of time trying to photograph it. It has been modified to carry six rockets, of which three are armed with nuclear warheads. It also has the latest Soviet surface-to-air missiles in case anyone gets nosy. The Volga river delta provides an ideal entry, leading straight to Stalingrad, the underbelly of Russia. Not every channel is sufficiently wide for our purpose, but we have now established the perfect route into the main river—the very one, in fact, down which the Ekranoplan was launched. From Noshahr to Astrakhan is a little over six hundred miles and from there it is a further two hundred miles to Stalingrad. Even allowing for possible refuelling stops from a tanker, the immense speed of the Ekranoplan means it can make the entire journey, beneath the radar, in four hours.

"As it comes to the outskirts of the city, the Ekranoplan will open fire as a hostile act against the Soviet Union. The craft herself will sail under the colours of the United Kingdom. All the crew will be carrying British passports. They will, however, be disposed of by two of my people on board as soon as the job is done. The Russians will find only dead British citizens responsible for the attack. My two men will make their own way back."

Bond looked up from where he knelt. "And where did you get the warheads?" he said.

"I bought them," said Gorner. "They are of American manufacture. There is a market in such things. Of course, they're relatively small . . . much smaller than those with which your friends the Americans burned alive the civilians of Japan in their wood-and-paper houses. But three together . . . I have high hopes. Our tests predict devastation of the city. The Ekranoplan, incidentally, was modified for me in Noshahr by Soviet technicians who had defected at my invitation."

A look of self-satisfaction flickered briefly over the Slavic features. "I've previously used the Ekranoplan only as a cargo transport and there's no reason for the Soviet authorities to suspect anything else tomorrow. On the contrary, I have many friends in the Soviet Union. The gentlemen in SMERSH have been kind enough to facilitate the passage of heroin through their country to the West. They understand its strategic importance."

Bond winced at the name. SMERSH, a contraction of *Smiert Spionam*—"Death to Spies"—was the most secret and feared department of the Soviet government. Even its existence was known only to those who worked for it—or, like Bond, had crossed its path.

Gorner stood up and walked round the desk so that he towered over the kneeling Bond and Scarlett. He lowered his white-gloved hand to Scarlett's chin and jerked her head up. "Pretty little thing, aren't you? The early shift is in for a rare treat tomorrow evening."

He sat down again behind the desk. "So much," he said, "for the diversion. Now, perhaps, you'd like to know where the main thrust of the attack will fall. Come with me."

He nodded to the guards, who pulled Bond and Scarlett to their feet and followed Gorner down the corridor. They went to the circular open elevator and rose to the ground-floor level, where an electric cart took them to a steel side door. At the command of a laser beam fired from a remote control in the cart, it rose vertically into the roof to reveal the blinding desert sun.

In front of them, however, not all was sand. Shimmering in the heat haze was a mile of tarmac runway, marked with yellow grids and flanked by electric landing lights. To one side of it were the two helicopters Bond had seen the day before. On the other side was a small unmarked Learjet and a twin-engine Cessna 150E.

And next to them, glistening brightly in the morning sun—huge, white and out of place—stood a brand new British airliner: a Vickers VC10 painted with the BOAC livery and with extra Union flag markings on the tail. Several mechanics were working on its cargo bay with welding machinery.

"Aviation," said Gorner. "A little hobby of mine. And in a big country like this, you need to be able to get around fast. The VC10 is a new acquisition. It was headed for life in Bahrain with a commercial airline flying oil men and their families on holiday. But on its maiden flight from Britain it turned out that two of the executives from Vickers were not what they seemed. They were working for me. The pilot was 'persuaded' to make a detour. He put the plane down here three days ago. I must say, for a man under pressure, it was a textbook landing."

Bond glanced at Scarlett to see how she was managing. She was looking round the airstrip and its small hangar, and beyond it to the desert. She had rallied a little, he thought.

"Tomorrow," said Gorner, "the flight of the VC10 will take it seventeen hundred miles due north to the heart of the Ural mountains. To Zlatoust-36. The plane will have only just enough fuel to reach the destination, where the adapted cargo bay will open and she will drop a bomb. Together with the fissile material on the ground, it will generate enough power to obliterate the site and much of the surrounding countryside. The total destruction will be as great as that inflicted by the RAF on the civilians of Dresden. I presume, incidentally, Bond, that you know what happens in Zlatoust-36."

Bond knew only too well. Zlatoust-36 was the code-name given to the Holy Grail of Soviet nuclear weapons: the "closed city" of Trekhgorniy, established in the 1950s to serve as the principal site for Russia's nuclear-warhead assembly and as a warhead-stockpile facility. It was no exaggeration to say that it was the engine room of the Soviet Cold War effort.

"You'll never get there," said Bond. "The radar mesh over Zlatoust-36 must be as tight as a crab net."

The faint look of smugness, which was the closest Gorner came to a smile, crept over his features. "That's where the diversion comes in," he said. "If Stalingrad's in flames, all eyes will be there."

"I doubt it," said Bond. "They'll think it's an all-out NATO attack and go on red alert."

"We shall see. The beauty of the plan is that it doesn't really matter whether the plane gets there or not. If Russian fighters down it in the southern Urals it will still have done its job. Soviet crash investigators will find a British plane stuffed to the flaps with charts of Zlatoust, with a cargo full of explosive and a dead British pilot in the cockpit. It will be enough, Bond. With what the unstoppable Ekranoplan will do by water, it will be enough."

"And what's the point of all this?" said Bond.

"I'm surprised at you, Bond," said Gorner. "It's obvious. The point of it is to precipitate Britain into a war that—finally—it cannot win. The Americans saved your bacon twice, but your failure to support their crazed adventure in Vietnam has made them angry with you. They will not be so generous on this occasion. And in any event they will have no time. Within six hours of my strike, you can expect a Soviet nuclear attack on London. This is it, Bond. This is justice at last."

Bond looked at Scarlett, but she was staring into the distance. The blood had drained from her face and she was swaying as though she might faint. She had borne up unbelievably well so far, thought Bond, and it was hardly surprising that she had reached her limit.

Gorner's eyes shone with the quiet pleasure of a bridge-player who, after a killing finesse, lays down his cards face up and says, "The rest, I think, are mine."

"Yes, indeed," he said. "London going up in nuclear smoke. The Houses of Parliament, jolly old Big Ben, the National Gallery, Lord's cricket ground . . ."

"This VC10," said Bond, "who's going to be the fool to fly it?"

"Why, that's very simple, Bond," said Gorner, taking a few paces towards him. "You are."

"Me? I can't fly something that big. Certainly not with a dislocated shoulder."

Gorner looked at Bond, then at Chagrin. "Fix his shoulder."

Chagrin came towards Bond. He pointed to the ground. Bond lay down on his back and Chagrin put his boot on his chest and grabbed Bond's left hand and upper arm. With one brutal heave, he yanked upwards and across, so Bond felt the end of the upper proximal humerus grinding back into its socket.

"You'll have plenty of help on board," said Gorner. "Take-off will be effected by the original pilot. Then he'll hand over to you, and my best man will sit next to you all the way. It's not difficult."

Bond knelt panting on the sand, grinding his teeth, the sweat of pain sheeting into his eyes.

Gorner walked back to the electric cart. "After all," he said, as the driver engaged the forward gear and they set off towards the open steel doors, "you won't have to do the difficult bit. You won't have to land it."

Bond was relieved to be back in the cell. He checked with his fingers that the slivers of windscreen glass were still under the sand, then turned to Scarlett.

He said, "I'm sorry about the parade. The walkway."

Scarlett looked down. "It's all right. I . . . I survived."

"We need to make a move now," said Bond. "Before it's too late. Come closer so I can talk to you quietly. We should make it look as though I'm comforting you."

Scarlett crawled across the sand and leaned against his chest. She turned her face up to his. She looked exactly as she had on the first night he had seen her in Rome. She said softly, "Did you see me? You know. On the walkway?"

"No. I turned my back. I didn't want to look. One day, Scarlett."

"If we get out of here, my darling, you can look all you want."

Bond smiled. "Where do you think Gorner's keeping Poppy? Did she ever say anything about her quarters or where they are?"

"No. But I'm sure that as soon as he saw me, he decided to keep her out of sight. He clearly doesn't want to talk about her."

Bond drew in a deep, tight breath. "Scarlett, we're going to have to leave Poppy behind. We won't have time to find her. I'm going to go on that plane and you have to be with me. If I leave you, Gorner will throw you to the workers."

"No, I can't do that," said Scarlett. "I came here to rescue my sister and I'm not leaving without her."

"No, you didn't," said Bond. "You came here to be near at hand while I rescued her."

"Don't split hairs with me, James. Poppy is my twin, my own flesh and blood, and I'm not leaving here without her."

"Please try not to be emotional, Scarlett. Just consider the facts. If we can stop Gorner today, then as early as tomorrow we can get people in here to close the plant and rescue her. Police, the army, everyone."

"No, James, I—"

"Be quiet." Bond raised his voice. "In the mayhem, Gorner's not going to be thinking about Poppy. She's just another girl on the walkway to him. He'll have bigger fish to fry. He'll be thinking of his money, his plant, his machinery, his future. He won't have time to worry about one girl, however dear to you she may be."

Scarlett turned her back on him. "You cold bastard," she said. "I should never have trusted you."

She lowered her face into her hands, knelt down on the sand and sobbed.

"The fact is," said Bond, flatly, "that Poppy's best chance lies with you and me. If we can get out safely and bring down Gorner, she'll be all right. But tonight, my dear Scarlett, we have to leave without her."

Almost five minutes passed in silence before Scarlett finally lifted her head and turned her tear-streaked face up to him. He saw submission in her swollen features and lifted her gently to her feet.

She put her mouth to his ear. "I suppose you may be right," she said sullenly, "but do you have any idea how to do it? How to get me out before they . . . before the workers take me and—and—kill me?"

"Move slowly round and put your fingers against mine," said Bond. "Can you feel something sharp?"

"Yes."

"Twist yourself so it's against the rope on your wrist, then slowly start to rub. I don't know if there really is a camera up there—I suspect not—but we can take no chances."

It took Scarlett almost two hours of imperceptible movement to fray the nylon cord sufficiently to break it before she set to work at the knots that secured Bond's wrists.

"Do you have an ear for music, Scarlett?"

"I used to play the violin and the piano. My father was very keen on it. Russians love music. It makes them cry. Why do you ask?"

"If I could sing to you or hum a sequence of five notes, could you work out what numbers from one to nine they might represent?"

"I might."

"Lay your head on my shoulder."

In the course of the next hour Bond transferred into Scarlett's mind the sequence of sounds he had heard from the door that had led him out to the helicopter. She repeated them and sang them to herself, interspersing the tune with a spoken commentary, using terms that meant little to Bond—intervals, semitones and so forth.

Eventually, she had loosened the knots enough for Bond to slide one hand free.

"It doesn't quite make sense, James. I've almost got it, but it won't quite work. Unless, unless . . ." She began to laugh. "James, you are absurd."

"What?"

"You forgot the zero. Wait." She hummed to herself again. "Now it works. Listen." She placed her lips against his ear. "Was that the sequence?"

"Exactly," said Bond. "And what are the numbers?"

"One, zero, six, six, nine. Don't ask me what it means."

"I won't. Listen to me, Scarlett. If you get out, you won't be on the right side of the plant. You'll still have to make your way round to the plane. And then . . . Well. I'm going to have to leave it to your ingenuity. Just get yourself on board and hidden. I calculate it's early evening. We'll make our move at about two in the morning. You may be lucky. At any rate, it's our only chance."

Scarlett nodded. She said nothing for a while, but Bond could see that she was warming to the idea.

"Are you hungry?" said Scarlett, eventually.

"Ravening."

"What would you most like to eat?"

Bond thought. "Something easy on the digestion to start with. Eggs Benedict. Then some caviar, perhaps, the one Darius gave me in his garden. A sole meunière. Then a roast partridge. A bottle of Bollinger Grande Année 1953 and some red wine—Château Batailley. A friend of mine introduced me to it in Paris."

"Anything else?"

"I'd like to have it in a hotel room. With you. Sitting naked on the bed. Now, come and lie close here till I tell you it's time to move. Think about that hotel room and try to sleep."

"Mmm. I'm there," said Scarlett. "The smell of gardenia bath essence floating through the open door . . ."

When Scarlett slept, Bond's eyes scanned the ceiling for any sign of a camera lens. It was dark in the cell, with only a little light filtering through the half-closed grille in the door from the sodium lamp in the corridor outside. So much the better, thought Bond. He was satisfied that the girl had understood his instructions and she hadn't let him down yet.

When he judged it was about two in the morning, Bond stood up carefully and helped Scarlett to her feet. She massaged his replaced shoulder and kissed the deep cut in his cheek where the glass had gone through to his gum. "You're going to have a good time at the dentist, aren't you, my love?"

He grimaced.

"One last thing," said Scarlett. "Promise me the first thing we do if we make it out alive is get some-one here to bring out Poppy."

"I promise." Bond kissed her lightly on the lips, turned to the door and levered his aching body up the rocks till he was wedged above the lintel. "Now!"

Scarlett put her mouth to the grille and let out

a long shriek. There was no sound from the other side, though Bond knew that the factory was at work and that there must be guards in the vicinity. Still, no footsteps were better than too many.

"Try again."

"Ssh. He's coming."

Bond could hear someone approaching. A torch shone through the grille.

Scarlett opened her grey workshirt to show her breasts. "Do you want me?" she said.

"Where is he?" said the guard.

"Sleep. He's hurt. Shoulder." Scarlett mimed exhaustion and pointed to a corner beyond the range of the guard's vision. "Come quick," she said, tugging at the waistband of her work trousers.

Still the man hesitated. Scarlett took her breasts in her hands and lifted them into the middle of the torch beam. There was the sound of a key in the lock. The door opened and the guard came in. As he turned to shut the door, Bond fell on to the man's shoulders, put his hand across his mouth and his other forearm across the windpipe. Scarlett slid the guard's gun from its holster on his hip. Bond used the carotid takedown he had used on the man at Noshahr, but this time he finished the job.

When the guard was dead, Bond led Scarlett down the passage from the cell and out into the labyrinth. They ran along the corridor away from Gorner's office until they came to the open elevator. Bond pointed Scarlett in the direction of the door on the top level, pressed the button and watched her slim figure rise up into the darkness with the dead guard's gun tucked into the waistband of her trousers.

He waited till Scarlett, he calculated, was within range of the door, then ran down the corridor to Gorner's office. He tapped numbers at random into the entry pad, and stood in full view of the security camera. It was only a few seconds before a red bulb began to flash above the door. At once, the corridor was flooded with harsh light and he heard the screech of a siren, then the barking of furious Alsatian dogs and the sound of feet pounding towards him.

Diversion successful, he thought. Now to survive. He placed his hands high in the air above his head.

16. "SHALL WE PLAY?" (II)

Within a few moments, Bond had six semi-automatic rifles against his head and three Alsatian dogs, barely restrained by their handlers, leaping at his face. He stood completely still with his back to the door of Gorner's office and his hands above his head, hoping that his calculations had been correct.

He believed that Gorner's men were under orders to keep him alive. In the absence of Bond, Gorner could still have a British passport holder at the controls by coercing the pilot of the hijacked VC10 back into the cockpit. But with his eye always on maximum provocation, Gorner would never use an unknown as the instrument of attack on the Soviet Union if there was a chance of using a known enemy of long standing. The grand symbolic gesture, Bond thought, was a key element of Gorner's operating method and of the revenge he craved.

Then, at the end of the corridor he saw a burly shape, silhouetted in the night lights as it approached. On its head was a Foreign Legion cap, and Bond felt a new and strange emotion at the sight of Chagrin: relief.

Chagrin barked two words in Farsi as he approached. The guards backed off a little and made room for him.

"Where is girl?" said Chagrin.

"I don't know," said Bond.

They would see the open door and search outside the building. His gamble was that the last place they would imagine a young woman to hide was on board an airliner that she knew was destined to crash the next day. The odds were not great—but it was the only play left open to him.

Chagrin jerked his head down the passageway, in the direction of the cell, and gave a brief order. As Bond was frogmarched away, he became aware of the commotion in the building. Alarms were wailing and hundreds of footsteps seemed to be pounding the floor. "Go on, Scarlett," he muttered to himself.

The picture of the slim figure rising silently into the darkness flashed across his mind.

Two men stayed with him in the cell, where they retied his hands, and two more guards were stationed outside. After a few minutes, when the alarms and sirens had been stilled, the door was opened and Chagrin came in.

"Get down," he said, pointing to the floor.

Bond knelt down, placing his knee on the sand where the two shards of glass had been reburied.

"Where girl?" said Chagrin.

"I've told you," said Bond. "I don't know. A guard opened the door because she felt ill. She ran away, but I don't know where she went. I went down the corridor to inform Dr. Gorner that one of his guests was missing. I seem to have misremembered the code to his office."

"Liar!" Chagrin screamed at him. "Liar!"

The side of his face that moved normally was contracted in fury, while the other side remained unnaturally still. There were flecks of foam at one corner of his mouth.

And this, thought Bond, was the sight that had greeted the eyes of schoolchildren when they had been sitting cross-legged in a circle in a village clearing to listen to the parable of the Good Samaritan.

"Tell me where girl go. Tell me!"

Bond looked at the torturer with contempt. A verse from long-ago scripture lessons came into his head. " 'Suffer the little children to come unto me,' " he said, " 'and forbid them not: for such is the kingdom of—' "

Chagrin kicked his boot into Bond's ribs and Bond heard a crack of bone. Then, from his shirt pocket, Chagrin withdrew a leather case, and, from inside it, two ivory chopsticks with scarlet Chinese lettering.

One guard jerked back Bond's head by the hair and the other gripped him under the jaw while Chagrin inserted a chopstick slowly and deeply into his left ear.

The guard held Bond in a headlock while Chagrin, with equal care and precision, inserted the second chopstick. Bond could feel the tip work through to his eardrum.

"You hear bad things you no tell," said Chagrin. "This what Pham Sinh Quoc do when man hear bad thing."

Bond braced himself as Chagrin moved closer and spread his feet. He could see the army boots worming their way into the sand for better purchase as Chagrin spread his stubby arms wide.

As he breathed in deeply, Bond closed his eyes

and did not see the face from whose mouth came the single word "Stop."

He looked up, and could see at the open grille of the cell door the long fingers of an outsized white glove. The door was opened and Gorner came in, wearing a crimson silk dressing-gown.

"Thank you, Chagrin. You can go. I want Bond to be able to hear instructions when he's flying. Stand up."

Bond got to his feet. "So," said Gorner, "the bitch has escaped. The workers are going to be disappointed if I don't get her back. But I think we'll manage something even without her, don't you?" He smirked.

Poppy, thought Bond. He would make her stand in for her sister, and the workers would never know the difference.

"Well," said Gorner, "I suppose I had to expect to sacrifice a pawn in this game. To win a war, you may occasionally lose a skirmish—and, frankly, the girl was a nuisance. The big fish is still in my net. Aren't you, Bond?"

"What time do we take off?"

"I see no reason to change my plans," said Gorner. "Not for the sake of a girl my men will find within the hour. You board at nine. Your navigator is one of my best men, a former thick-neck from a Tehran bazaar that I've trained up. His name is Massoud. He speaks English—or enough to tell you what to do. The plane has fuel to get to Zlatoust-36, but no more. When you've lost height and dropped the bomb, under Massoud's instruction, you will lose height further and he will leave the plane by parachute. You, Bond, will fly on until there's no fuel left, and then . . ." He spread his arms wide.

"I see."

"British planes. Very unreliable. And in case you think you can do something heroic when Massoud has left you, there are three armed guards as well. They won't know about Massoud's departure. Or the shortage of fuel. They are men who have displeased me. They're desperate to get back into my good books and think this is their last chance. They imagine Massoud will turn the plane round and fly home. But they have British passports and they're going down with you. So you can forget about some story-book crash landing on a Russian highway."

Gorner looked at his watch. "It's nearly four o'clock. I'm going back to bed. Then I shall rise at six and take breakfast. Poached egg, bacon, coffee."

"I should like black pepper on mine," said Bond. "Cracked, not ground."

"Remember the starving Irish," said Gorner. "A

cup of water at eight for you. Sleep well, Bond. Big day tomorrow."

The cell door clanged shut. Bond lay down and began to search with his tongue in the sand for the shards of glass.

At the same moment, Darius Alizadeh was woken by a telephone call in his room at Jalal's Five Star in Noshahr. He was dreaming of Zohreh in the mixed hammam.

"Hi, Darius. Sorry to wake you. This is Felix Leiter, CIA. Something very big's going to go off. I need your help."

"How did you find me?" said Darius, reluctantly pushing away the image of Zohreh, hot from the steam.

"Relations haven't completely broken down in the old alliance. I've spoken to people in London. To hell with the politicos. This is the real thing."

"Have you seen J. D. Silver?" said Darius.

"Carmen? Yup. Saw him in Tehran. Think he's on his way here."

"Where are you, Felix?"

"I'm right across the street, Darius."

"Are you a friend of James Bond?"

"*Santiago!* That's our battle cry. Same as Cortez.

James Bond is my blood brother. Shame about his taste in automobiles. Apart from that, he——"

"That's good enough for me," said Darius. "Come up to my room. Number two three four."

"You got it."

Leiter replaced the receiver in the waterfront telephone booth and limped the short distance to Jalal's. When he got up to room 234, he found Darius Alizadeh already dressed with a tray of coffee and fruit waiting on the table.

Also in the room was a portly man with a boot-brush moustache. "This is Hamid," said Darius, as he shook hands with Felix. "Driver. Part-time spy. Expert on dead drops and safe-houses."

Hamid smiled diffidently.

"Boy, that stuff takes me back," said Felix.

"And Hamid knows where the Monster lives."

"Did Bond trust him?"

"With his life," said Darius.

"All right," said Leiter, taking the cup of black coffee Darius held out to him. "Tell me what you know."

When Darius had finished giving him the details he'd received from London of the modified Ekrano-plan, Leiter said, "Okay, at least we know where she's starting from. But the rate that baby moves across the water we're going to have about two hours from

Scramble to Bombs Away. After that our planes will be in Soviet airspace. And that's not a place where a US plane can be for more than five minutes."

"Where's your nearest base?" said Darius.

"Officially, it's miles away. Timbuctoo for all I know. But unofficially we got planes in Dhahran in Saudi, and something in eastern Turkey. Fighter-bombers. I don't know for sure. I'm on a need-to-know ticket here, Darius. I just pass on the good news. It's going to be tight as hell. And that's just half the problem."

"What's the other half?" said Darius.

"This is what I got. That British airliner went missing a few days ago, it's due to reappear any day, heading north."

"Towards the Soviet Union?"

"Yup. We don't know where, but we're sure it's up to no good. We got some intercepts out of Istanbul. Probably been converted to carry bombs of some kind. The Soviet radar's pretty good and I think we can rely on a whole bunch of Mig-21s swarming all over this airliner soon after it enters Soviet airspace. Bam. Down she comes."

"But the fallout from that," said Darius. "Politically. If it appears to be part of an orchestrated attack by Britain, or NATO."

"You got it, Darius. We gotta get that bird down

before the Soviets do. And we don't even know where she's taking off. All our air-force bases are on full alert—but, hell, the sky's a big place. Carmen Silver's got his ears burning off with updates every minute out of Langley."

"That bad?" said Darius.

"Yup. The president's cancelled all engagements. They're following the protocols they laid down after the Cuban missile thing. They think this is the big one. Any moment."

"But what can we do?"

"Nothing right now. Just await instructions. Silver may have more news."

Darius sipped his coffee and sighed. "There must be something I can do," he said. "If it's Gorner, then Savak had a rough idea where he's based in the desert."

"Yeah, but the plane won't be coming out of the desert, will it? Must be at some airstrip. Or an airport. It's a big plane."

Darius stood up and walked round the room, scratching the back of his head. "Mmm . . . Airports. Yazd. Kerman . . . While I'm turning this over in my mind, Felix," he said, "just tell me one thing. Why do they call him 'Carmen'?"

"What d'you hear?"

"He told me some story of his first job in

Guatemala," said Darius, "and how he helped to start a mutiny to get the strong man thrown out, and that was what the character Carmen did in the opera—caused a mutiny."

Felix Leiter laughed. "What a load of bull. JD's a man doesn't like women, if you know what I mean. One of those. He fixed some cover with General Motors in his last posting. Forget where. One night he boasted in his cups that he'd seduced three of the General Motors sales force. Car men are what he likes best. Carmen Silver."

Darius laughed richly. "So long as he keeps us in the picture."

"You got to do the same for him. You call this number if I'm not around." Felix passed him a card. "Now don't you think we should go down to the docks and keep an eye on the Monster?"

Darius looked hard at Felix, as though summing him up one last time. He made up his mind. "We don't need to go," he said. "We stay here. I have a man on board."

"You what?" said Leiter.

"I've not been idle," said Darius. "I couldn't wait all day for the US cavalry. I got to one of the Russians who defected and made the modifications to the Ekranoplan. He's radioing to my office in Tehran the exact co-ordinates that they're feeding into the navigation system. Babak, my man in Tehran, is going to telephone through here."

"You are one smart guy," said Felix. "How did you persuade him?"

"The usual," said Darius. "US dollars. Plenty of them."

"Okay, so when we hear, I call Langley and they scramble whatever they got."

There was a bleep from the bedside telephone. It was the desk clerk.

"Mr. Silver here. I send him up?"

Shortly before eight, Bond, shoeless and still in his worker's clothes, was taken from his cell to the washroom and thence to Gorner's office.

An air of almost palpable excitement was coming from the man in the linen suit. He had a fresh scarlet carnation in his button-hole and wore what looked like a new shirt and blazing crimson tie. The lank fair hair had been combed back from the high forehead. Even the white glove had been freshly laundered.

Gorner held up a BOAC uniform with the rank of captain.

"Five minutes before the end," he said, "you will change into this. It will be stowed on board. How splendid you will look, Bond, in your captain's uniform. As swell as an old Etonian. Enjoy your brief moment, won't you? As the French say, *'Aujourd'hui roi, demain rien.'* Today a king, tomorrow—"

"I know what it means," said Bond.

"Of course you do. Very unusual to speak a foreign language. Most of your fellow countrymen expect the 'lesser races' to understand English if they shout it loud enough. But by this time tomorrow their arrogance and duplicity will be crushed. For ever. Your capital will be a smouldering wreck, your charming 'home counties'—Kent and Surrey—a radioactive fallout zone."

Gorner walked round his desk so he was standing next to Bond. "I shall watch you take off in a few minutes, then I shall await the inevitable. Do you have any farewell message to your countrymen? Your queen? Your prime minister?"

Bond bit his lip. Poppy's words went through his head. "Kill Gorner."

"Very well, then," said Gorner. "Shall we play?"

The familiar guards took Bond along the corridor and rammed the muzzles of their guns into his ears as they rose on the telescopic elevator. The electric cart was waiting to transport them to the main doors, where the driver operated the laser beam release.

It was not yet nine o'clock, but the heat of the Persian sun was already intense as they crossed the runway to the brilliantly shining VC10. The high tail, with the four rear-mounted Rolls-Royce Conway jet engines, gave the aircraft a superbly sleek silhouette, and at any other time the prospect of its "hushpower" ride would have lifted Bond's spirits. But he knew on this occasion that his only chance of getting out of the plane alive depended on the remote possibility that a slender female investment banker with shining black hair and a Soviet pistol she had not been trained to fire had somehow hidden herself on board.

Bond breathed in deeply and set his foot on the steps up to the main passenger door. Once on board, he was hustled down the gangway and pushed into a window seat towards the back of the first-class section. As he bent his head beneath the overhead locker, he allowed the shard of glass he had secreted in his mouth to drop on to the seat ahead of him. One guard sat next to him, another in the row in front and a third behind. The engines were already turning slowly.

A dark, thick-set man in combat trousers and a white T-shirt leaned over from the aisle. "I am Massoud," he said. "We do checks with pilot. We leave in half-hour. You stay where you are. If you move, we kill you."

"Worse than Dan Air," said Bond. "Do you have a cigarette?"

"Be quiet. No smoke. Fasten seat-belt."

Bond did as he was told. This was the moment in a flight he normally enjoyed, knowing that he would have a few hours to himself, unreachable by the demands of M or any of the women in his life—time in which he could read a few pages of Ben Hogan on *The Modern Fundamentals of Golf*, then watch the sun glinting on the wings as he sipped a Bloody Mary over the Arctic cloudscape.

Bond looked up to see another man staring down at him from the aisle. He wore a grubby BOAC shirt. He looked English, and afraid. "My name's Ken Mitchell," he said, in the tones of the Surrey golf course. "I'm the pilot of this crate for my sins. I'm just here to tell you not to try anything funny. It's our only hope. I do the take-off and get us most of the way. Then they're going to bring you up to the flight deck for the last bit. They've promised me that if I play ball with them, they'll let me go. Don't muck it up for me, Mr. Bond. It's my little girl's birthday tomorrow."

"All right," said Bond. "Any tips on how to fly it?"

"To keep her level, don't look at the instruments. Pick something on the horizon, the edge of a cloud or something. Orientate yourself by that, not by the instruments. But we'll be on autopilot most of the way. She flies herself."

"Thank you. Now sit back and enjoy your flight, Ken."

Mitchell gave him one last imploring look as he was grabbed by the arm and pushed back towards the cockpit.

A few minutes later, Bond felt the jolt of the engines engaging as the plane began to taxi. Through his window he could see the green light winking on top of the simple control tower, half a mile distant. At the end of the runway, the big plane turned and stopped.

Bond heard the Rolls-Royce engines roar from the back of the fuselage, and then they were moving forward purposefully, rapidly accelerating. He felt the small of his back pushed against the padded first-class seat as the nose lifted and the rear thrust drove the great plane up through the thin air into the burning desert sky.

In the steel hangar in Noshahr, the last of the camouflage nets was cleared from the nose of the

Ekranoplan and the engines were started. The fourteen-man crew all carried fake British passports, though eight were Persian, two Iraqi, two Turkish, one was a Saudi and the last, who sat at the radio console wearing headphones, was a Farsi-speaking Russian.

It was the first time the Ekranoplan, modified by the addition of four extra fuel tanks, six rocket launchers and four surface-to-air missiles, had left the hangar, and there was tension among the men as the mighty engines opened up on the calm sea. The drag created by the bow wave meant that more power was necessary to achieve the initial lift-off from the sea than to run at full speed. The maximum drag came well before take-off speed, as the craft needed to climb its own bow wave to get clear of the water.

As the screaming of the engines rose and the Ekranoplan remained stuck to the ocean, the Russian looked at the anxious faces around him. "Don't worry," he said in Farsi.

The pilot reached out and pulled down the switch in front of him that activated the PAR—Power Augmentation of Ram—which briefly diverted the engine thrust to force air beneath the wings.

Suddenly, there was an upward surge, and they were skimming clear above the water on a cushion of air. The pilot was able to drop the engine revs even as the speed increased, and spontaneous applause went round the cramped crew area.

The traffic stopped along the sea-front at Noshahr and Chalus, and hundreds of local people stood and stared at the breathtaking sight.

Oblivious to the spectacle the Ekranoplan was creating, the Russian bent to his radio set.

"This is the strangest war room I ever saw," said Felix Leiter, looking at the bowls of pomegranates and barberries on the table and the ocean view through the window of Jalal's Five Star room 234.

J. D. Silver held his cup of tea to his mouth while his eyes swivelled round to take in his surroundings.

The bedside telephone bleeped, and Felix picked it up. "It's for you, Darius," he said. "Your man Babak in Tehran."

Darius leaped over the bed and grabbed the receiver.

"Babak? Have you got the details? Good. Let me have them."

On the pad of paper by the bed his pen scribbled furiously—"Latitude 46.34944. Longitude 48.04917. Latitude 48.8047222. Longitude 44.5858333"—and other words in Farsi illegible to Leiter and Silver, who looked over his shoulder.

After about five minutes, Darius replaced the receiver and handed the piece of paper to J. D. Silver. "This is where the Ekranoplan is heading," he said. "These are the speed calculations and this codeword means it's nuclear-armed. You're going to have to move fast."

"Sure," said Silver. "How secure is this line?"

"Who knows?" said Leiter. "But it's the only one we got, pal."

Silver hunched over the phone. "Just cut me a little slack here, guys. There's one or two codes I have to put in when I get through that even you guys . . . No offence."

"None taken," said Leiter. "Let's admire the view, Darius."

"Hamid," said Darius, "will you wait in the corridor outside?"

Felix and Darius stood in the window and looked towards the sea. Felix raised the metal claw he used for a right hand. "I'd cross my fingers if I had any," he said.

Darius, large and bear-like, put his arm round Felix's shoulders. "It's all destiny," he said. *"Kismet."*

"Double four six," Silver's voice was saying.

"Eight seven. Callback." With his right foot, he gently pressed down on the telephone line where it went into a wall fixing under the bedside table.

One by one the small internal wires became disconnected under the pressure of his foot. Finally, the entire cable came free from the skirting-board and Silver pushed the frayed end quietly out of sight beneath the bed.

"You got it, Langley!" he said enthusiastically. "Here we go. Latitude 46.34944. Longitude 48.04917. Latitude 48.8047222. Longitude . . ."

"Looks like we're in good shape, Darius," said Felix. "Now for the airliner."

17. CARMEN'S SONG

The VC10 levelled out at thirty thousand feet, some-where east of Tehran, and continued on its smooth, level progress north, towards Kazakhstan in the southern Soviet Union. In any other circumstances, thought Bond, as he looked from his window down on to the Elburz mountains, it was a perfect day for flying. Holding the piece of glass in the tips of the fingers of his right hand, he continued the friction against the rope on his left wrist—gently and, with luck, imperceptibly. Thank goodness, he thought, for the space between the first-class seats. In economy, a small vibration would almost certainly have been relayed to the guard in the aisle seat to his left.

Bond twisted his body towards the aisle, lowered his head and closed his eyes, as though he was exhausted by his desert ordeal and had submitted to his destined end. He estimated the remaining distance to Zlatoust-36 to be approximately fifteen hundred miles, depending on where exactly in the desert Gorner's lair was located. He knew the VC10 could cruise at over five hundred miles per hour—a figure well publicized in the political squabbles that had surrounded the commissioning of the plane by the British government for BOAC.

They had already been airborne for an hour, he guessed, and if Scarlett didn't appear within the next sixty minutes, he would have to try to take on four armed men single-handed. Unless, of course, he could do something to enlist the help of Ken Mitchell on the flight deck. It seemed unlikely. Mitchell looked like the kind of man whose idea of action was eighteen holes in the monthly medal at Woking.

Bond twisted his right wrist within the burning constriction of the rope until he could feel the extent to which he had managed to fray the nylon cord. Sharp though the glass from the jeep windscreen was, it had as yet made little impression.

He had no idea when they might summon him

to the controls. Presumably at some juncture they would have to untie his wrists to make it seem that he was in charge of the attack on Zlatoust-36, but by the time he was on the flight deck it would be far too late. He needed to make a move before then.

Glancing at the man beside him, who stared blindly ahead, Bond increased the rate of friction. It was his only chance.

When J. D. Silver had replaced the receiver on the telephone in room 234, he told Darius and Leiter that he had to go back to his car. "I won't be five minutes," he said, "but we're getting a call back from Langley, so don't use the phone while I'm away, okay? We need to keep the line free."

"Sure thing," said Felix.

"Good man," said Silver, as he went out and shut the door.

"Well," said Darius, "I suppose we can expect a big wave in the Caspian some time in the next sixty minutes."

"Sure. Silver's through to Langley. They get on to the Pentagon. USAF scramble . . . Goodbye, Ekranoplan."

"But what about this airliner?" said Darius. "Do you think there's nothing we can do?"

"Well, we know it's likely to attack at the same time as the Ekranoplan, so it must be up in the air right now. We also know that every USAF plane in range is sniffing round the edge of Soviet airspace. More than that, Darius . . ."

"Nothing?"

Felix spread his arms wide. "Three days ago I was doing a missing-persons in LA. I can't work miracles. What I really need is breakfast. Do you do eggs easy over in your country, or is it just fruit?"

"I'm sure they could do an egg," said Darius, "but we can't phone down because we're meant to keep the line free. For Langley to call back."

"Well, I guess I could go down to the kitchens and ask," said Felix. "Or I could fry it myself. A Texan doesn't go to work on an empty stomach."

"It's infuriating," said Darius. "I should call Babak so he can radio through to London. They should be updated. We need RAF planes as well in case your men don't make it. Belt and braces." He sat on the end of the bed, shaking his heavy, handsome head in frustration.

A few feet away, Felix sat on the little hardwood chair and scratched his cropped hair with his left hand.

Three minutes passed as they stared into space, occasionally catching one another's eye.

Eventually, Leiter said, "Where the hell's Silver? He said he'd be five minutes." He glanced at his watch. "It's ten already."

Darius looked hard at him. Felix stared back.

Another minute passed in silence as Darius's eyes gazed deep into Felix's. It was almost as though two half-thoughts were becoming one in the air between them.

"I'm getting a feeling," said Felix.

"Yes," said Darius. "When did Langley ever use a telephone line to call back?"

"Oh, my God."

In the same instant, both men dived for the telephone. Darius was closer, and it was his hand that lifted up the disconnected cord.

Felix swore loudly.

Darius was already at the door. "Hamid!" he yelled down the corridor. "Let's go!"

There was no time to wait for the lift. The three men went as fast as they could down the stairs, Felix limping in the rear, and out to Hamid's grey Cadillac.

Darius was shouting in Farsi as they piled in and Hamid smacked the car into gear. As he let in the clutch and laid a long black streak of rubber down the Noshahr waterfront, Darius turned to Felix. "I've told him to get us back out of town to an isolated call box I saw. I'm going to get on to Tehran. Babak can radio through on a secure wavelength to London and they can scramble whatever the RAF can manage. I don't think we can go via Langley."

Felix swore again. "That way is sure enough shot for the time being. I don't know if Carmen's doing what he's told from Washington or if he's at some rodeo all his own."

"At the moment," said Darius, "it doesn't really matter. We just know we're on our own. In any case, we may find out soon enough about Silver. There's someone following."

As Hamid screeched round the corner into a palm-lined residential street of white villas, Felix looked through the back window. A dusty black Pontiac was closing in on them.

"That's all we need," said Felix. "I only got this." He took a Colt M-1911 from inside his jacket. "Accurate to seventy-five yards, but feeling its age."

"Give him a warning," said Darius.

"Another thing," said Felix, holding up his hook. "This was my firing hand."

Darius took the gun, knocked out the rear window and fired a shot at the black Pontiac, which swerved wildly, ran up over the pavement, but then regained the road.

"Allahu Akbar!" said Hamid.

"Just drive, pal," said Felix, ducking down below the open rear window. "Is it Carmen?"

"I couldn't see," said Darius. "Faster, Hamid! Go, go, go!"

The Cadillac came to a small street market where its front wheel clipped an overflowing barrow, sending a cascade of oranges across the street. Hamid sank his right foot and the big car roared on, over an ungated railway crossing and up into the shallow hills behind the town.

Darius raised his head and looked back through the rear window. Holding the Colt carefully in both hands, he let go another round.

It shattered the windscreen of the Pontiac, but the stock of a handgun punched swiftly through the glass, revealing a pale, sweating face of terrier eagerness with reddish hair plastered to its forehead.

"It's Carmen," said Felix. "Let him have it."

Darius shot again, and the bullet whined off the bonnet of Silver's car. "How many shots have you got?" he said.

"Seven plus one in the chamber," said Felix. "Five left."

"We'll have to keep those in reserve," said Darius. "You're going to have to cover me while I make that call."

"Better try and lose him, then."

Darius barked at Hamid, who dropped the wheel to the right so the car, as it drifted and screeched through a right-angle turn, laid a towering dustcloud behind it. Hamid shouted back at Darius over the noise.

"We're nearly at the call box," said Darius to Felix. "He's trying to kick up more dust. Hold on tight."

They were off the tarmac and on to a dirt road, where Hamid swung the car from side to side, violently, so they could hear the steel frame groaning against the whipping G-forces and the tyres screaming as they tried to grip the surface. But the big sedan was built for cruising, not for stunts, and as Hamid tried to correct the heavy understeer he hit a white rock and the car flipped over on its side, slewing hard across the road on its doors.

Darius, his head cut, climbed out of the upper rear door and pulled Felix up after him. Felix cursed as he dropped down on his good leg and Darius handed him the gun, then ran ahead to where the track rejoined the tarmac road and they could see the lonely call box.

"Cover me," he shouted to Felix.

Through the swirling dustcloud came a labouring-engine noise, then the black Pontiac appeared, and Felix, from behind the barrier of the steaming Cadillac, fired straight through the open windscreen. The

Pontiac braked, swerved and stopped. Silver, bleeding from the shoulder, threw himself out and rolled behind the vehicle.

Felix knew he had only to keep him there long enough for Darius to get through to Tehran with the co-ordinates. But who knew how long that would take? How good was the Persian telephone system?

In the box, Darius was talking to Babak. "Listen hard. Get on to London on fourteen megacycles. And there's an airliner . . ."

Felix, holding the gun in his left hand, watched for any sign of movement from the Pontiac. He had four shots left and didn't want to waste any. If Silver was playing some cat-and-mouse game, that was fine by him—though it was unlikely, since Silver would have guessed that he and Darius were rushing to make contact with London.

From near his feet, he heard groaning. "Are you all right, Hamid?"

"I think so. Cut hands. But all right."

"Keep down."

A bullet cracked off the side of the Cadillac. Hamid began to pray noisily. What alarmed Felix was that the bullet came from above them on the upper road, where the call box was. Somehow Silver had sneaked out from behind the Pontiac and climbed through the bushes above.

Felix cursed noisily and began to run as fast as his artificial leg would let him.

"Got that, Babak?" Darius was saying into the mouthpiece. "And the VC10. Good man, Babak. Now as fast as you—"

But Darius Alizadeh could not complete the sentence as two rounds of pistol fire went through his heart. His big body crumpled at the knee and fell forward into the dust of his homeland.

Felix came toiling up the hill, dragging his leg behind him. He was too late to see Silver replace the smoking gun in his waistband as he knelt down behind a bush.

Felix let out a cry when he saw Darius and the telephone receiver swinging by its cord. He got down beside him and put his ear to his chest. He was still just breathing, and he opened his eyes. "I got through," he said. "To Babak. The whole lot. Everything we know."

He closed his eyes as Felix lifted his head and cradled him in his good arm.

"J. D. Silver," said Darius weakly, and the glimmer of a smile passed over his face. "Not what my father called a 'citizen of eternity.' "

"Not like you, my friend," said Felix. "No. JD's what *my* father called a sonofabitch."

As Darius's body went limp, Felix heard a pistol being cocked.

"Don't move, Leiter."

Silver stepped out, both hands steady on the gun. "Put your hands up. You don't have to die. You can go back to your matrimonials and your missing girls. Just do as I say. Put both hands on your head."

"Who are you working for?" said Felix.

"Same as you. I just got new orders. We want the Brits in Vietnam. We need some help. If this is what it takes. A little reminder from the Russians . . ."

"You're out of your mind," said Felix.

"Shut up," said Silver, beginning to frisk him, and stopping when he came to the Colt in Felix's waistband.

"Big old thing," he said, hauling it out and putting it into his jacket pocket. "Now get down on the ground. Face down."

Felix did as he was told. "Did you tell Langley about the goddam plane?" he said. "The airliner full of explosive?"

"I don't know it's full of explosive," said Silver. "Neither do you."

"What the hell you think it's got on board? Kids' toys?"

"I tell them all I know," said Silver. "They decide

what to do with it. When the chips are down, Leiter, it's the man in the White House makes the call. He's looking at the whole picture. Russia takes a hit, he can live with that. London takes a hit—that's not so good. But if it gets the Brits off their backside and into Vietnam and makes them take this whole war seriously, then, hey, that's tactical. Once in a while you take a punch. And if it helps you win the bout, it's worth it."

Felix levered himself up on to his elbow. "But if you're not letting them have all the detail they need . . ."

As he spoke, he saw a shadow on the dusty ground behind J. D. Silver's black penny loafers. Felix's CIA training, many years ago but wired deeply in his reflexes, stopped him reacting in any way.

But he knew he needed to keep talking. "I don't think you're telling me the whole truth, Carmen. Sure, we want the Brits in Vietnam, sure I think those guys in the State Department would absorb a small attack if they thought it would help us in the long run. But not this. This is a big one. A very big one. Know what I think, Carmen? I think someone told stories about you. You and your car men. I think you got turned. Blackmail. I think someone from the Soviet Union had a little word with you, my friend, and—"

Silver screamed in anger and raised his gun to fire at Felix's heart, but before he could pull the trigger, part of the contents of his head shot through his nose, as Hamid crashed a heavy white rock down on to his skull, with a crack that echoed round the foothills of Noshahr.

Felix climbed shakily to his feet. He put his good arm round Hamid's shoulder. "Thank you, Hamid."

"Allahu Akbar."

Felix took a moment to regain his breath. "Yes, I think he is. I think you may be right there, Hamid. Now let's get Mr. Alizadeh home."

Bond calculated that they had been airborne for nearly three hours. He could see in the clear sunlight that they were over the Ural mountains.

"Can I talk to the pilot?" he said to the guard in the aisle seat. The man shook his head. He probably didn't speak English, Bond thought.

"Get Massoud," he said.

The man shook his head again.

"I need to know how this plane works," said Bond. "Get Massoud, will you?"

The guard made guttural noises to the man in the seat in front of them, and this guard, who wore an American cap of the Chicago Bears, got reluctantly to his feet and went forward. A minute later, he returned—not with Massoud but with Ken Mitchell.

"They want you up front now," said Mitchell. "Don't try anything funny."

"Who's flying this thing at the moment?" said Bond.

"It's on autopilot. You don't have to do a thing. Not until we get close. Then we have to lose height."

"Do you know why?" said Bond.

"No. Funnily enough, when I have a gun at my head I just do what I'm told."

"I think it's time you knew," said Bond. "In the hold of this plane is a large cargo of explosive. We're going to drop it on Zlatoust-36, Russia's biggest nuclear stockpile."

"Dear God." Mitchell slumped forward against the seat in front of him.

"Now, Ken," said Bond, "do you still want me not to try anything funny?"

The guard next to Bond slapped him in the mouth with the back of his hand. "No talk."

"What going on?" Massoud came down the aisle from the now empty flight deck.

He withdrew a Colt .45 from his waistband. Big stopping power, thought Bond, but dangerous at this altitude.

"Get up," said Massoud, pointing the gun at Bond's head.

"I'm not moving," said Bond.

"Get up!" screamed Massoud. He leaned over the guard and grabbed Bond by the throat. Bond could see how this "thick-neck" had controlled the protection and racketeering of a whole bazaar. The guard undid Bond's seat-belt and Bond kept his hands tight behind his back, holding the recently severed rope in them.

He allowed Massoud to manhandle him over the guard in the aisle seat, but as his hand trailed over the man's neck, Bond dropped the cut ropes and sliced down with all his strength into the jugular vein with the shard of glass. Blood spurted on to the seat in front as the man screamed. As he fell forward, Bond grabbed the gun from his holster, and, swivelling powerfully on his heel, smacked the butt of it into Massoud's face. Massoud fell back across the empty row of seats opposite, momentarily stunned, while Bond threw himself to the floor of the aisle.

At the same moment there was the magnified explosion of a Soviet pistol going off, and Bond saw the face of the guard in the seat in front of him blown away as the bullet entered his head below the eye socket. The Chicago Bears cap was blown ten rows up the aircraft.

From the floor, Bond looked back down the aisle. Half-way up the economy section, her feet planted, and a Makarov 9mm semi-automatic held at the apex of the triangle made by both hands joined, her long dark hair pinned neatly up beneath the cap, stood a woman in a brand new, pressed uniform of a BOAC hostess.

The guard from the row behind Bond's leaned out into the aisle and fired at Scarlett. As he did so, he presented a simple target to Bond, who fired up from the floor with the Luger he had taken from his neighbour. The man's body fell back across the seats.

Massoud, meanwhile, had gathered himself and struggled to his feet. Scarlett saw him coming and fired again with her Makarov as Bond threw himself at Massoud's ankles. Bond was on top of him in the cramped space of the legroom in the row opposite. He got his hands round Massoud's throat, but found himself thrown back across the gangway as Massoud's big Colt went off once.

The bullet went straight through the reinforced Perspex window next to the guard Bond had just shot. The immediate decompression sucked the man's corpse towards the small jagged hole, where for the time being it made an effective plug.

There was a shout from Mitchell. "Stop shooting! Something's screwed up the bloody autopilot!"

The big new aircraft, so powerful and smooth on its flight thus far, suddenly lurched, fell about a hundred feet, stopped as though it had hit a solid floor, sending a shudder through every rivet of the airframe, then howled and began to dive.

Bond, Massoud and Scarlett were all thrown to the floor.

"Get to the flight deck, Ken," Bond shouted. "For God's sake, we're going down."

Bond's face was drenched in the blood from the jugular of the man he had stabbed, while all around them the first-class seats were spattered with the red brain and muscle of the other two thugs. Bond was shouting and swearing at Ken Mitchell, but Mitchell seemed paralysed by panic as he merely gripped the edge of one of the seats. Bond crawled over and shoved the muzzle of his gun into Mitchell's ear.

"If you don't get on that flight deck right now I'm going to blow your brains out. Go! *Go!*"

Mitchell began to slither and slide down the bloody, plummeting aisle. Bond could see his face screwed up in tears.

"Get in there!" roared Bond.

Massoud managed to find a foothold long enough to fire at Bond, but the buffeting of the turbulence as the plane continued to dive caused the bullet to go upwards into the ceiling.

Further back in the plane, Scarlett had taken a handhold on a seat leg. But it was evident she had no clear view of Massoud and was holding her fire.

Mitchell staggered towards the flight deck as the other three held on to the sides of the seats. Bond could see Massoud's legs about five rows back, but hesitated to fire in case, even with the under-powered Luger, he caused further decompression.

The next thing he knew, the plane took another gigantic buffet, and pitched downwards. Mitchell crashed against the bulkhead and fell to the floor. Scarlett screamed and Bond saw her body sliding down the aisle. Massoud caught her as she went past and held on to her arm. Bond watched as he drew her into his row, with his arm round her throat. She had lost her gun.

Somehow in the yawing and pitching aircraft, Massoud managed to get to his knees, dragging Scarlett with him for cover. His strength was extraordinary, thought Bond. He was like a caveman dragging off his woman by the hair as he manoeuvred them both towards the front of the plane with one free hand. As he went past Bond, their eyes met and Bond saw the muzzle of his gun in Scarlett's ear. There was no need for words. Once Massoud hit the blood, he was almost able to slide down to the flight deck—where he took the empty pilot's seat.

314

The plane levelled out, and Bond surveyed the damage. The holed window was continuing to cause decompression, and it was hard to move against the sucking force. Some of the seats had been shaken free of the floor, and Bond knew that if the guard's body finally succumbed to the pressure and broke through the Perspex, the situation would worsen dramatically.

Mitchell seemed to be unconscious, and his body lay where it had fallen across the aisle just short of the flight deck.

Bond made his way down, stepped over Mitchell and opened the door. Scarlett sat at the controls with Massoud's gun against her head.

Massoud looked at Bond calmly. "Drop your gun. Or I kill her."

"You wouldn't risk firing again," said Bond. "Not with that big thing."

Massoud dropped his arm and pulled hard across Scarlett's windpipe. "This what we do in bazaar," he said. "To traders who don't pay. No need to fire."

"All right, all right," said Bond.

"Sit down." Massoud pointed to the co-pilot's seat. "Give me gun."

Bond saw Scarlett's wide and frightened eyes pleading silently with him and did as he was told.

Massoud glanced rapidly at a chart he had taken

from the central console and, more carefully, at the forest of dials in front of Scarlett. "Six minutes," he said. "Take plane down." And he demonstrated to Scarlett how, when he moved the control arm forward, the plane lost height.

Beside him, beneath his right hand, was the switch that Gorner's engineers had installed. It connected to the bomb rack and the door-release mechanism in the adapted cargo bay. Massoud was fingering it impatiently.

At the same moment, the Ekranoplan was taking on fuel from a tanker at a prearranged stop off Fort Shevchenko on the westernmost tip of Kazakhstan.

The target was thus a static one for the pilots of the three RAF Vulcan B.2s coming in at five thousand feet at just below the speed of sound—a velocity they had maintained since departing from their secret location in the Gulf, scrambled by an emergency order from Northolt, based on information from a Noshahr call box via Tehran and Regent's Park.

One of the planes was loaded with a Blue Steel missile, a rocket-powered stand-off bomb armed with the 1.1 megaton yield Red Snow warhead. The other two carried twenty-one 1000-pound conventional bombs.

The nuclear-armed aircraft was instructed to attack only if the first two planes were unsuccessful and stood off at a distance of some twenty miles. As the British pilots closed in for the kill, the airwaves crackled with anticipation. They began the operation with both leading Vulcans on a classic "laydown" attack, releasing ten bombs each in a long, wavering trail.

The sea around the Ekranoplan rose up in towering sheets of salt water that swamped the tanker as well as the hybrid craft herself, which shook to the limit of her stress equations. But she remained intact as the bombers climbed up into the sun, banked and regrouped.

Neither pilot was trained for a second pass, as the slow delivery speed of the aircraft made it vulnerable to Triple "A" and surface-to-air missiles. "The kitchen sink first time" was the pilots' rule of thumb, but these were no ordinary circumstances.

After brief radio contact, both planes came round for a second attempt, but this time the Ekranoplan was ready for them and fired one of its missiles directly into the flight path. Seeing its approaching white vapour trail, the pilot of the first plane fired chaff and went into a sharp emergency climb. The second plane was slower to react, and the missile, rising like a lethal white firework, tore a section from the starboard wing. Unable to control the plane, the pilot was forced to climb as high as he could before ejecting, his co-pilot following suit, their parachutes opening five thousand feet above Fort Shevchenko. The stricken plane spiralled back into the sea with three crewmen still on board.

The first Vulcan, meanwhile, levelled off, and, after a steep banking manoeuvre, ran in at nine hundred feet for a seemingly suicidal third pass. This time, however, its angle and low altitude were too much for the stranded amphibian's defences, and the plane dumped its remaining bombs with geometric precision. As they hit the side of the fuel tanker there was a calculated delay before detonation to allow the aircraft to escape the blast.

The astonished Vulcan pilot looked down from his climb to see the Ekranoplan lifted clear of the water and disintegrating into a million particles as the giant explosion shook the Caspian Sea to its bedrock.

18. ZLATOUST-36

"One minute," said Massoud.

Below them, the Ural mountains towered grey and jagged. They could make out the sprawling city of Chelyabinsk in the eastern foothills to their right. Away to the left a large expanse of water stretched to the western horizon. The bright sun and clear, sparkling air made navigation childishly simple.

Under Massoud's instruction, Scarlett continued to move the control arm forward so the needle in the altimeter whirled anticlockwise and the big plane tilted steeply down towards the nuclear city of Zlatoust, cradled in its secret folds of rock.

The door of the flight deck burst open, and a Luger pistol pointed at Massoud's head. It was all that Bond needed. As Massoud turned his gun away from Scarlett, Bond threw himself across the cabin and grabbed his arm.

The roaring sound of a shot reverberated round the small area, and Ken Mitchell pitched forward, the Luger falling from his hand. Bond and Massoud were now locked in a struggle to the death, with Scarlett tangled between them.

The combined weight of their bodies on the control arm had sent the plane into a nose dive, and Bond's knee was jammed against the throttle levers, making the Rolls-Royce Conway engines howl.

Bond felt Massoud's fingers on his neck, digging down for the arteries. He thought of the slave workers in Gorner's plant and of the girls paraded for them. He smashed his forehead into Massoud's face, and, as the thick-neck reeled back against the side of the cockpit, Bond drove his knee into the unprotected groin.

Scarlett freed herself from the seat and grabbed the Luger from where it had rolled against the co-pilot's seat. She handed it to Bond, who whipped it across Massoud's temples. Massoud lashed up at Bond with his foot, but Bond had anticipated the move. He caught Massoud's ankle in two hands, stamped his foot down into the groin for leverage and gave a sudden twist. He felt the ligaments tear and heard the scream.

"Get the controls!" he shouted to Scarlett, who pulled back hard to try to stop the dive.

Bond climbed on top of the disabled Massoud, turned him face down and smacked his head repeatedly into the floor of the flight deck until he stopped moving. Then he grabbed the throttle levers and eased them back, before trying to help Scarlett level out the airliner. The man who might have managed the manoeuvre, Mitchell, lay dead at their feet.

"I can't do it!" Scarlett was screaming. "It's too heavy. It won't respond."

"The controls are shot to hell," shouted Bond, wiping Massoud's blood from his face. "And we're decompressing. The guard must have gone through the window. Let's go. Where's the parachute?"

He pulled open the crew locker and found what he wanted.

"Strap it on!" he said, handing the parachute to Scarlett.

"But what about you?"

"Do it!" Bond yelled.

Scarlett did as she was told, feeding the straps up

through her legs and round her waist into the central lock, leaving the packed parachute itself hanging and bulging from behind.

Bond climbed up the sloping aisle to the passenger door, with Scarlett clinging on to him.

"Put it to manual," she said.

With shaking hands, they tried to wrestle the door open.

"We're still too high," said Bond. "The pressure's too great."

In her torn uniform Scarlett looked at him with desperate eyes.

"We need water to land in," said Bond. "Stay there."

Back on the flight deck, he throttled back to minimum, just above stalling speed. He picked up the Luger from the floor, put the safety catch on and stuck it in his waistband. As an afterthought, he slipped off Ken Mitchell's shoes and buttoned them inside his own shirt. Then he gave one last heave to the controls, to set the plane on a course over the long expanse of water to the west. It levelled out enough to allow him to climb back to the door, where Scarlett was clinging on.

"Try again," he shouted.

They fought the door release, and as it began to give, Bond said, "I'm going to hold on to you."

He put his arms through the harness and locked his hands together under Scarlett's breasts.

"Don't do anything. Let me pull the cord," said Bond, and at the same moment kicked the door.

Scarlett was sucked out at once into the slipstream, with Bond on her back. The plane was at such an angle that the engines and the tail passed above their heads as they rolled and rolled through the thin air above Russia, Bond half crushing Scarlett's ribs with the strength of his embrace, she digging nails and fingers into his wrists to keep him with her. The air rocketed into their lungs as they tumbled in freefall.

Bond waited as long as he dared until, gripping Scarlett still harder with his left hand, he slid his right over to the rip-cord lever and pulled. There was a short delay, then a bang and flap and Scarlett's body was jerked upright with such violence that Bond was almost shaken from her back. She screamed as she felt his grip slipping, and grasped his wrists. But his elbows were caught in her harness, and, as the parachute filled and their speed decreased, he was able to lock his arms round her again.

Bond tried to manoeuvre them towards the water he could see about two thousand feet below. The maximum weight allowed on a military parachute was somewhere near two hundred pounds. He calculated rapidly that even though Scarlett was a slender girl, they were nearer three hundred pounds between them. For a moment there was a kind of peace as they floated down. Then they heard a sound like an earthquake and twisted to look away behind them.

The Vickers VC10 had veered right in its descent and had exploded on the face of the mountain.

"The Urals have lost a peak," Bond shouted into Scarlett's ear.

He looked down at the water, now no more than five hundred feet below.

"The second you hit the water, smack the release. Got it? Otherwise the chute'll drown you."

"Okay," Scarlett shouted back.

The water, Bond could now see, was not a lake but part of a wide river. It didn't matter, he thought—so long as it was deep enough.

Fifty feet above the surface he disentangled his arms from the harness and kissed Scarlett on the ear. At twenty feet, he pushed back and let go.

With his hands placed protectively over his groin, Bond sliced the surface of the water like a dead duck and sank to the depths of the Volga. For a few moments, he saw weed and cold darkness reeling up past him. Then, with a shock that jarred his spine, he felt the riverbed beneath his feet and on his knees and hands, as he bent double with the impact. He pushed up hard, and saw reed and fish and water rewind past his thrashing feet and hands until he broke through into sunlight.

At first he saw only a floating canopy on the surface of the river. Then he saw a dark, wet head coming through the water to meet him.

Scarlett climbed into his arms and covered his dripping face with kisses. "My God," she said, laughing as she spluttered and coughed the water from her mouth. "You are quite something."

"Thank you for the lift," said Bond.

On the riverbank, they sat for a while to gather themselves and check their injuries.

"Poor Ken," said Scarlett.

"He was a better man than I gave him credit for," said Bond. "What happened to you after I last saw you?"

"The door code worked fine. There were quite a few guards but they were all running to Gorner's office."

"And outside?"

"Nothing much. Gorner's lair is just a lump in the desert. I suppose they didn't want to draw attention to it, so there's not much in the way of lights. But I

thought I should move fast, while they were still con-
centrating on you. I got round to the airliner. The
cargo doors were open because they hadn't finished
working on the modifications. I was able to climb up
into the hold from a sort of baggage-handling truck
alongside and, once I was in there, I saw a flap that
led up into the main part of the plane. They'd had to
cut it out to feed all the cables for the bomb release.
It was big enough for me to crawl up through. It
came out just behind the flight deck. Then I found
this uniform in the crew locker, changed in the lavatory between first and economy and just waited for
you. Not a very comfortable night."

"Didn't they search the plane?"

"I heard someone sniffing about in the hold later
on. But I suppose once they were satisfied the bombs
were in position they left it at that. They probably
forgot about the flap they'd cut or didn't think it
was big enough. And there were no passenger steps
in place outside, so I suppose they thought no one
could be in the main part of the plane."

"Well, you did a good job," said Bond. "I knew
you had it in you."

"Yes," said Scarlett. "My professional expertise."

"I was banking on it."

"Now what do we do?"

"Try and get help to Poppy. We'll need to find a telephone. I suggest you do the talking. Then when we get a connection I'll speak to my people in London. I'll give them all the information we have."

"All right. And what do we do in the meantime?"

"Go home," said Bond.

"How?"

"I reckon we're due east of Moscow. Probably seven or eight hundred miles. In view of what's been going on, it's too risky to take a train. They won't expect survivors from the plane, but they'll be jumpy. We'll drive. You can navigate. I'm sure your Russian's up to asking the way."

"I'm sure it is," said Scarlett, "though my accent may be a bit old-fashioned. Pre-revolutionary. I learned from White Russians."

"Well, even Communists respect a lady, don't they? First we need clothes, money and a car. You may need to avert your eyes for the next few hours, Scarlett. Sometimes a secret agent has to do undignified things."

"To tell the truth, James, I don't mind what you do, so long as I can have something to eat soon. Anything else I see, I shall forget at once."

"First, you need shoes," he said, as he pulled Ken Mitchell's wet loafers on to his own feet.

"Yes. There were no shoes or stockings with the uniform. The hostesses supply their own. Poppy told me. And—another thing—I have no underwear."

"I know," said Bond. "Let's see what we can find."

He held out his hand and pulled the weary girl to her feet.

They walked over the plain until they found a small road and, after half an hour of trudging, a village. At a farmhouse, Scarlett secured them water, bread and something half-way between curd and cheese.

The puzzled peasant woman who fed them couldn't keep her eyes off Scarlett's bare feet. She warned them they would need to walk for another half an hour before they came to a road of any size. She gave them more bread and two wrinkled apples from a store.

At the roadside, Scarlett waved down an agricultural lorry. By the time the driver realized there was a male hitch-hiker as well, it was too late and they were on their way west. He took them to a market town and pointed out where they could find a junction with a main east–west road to Kazan, the Tatar capital, then on to Gorky, the industrial city at the centre of the Volga-Vyatka region. From Gorky, he said, it was only five hours by road to Moscow.

When the driver had dropped them off, Bond

helped Scarlett to tidy up as best she could. Their clothes had dried, but the jacket of her BOAC tunic was torn, and in any case looked suspicious with its braid and insignia, so they discarded it. Barefoot, in the navy skirt, which they pinned up with a hair grip to make it look short enough to catch the eye of passing drivers, and with her hair tied back as neatly as possible, Scarlett looked like a beautiful but dishevelled schoolmistress, Bond told her—just the sort of woman men would want to stop and help.

More than a dozen vehicles of varying kinds slowed and pulled over for her, but none met Bond's requirements. From his concealed position behind a fir tree, he shook his head in answer to Scarlett's interrogative glances.

Bond was beginning to wonder if there were any decent cars in this totalitarian country when at last he heard the sound of a 2.5-litre, four-cylinder engine and saw a black Volga M21, the "Russian Mercedes," approaching down the avenue of birches. It was the vehicle favoured by the KGB and thus the car most Russians least wanted to see outside their door at night. So much the better, thought Bond, for his purposes.

Scarlett stood in the road, and the car slowed down. A single man was at the wheel, and leaned across to open the door. He was in his fifties, grey-haired, plump and wearing a suit without a tie. Not KGB, Bond thought, but probably an illegal dealer of some kind. Either that, or a favoured Party functionary.

As Scarlett got into the front, Bond climbed into the back. Scarlett explained to the disgruntled driver that he was her brother and that he was soft in the head, which was why he never spoke.

They drove west towards Kazan for an hour, and when they had reached a desolate stretch of road, far from any habitation, Bond pulled the Luger from his waistband and put it to the driver's ear.

"Tell him to slow down and stop."

All three climbed out of the car and walked to a clump of trees so they would be out of sight.

"Tell him to strip to his underclothes."

Scarlett looked away while Bond stripped naked and put on the man's suit. There was a wallet in the inside pocket, from which he extracted the cash.

"How much is this?"

Scarlett counted it. "Enough for food and drink."

"Petrol?"

"Yes. But not clothes."

"Tell him to wait here for ten minutes before he moves. Tell him we'll leave his car in Moscow. And say I'm sorry."

Bond and Scarlett ran back to the Volga and took off with a screech.

"When we get to Moscow," said Scarlett, "will we go to the British embassy?"

"No," said Bond. "As far as the embassy's concerned, the Service doesn't exist. Especially in Moscow. I can't use their protection. You can, though."

"But without my Russian, you won't make it."

"I might."

"I'm not leaving you, James. Not now."

"All right, but if so you'd better get some sleep. This bench seat can turn into a double bed. The Russians are very proud of it. They've shown it often at the London Motor Show."

An hour later Bond woke her. They were at a petrol station, where an old man came out to work the pump.

Inside the car, Bond said, "Get out to stretch your legs and tell him I'm going inside his hut to pay."

The man nodded as Scarlett spoke to him, and Bond walked inside the building. A woman in a headscarf sat behind a counter.

Bond took the Luger and pointed it at the cash drawer, at the same time raising a finger to his lips. The terrified woman pulled open the drawer and Bond filled his pockets with the notes inside as well as some loose change for the telephone. He motioned to the cashier to take off her headscarf, cardigan and shoes and to hand them over.

Then, raising his finger once more warningly to his lips, he ran back to the car and called to Scarlett to get in.

As she closed her door, Bond engaged the clutch and drove off, leaving the old man holding his still-dripping pump in amazement.

Bond drove fast for two more hours, till it was starting to grow dark.

"Look!" said Scarlett. "There's a telephone box. Let's try it."

Bond watched from the car while she wrestled with the primitive Soviet system. After ten minutes, she returned, downcast and frustrated.

"I managed to speak to an operator, but the idea of making an international call was completely out of the question. She didn't even seem to understand the idea of it."

"You'll have to go to the embassy in Moscow after all. It's the only way. I'll get us there as fast as I can. We won't be able to find petrol at night, so we'll have to stop somewhere and start again in the morning. But we'll try to find some food once we're past Kazan."

Scarlett nodded unhappily, and snuggled down against Bond on the bench seat. He had to wake her for help with the Cyrillic signposts at Kazan, but once they were on the western outskirts they saw a truck-drivers' restaurant set back from the road.

They sat alone beneath a strip-light, while a large woman brought them soup and black bread with tea. There was some stew afterwards, though neither of them could manage much of it.

"I can see why there are no other patrons," said Bond.

"It's not quite what you fantasized about, is it?" said Scarlett.

"Not quite."

"Will you come and see me in Paris, James? I'll cook you that dinner you described."

"I thought it was meant to be in a hotel."

"All right. Do you know what day of the week it is?"

"No. Why?"

"Let's make a date for the first Saturday we're free. You call my office on the Friday and tell me which hotel."

"It's a deal. Look. There are two lorries stopping outside. Time to go." Bond threw some notes on the table as they left.

When it was night, and they were deep in the Russian countryside, miles from any town, Bond turned off the main road on to a minor one for a mile or so, then on to a cart track. He pulled over and turned off the engine.

He took Scarlett by the hand and opened the boot of the car. Inside was a small suitcase which contained a clean shirt and men's underwear. There was also a razor and a sponge bag with a toothbrush and paste.

"I don't want to risk a farm building," said Bond. "It'll just mean dogs. We'll try to sleep in the field over there. It's not too bad. Put on that nice cardigan if you're cold. If you get really freezing, you can get back into the car and try out the famous double bed."

It was a beautiful summer night, and the sky above them was dense with stars. Bond made himself as comfortable as he could on the grass, folding up the suit jacket for a pillow.

He stroked Scarlett's hair as she rested her head on his shoulder. He bent down to kiss her, but she was already asleep.

How strange, thought Bond, to find himself at last in the country against which he had spent the greater part of his adult life conspiring and fighting. Now that he had finally set foot there, it seemed— with its European faces, straggling roads and poor farms—less alien and somehow more normal than he had pictured it. Then, deep in the heart of the

Soviet Union, James Bond fell into a light but restful sleep.

As they neared Moscow towards noon the next day, Bond noticed a burning smell coming from beneath the Volga's bonnet. He had driven it hard for several hours, and it seemed to be resenting it. A dim memory of a London Motor Show came back to him at which the men on the Volga stand had extolled its high ground clearance, cigarette lighter, integral radio and . . . Yes, that was it: its pedal-operated lubrication. In the footwell, Bond saw an auxiliary pedal and pumped it hard, oiling not only the big end but large parts of the main road to Moscow.

"Once we get to Moscow," he said, "we'll go by train. Do we have enough money for tickets to Leningrad? Then we'll get a boat to Helsinki."

Scarlett counted the roubles from Bond's pocket. "We may have to do another Bonnie and Clyde at a petrol station," she said.

"Another good reason to dump the car in Moscow. The police will probably have its number by now."

"Good," said Scarlett. "We'll take a tram into the middle of town. I need some clothes. These shoes . . . We'll go to GUM, the state department store."

"Isn't that right next to the Kremlin?" said Bond.

"Yes, but I'm not sure where else to go. I think most of the other clothes shops just have empty shelves. You don't have to come in, James. I know what men are like about shopping."

"It's not the tedium, it's the—"

"I know."

"Get me a clean shirt and underwear while you're there. And food. We don't want to risk a restaurant."

They left the car near a tram terminus on the east side of the city and travelled into the centre. Bond carried the small suitcase from the boot of the Volga and hoped he looked like a middle-ranking Party functionary. Scarlett wore the BOAC hostess skirt and blouse with the garage woman's cardigan and shoes. Most of the others on the tram were dressed in a similarly improvised way and no one seemed to give them a second look.

While Scarlett disappeared into the labyrinth of GUM—a green-roofed, turreted monster almost as big as the Louvre—Bond walked round outside, not wanting to stop in case anyone came to speak to him. He made several long circuits before he eventually saw Scarlett emerge with two full bags.

"That was the longest half-hour of my life," he said.

"You wait till you see what I've got. A little straw

hat to make you look like a maths teacher on his summer holiday. Short-sleeved shirt. You like those, don't you? Socks that Ivan would be proud of on his collective farm."

"And for yourself?" said Bond, hustling her away from the shadow of the Kremlin towards the tram stop.

"Two pairs of babushka knickers and a reinforced bra that could support the onion domes of St. Basil's. A clean blouse. And some bread and cheese."

"Good girl. Now let's go."

They took a tram to Three Stations Square in the north-east section of the city and went up the steps of Leningrad station. Bond felt safer in the purposeful comings and goings of the concourse than he had while killing time outside GUM.

Scarlett bought two tickets for the Krasnaya Strela, the Red Arrow overnight train to Leningrad, leaving at eleven fifty-five. Then they walked to a small park and changed into their new clothes in the public conveniences.

"And now," said Scarlett, "I'm going to the embassy."

"Do you know where it is?" said Bond. "A grand building near the river—on Sofievskaya Quay, I think."

"I'll manage. The taxi driver will know. Will you stay here, in the park?"

"Yes, this is as discreet as I can be. I wish I could come with you, but I wouldn't be welcome. Who will you ring?"

"My office in Paris to begin with. I'll speak to the head of my department. He'll know what to do."

"All right. Before you go, Scarlett, remember one thing. Gorner has connections with SMERSH and the KGB. We've left a trail of havoc across the Soviet Union. A crashed airliner, armed robberies, a hijacked car. Soviet communications may be bad, but we're still almost certainly being watched. Watching's one thing they're good at. Remember, too, that if Darius has somehow managed to get details of the location of Gorner's factory back to London, a rescue operation will be under way already."

He took her hands between his own and looked deep into her eyes. "I want you to ask yourself one thing, Scarlett. Is a single telephone call from you going to make any difference? Is it really worth the risk?"

Scarlett returned his gaze without blinking. "James, she's my sister."

Bond released his grip. "For God's sake, make sure you're back here by nine at the latest." He watched the slim figure walk off in the new blouse at a determined pace towards the main road.

He spent the afternoon and evening in the park,

where he tried to sleep. He ate some bread and cheese and drank water from a fountain.

When darkness fell, he was able to breathe more easily. In the morning they would be in Leningrad, only a short boat ride from freedom. His body ached for the West: for iced cocktails, hot showers, clean sheets, good tobacco ...

His head grew heavy as he rested it against the rough bark of the plane tree behind the park bench.

Meanwhile, between two of the yellow-and-white columns that held up the great portico of Leningrad station, an urgent transaction was taking place.

A thick-set Soviet man, whose fleshy face bore the marks of a razorblade long past its best, was holding out his hand and nodding in agreement. The sleeves of an ill-fitting suit rose up to reveal grimy shirt cuffs.

Into his hand were pressed five US twenty-dollar bills, and the eyes widened with uncontrollable greed above the raw, red cheeks.

His interlocutor spoke bad English, as did he, but it was easy enough to understand what was meant. There were two photographs: one of a man with hard eyes and an unruly lock of black hair above his right eye, and one of a smart young woman, Russian perhaps, but more glamorous than any female he had ever seen in Moscow.

As for the man with the money, who could tell where he came from? He had the eyes of a Tatar or Mongol, but his skin was yellow, and the odd little hat he was wearing looked Spanish or French.

Two things were clear. One was a telephone number, underlined on a piece of paper pressed into his hand, and the other was that more money awaited a successful call.

19. A POINT OF SHAME

Scarlett returned to the park shortly before eight o'clock. She told Bond the embassy had been suspicious at first, but in the end a first secretary had taken pity on her and, having verified her *bona fides* by making a series of calls to Paris, had allowed her to use the telephone. She had then told her boss in Paris everything that might be helpful and he had promised to pass it on to the authorities. Bond smiled. He had no doubt that Scarlett had used all her feminine charm to persuade the hapless first secretary into permitting this irregular use of his telephone. The important thing was that she had got back safely.

At ten o'clock they left for the station. As they boarded the train, Bond, exhausted as he was, felt the excitement of the overnight journey and the never-failing romance of the busy concourse with its hopeful arrivals and tearful farewells.

"How did you manage to get us in here?" he said, looking at the wooden bunks of the private sleeping compartment, normally reserved for senior Party members.

"I gave the guard about three months' wages," said Scarlett, "out of the money you took from the garage. You saw his face, didn't you?"

"I did," said Bond. "It was unforgettable."

"He says if any Party bigwigs get on board, he'll have to move us—but I don't think that's likely to happen now. If they were going to get on, it would be in Moscow, not Klin or Bologoye. When we've been going for a bit, he'll bring vodka. Stolichnaya. And I asked for food. He said he'd see what he could find. Otherwise, there's just the remains of the cheese."

"It doesn't matter," said Bond. He felt a great weariness come over him as the Red Arrow pulled out of the station. Scarlett leaned her head against his shoulder as they watched the grey suburbs of northern Moscow eventually give way to the open fields. Surely nothing could go wrong now, Bond thought, as they hurtled through the summer darkness towards the old capital, home of the Romanovs and their great palaces.

An hour later, the guard knocked at the door and they sat up guiltily, as though they had been doing something wrong. With no expression of pleasure or concern, the man opened a copy of *Pravda* and spread it on the lower bunk next to them. Then, from inside a brown-paper parcel, he took half a loaf of black bread, a bottle of Stolichnaya, a bag of plums and two fillets of smoked fish.

Bond watched Scarlett as she smiled and proffered more money. She was an extraordinary woman, he thought, chatting away with this man who—clearly charmed by her—declined the extra cash.

When he had gone, Scarlett said, "I told him you were from the Ukraine, darling." Her eyes were alight with innocent mischief. "I hope you don't mind."

Bond smiled as he drank deeply from the Stolichnaya bottle and offered it to Scarlett, who shook her head. The meal was quickly done, and they each lit one of the cheap Russian cigarettes she had bought at the station. They were now sitting opposite one another, so Bond could watch her as she stared through the window.

He remembered returning to his hotel room in Paris to see her there, sitting in the gilded armchair beneath the looking-glass, her long legs demurely crossed and her empty hands folded in front of her breasts ... "I'm so sorry to startle you, Mr. Bond ... I didn't want to give you the chance of turning me down again."

Now, against the flashing Russian landscape, she looked tired, but no less beautiful. Her large brown eyes flickered and refocused as the fields went by. Her mouth was slightly parted, and he remembered that stiffening of the upper lip when she was aroused. She pushed a strand of black hair behind her ear. Did she know that he was watching? Why else reveal the perfect pink shape of her ear, so delicate and exactly formed that it was all he could do not to lean across and kiss it?

The rattle of the wheels on the tracks as the engine picked up speed, the gentle swaying of the carriage and the creak of the woodwork in the warm compartment all seemed to form an irresistible lullaby. Bond had not drunk alcohol for days, and the vodka had gone to his head. He remembered other journeys—the Orient Express with Tanya ... Soon, he thought, he should prepare himself for sleep and climb on to the bunk, but for the moment ...

Drowsily, he remembered the room at Jamal's

Five Star and the abandon with which Scarlett had kissed him, the light movement with which she'd stepped out of her skirt and sat on the end of his bed . . .

They were deep, deep in the darkness of the Soviet night, and the images became disjointed in his mind as the rattle of the wheels on the iron track brought back memories of childhood, a train in the Highlands, his mother's voice—then the glass walkway at Gorner's factory, the huge steel vats of somniferous poppy juice, drugging, drowsing . . . Someone he loved calling his name . . . Then, then . . .

He was staring into a face of half-dead flesh beneath a Foreign Legion kepi and Scarlett was screaming: "James, James, *James*!"

The fat hands of Chagrin were on his throat and Bond was fighting for his life. His deepest reflexes got his fingers jabbing into Chagrin's eyes, but he merely rolled his big head away. Bond lashed up with his leg and felt his shin drive into Chagrin's groin, but the jungle veteran didn't loosen his grip. Presumably he had brought no gun, thought Bond, because he wanted to do his work in silence.

Bond could find no reserves of strength. This was one struggle too many for a body that had been starved, beaten and tortured. In the heel of his own shoes was a blade he might have used to help himself, but he was wearing the useless slip-ons of a dead air-line pilot. The air was draining from his lungs.

Then he felt a slim hand move to the back of his waistband, and a discreet tug as the Luger was withdrawn.

With a roar of anger, Chagrin turned and swung his arm across Scarlett's wrist, causing the gun to clatter to the floor. It gave Bond enough time to move. He wrenched the little finger of Chagrin's left hand from his throat and, using both his own hands in a sudden downward snap, he broke it.

Chagrin stepped back, his noise now of pain as much as anger, and aimed a punch at Bond's face with his right hand. Bond ducked, and the blow glanced off his shoulder. Scarlett picked up the Luger.

"Don't fire," gasped Bond. "It'll bring the guard."

As the two men stood grappling on the rolling, swaying floor of the train, Scarlett climbed on to the seat. With the butt of the Luger, she knocked off Chagrin's kepi to reveal the shaved skull where the butcher-surgeons of Omsk had been to work.

She had found his point of shame. As Chagrin put both hands to his head to cover the botched osteo-plastic flap, Bond drove his head into the man's solar plexus. Chagrin doubled forward and Bond snapped his knee up into the chin, hearing the jaw crack.

"Pull down the window, Scarlett," he gasped. "Help me lift him."

Bond thought of the tame missionaries of the Vietnamese jungle—priests and spinsters from the Loire valley whose tongues this monster had ripped out with pliers for reading Bible stories to the children—and grabbed the gun from Scarlett. He stood on the seat and drove the muzzle with all his might deep into the concave dip in Chagrin's skull, feeling it pierce the unknitted bone and membranes beneath.

The torturer let out a terrible moan and fell against the bunk. Each taking a leg, Bond and Scarlett levered him bit by bit through the gaping window. They had got him half-way out and were holding on to his weakly kicking calves when the front of the train entered a narrow brick tunnel. When the entrance was opposite their compartment, the clearance was tight enough for the brick pier to whip off Chagrin's head, which ricocheted into the embankment. Once they were through the tunnel, Bond shovelled the rest of the wretched body out and fell back on to the seat.

Scarlett put her face into her hands and wept.

Bond awoke in daylight, with Scarlett's arms round him, lying on the bottom bunk. She had covered them both with a grey blanket and the garage woman's cardigan.

Scarlett's hair lay over his face like a dark shawl as she stroked his aching back and whispered in his ear, "We're nearly there, we're nearly there, my darling. Breakfast in Leningrad at the Literaturnaya Café on the Nevsky Prospekt. My father used to tell me about it. We'll have eggs with smoked salmon and coffee. Then a boat. Helsinki. And then Paris."

Bond smiled, rolled on to his back and kissed her on the lips. The sleep had partly restored him.

"Why is it that every time I'm about to make love to you," he said, "we get interrupted? Is it still 'destiny'?"

"No," said Scarlett, "it's so that when it finally happens it will be more wonderful."

Scarlett disappeared down the corridor with the Volga driver's sponge bag and Bond prepared himself for one more day. When they reached Helsinki, he would telephone M and find out what had happened to the Caspian Sea Monster. He smiled to himself at the prospect. The old man could never quite disguise the pleasure he had in hearing Bond's voice after a long radio silence.

When each had done what they could with Soviet toothpaste and brackish water, they settled back to watch the approach of Leningrad.

"As soon as we get to the docks," said Bond,

"you'll have to find an adventurous boat owner, Scarlett. Somewhere out in the Gulf of Finland there's a watery border between the Communists and the free world. I think we can be reasonably certain that it will be patrolled by armed frontier guards."

"You want me to find a pirate," said Scarlett.

"Yes," said Bond. "With a very fast boat."

"I shall need money."

"You're turning me into a cheap thief."

"You have such a flair for it, my love."

Bond sighed and checked the magazine of the Luger.

It was only a short walk from the Moscow station to the Nevsky Prospekt, and when they had breakfasted, Bond set about raising more money while Scarlett went to the docks. They had a rendezvous behind the Pushkin Theatre at one o'clock. Bond, rather to his shame, slipped a knitted balaclava from a market stall into his pocket and wore it while he removed a quantity of money at gunpoint from a van delivering cash before opening time to a bank on a quiet street off Moskovsky Prospekt. At least the security guard had been stupefied enough by the sight of the Luger to offer no struggle, and Bond had been able to put a good distance between himself and the scene before he heard a police siren. He threw the balaclava into a bin, put on the "maths teacher" straw hat from GUM and made himself as inconspicuous as he could in a municipal park near the Neva river.

When he was reunited with Scarlett, her news was mixed. She looked anxious. "I found a man," she said. "He's Finnish, in fact, and he speaks English, though not very well. He's prepared to do it, but he can't get us to Helsinki. It's too far. If he takes a lot of extra fuel, he can get us over the border. Then we transfer to a boat belonging to his brother. They do the run quite regularly, he says. This second boat will take us to a large port called Hamina, which is about a hundred and fifty miles from here. It's the best he can do. We can get a train from there, or there's a good road."

"All right," said Bond. "At least it's in Finland. A neutral country."

"There are Russian navy boats on patrol and part of the sea is mined, but he knows the way through. We do it at night. We leave at eleven. It'll take eight hours altogether. But he wants a hell of a lot of money."

"That's just what I have," said Bond.

"How did you—"

"You said you wouldn't ask."

———

At ten forty-five, Bond and Scarlett arrived at the appointed place. The docks were heavily guarded by Customs and police requiring paperwork and passports, so Scarlett had been directed to one of the small islands on the west of the city. At the end of a narrow street, there was a flight of old lightermen's brick steps going down into the sea.

At their foot, as he had promised, was Jaska, the man with whom Scarlett had made the deal. The boat was a converted fishing vessel with a sluggish inboard motor that was already turning over with a throaty, catarrhal sound. As they stepped aboard, Bond was relieved to see two 250-horsepower Evinrudes under canvas in the stern. There was a covered cabin of sorts in the bow, though most of the available deck space was taken up by fuel drums.

Jaska had about three days' growth of grey stubble and a blue cap. Most of his teeth were missing and those that remained were yellow or brown.

Bond handed him the money, which he counted carefully.

"He doesn't like the Russians," Scarlett explained. "His father died fighting them when they invaded Finland in 1939."

Jaska nodded to them, untied the single rope mooring, engaged the engine and began to move the boat as quietly as he could into the Gulf of Finland.

Bond and Scarlett sat together on a wooden bench on the port side.

"There's one thing we didn't think of," said Scarlett.

"I know," said Bond. "White nights. It's the worst time of year."

"Jaska says it will get a bit darker—like dusk. And at least it's clouded over."

Bond sat back against the side of the boat. "There are some moments, Scarlett," he said, "when you just have to place your life in the hands of others. Trust them."

"I know. And I like the look of this one."

"Mercenary and embittered," said Bond. "A good man to have on your side at a time like this."

Jaska steered the boat wherever he found shadows in the jagged archipelago, but after half an hour of creeping in the lee of the small islands, it was time to move into the open sea.

Scarlett had had time to prepare a basket of food, which she now unpacked. There was bread, sausage, cheese and vodka.

"It was the best I could find," she said.

Jaska helped them get through it, chewing hungrily at the wheel, his eyes never leaving the horizon.

An hour passed, then another, and the night grew as dark as it could manage—the shade of an autumn dusk, as Jaska had predicted. When they were well clear of Leningrad but also far from the border, he lowered the twin Evinrudes over the stern. He spoke to Scarlett in Russian.

"He says we'll use the outboards to make up some time," she translated. "They're too noisy near the land or the frontier, but we can blast on for an hour or so now."

Bond felt a welcome surge as the old fishing-boat began to part the water with more purpose. It was about a hundred and fifty miles to Hamina, and although they were now travelling at about twenty-five knots, they had previously been doing less than half that. He calculated that they must still be two hours short of the maritime border.

Jaska asked Bond to take the wheel while he decanted fuel from the drums into smaller cans with which he replenished the tanks.

When Jaska had resumed his position, Bond rejoined Scarlett on the bench. "How do you feel?"

She smiled. "Safe. And you?"

"I'm enjoying it," said Bond. It was true. "The strange light, the sea. The company."

Eventually, Jaska turned off the outboard motors and lifted them back in.

"He says we'll be making the hand-over in forty minutes," said Scarlett. "We have to go quiet again."

Jaska picked up a radio mouthpiece from next to the wheel and spoke into it. After a short pause there was a crackling reply.

The sailor's face remained impassive as he replaced the radio. He spoke again to Scarlett.

"There are Soviet naval patrol vessels to the north and south," she translated, "but one of them's been distracted by a tanker from Tallinn that's gone off course."

In the dusk ahead, like a ghost vessel, Bond saw the outline of a fishing-boat similar to their own. He pointed to it and Jaska turned his head. For the first time, the lined, weatherbeaten face broke into a smile. "Yes," he said in English. "My brother."

The two boats bore slowly down on one another in a light mist that rose from the sea. The night had grown cold, and Scarlett put on the garage woman's cardigan as she slipped her arm through Bond's.

Jaska slowed the engine as the two boats came alongside, miles from land in the middle of the great empty sea. There was a jolt as the sides of the vessels touched and Jaska tossed a line over.

Scarlett stood up and crossed to the starboard side. Jaska held out his hand to steady her and she threw her arms round him briefly. "*Spasibo. Ochen spasibo.* Thank you."

Bond shook his hand. "Thank you, Jaska."

Jaska held Bond's hand between both of his and for a moment the two men looked into each other's eyes.

Then Bond was gone, over into the second boat, while Jaska had pushed off and was already preparing his fishing-nets so that he could show a legitimate purpose for his night-time excursion if anyone should stop him on the way home.

Scarlett and Bond waved briefly in the mist, then settled in for the final part of the journey. Jaska's brother was called Veli and looked at least ten years younger. He moved vigorously about his small craft and smiled constantly.

He waited only a short time before engaging his outboard motor, and three hours later, after several refuellings from his onboard supply, they saw the port of Hamina, protected by its star-shaped fortress.

By eight o'clock they were on Finnish soil and by ten they were on the express train to Helsinki.

20. A WILDERNESS
OF MIRRORS

It was a rainy evening in Paris, and René Mathis was sitting at his desk, flicking through some police reports that had been forwarded to the Deuxième. Rumours were flying round his department of a spectacular development in the battle against drugs, but no details had yet been confirmed.

The green telephone rang, with its sharp, nagging note. There was a roar, an echo—then a familiar voice.

"Where are you, James?"

"I'm at the airport in Helsinki. I'm on my way to

Paris. My flight leaves in half an hour. I wondered if you'd like dinner tomorrow night."

"Tomorrow? Er . . . Friday? Fridays are . . . Fridays are always difficult for me, James. So much tidying up to be done at the end of a week. Maybe a drink? There's a nice bar I could show you. Or lunch one day? Are you here for the weekend?"

"We'll have to see what London says. And, René?"

"What?"

"Give her my love."

At the airport in Paris, Bond put Scarlett into a taxi with a promise that he would telephone her at work the next day. They had decided to spend some time apart to recover from what they had been through, and Scarlett was anxious to speak to her employers and find out if there was news of Poppy. Bond had not demurred at the thought of some time to rest and sleep: he was exhausted, and the poor girl seemed to be on her last legs.

As she kissed him goodbye, she said, "I'll be waiting for your call. Don't let me down, James."

"Have I ever?"

She shook her head silently as the taxi moved off. Bond watched the car receding into the rainy night, the girl waving from the back seat, her large brown eyes fixed on him till she was out of sight.

He took the next cab on the rank and ordered it to the Terminus Nord. He always stayed in railway hotels if he could, and the Nord was the least pretentious. An earlier call from Helsinki to Regent's Park had secured a wire transfer of funds to a bank in the Place Vendôme, where he could collect it the following day. Moneypenny, unable to keep the elation from her voice at the sound of his, had also booked him a time to speak to M on the encrypted line in the late morning.

There was a large room at the top of the Terminus Nord with a good shower and plentiful shampoo and soap. Bond had room service send up some whisky and Perrier, then poured himself a large glassful as he relaxed on the bed with a clean white towel wrapped round him.

He lay back on the pillows and let the events of the last few days replay in his mind. It had taken him some time to find the Service's man in Helsinki. He was new, and looked no more than twenty, but at least he had produced a couple of reasonable-looking passports in the course of the afternoon. Bond had given him the Luger to dispose of as he wished. He would get a new Walther PPK back in London.

Tomorrow, he thought, would be a wonderful

day. He could spend an idle morning buying new clothes, report to M, then lunch at the Rotonde or the Dôme and telephone Scarlett in the afternoon. After that, more sleep in his anonymous hotel room, then perhaps a film and dinner at one of the great restaurants, the Véfour or the Caneton.

As for tonight, the Finnish notes he had changed at the airport had given him enough money for a good dinner, but he didn't feel in the mood. He rang down again to Reception, told them to bring an omelette *fines herbes* and the rest of the whisky bottle.

When he had done it justice, he rolled naked beneath the covers and slept without moving for twelve hours.

Friday morning was brilliantly clear and sunny as Bond left his hotel and took a taxi to the Place Vendôme. On the rue de Rivoli, he bought a light-weight grey suit, a black knitted tie, three shirts, cotton underwear, some charcoal grey woollen socks and a pair of black loafers. He asked the shopkeeper to get rid of the Volga driver's clothes and Ken Mitchell's shoes.

It was time to make his call to M. He reversed the charges from a coin-operated box in the rue de l'Arbre Sec, then waited when he heard the switchboard in Regent's Park, the laborious clanking and the long silence that the inexperienced took for a lost connection before the strange hollow sound of the secure line.

"Bond? Where the devil are you?"

"Paris, sir. I told Moneypenny yesterday."

"Yes, but why?"

"I was escorting a young lady home, sir."

"Never mind that. I've had the PM on the line."

"How was he?"

"Well . . . He was extremely pleased as a matter of fact."

"Unusual," said Bond.

"Damn near unprecedented. The RAF took out that Ekranoplan. Somehow the VC10 also came down off-target."

"Yes, sir, I—"

"You can tell me all about it back in London. Give yourself a few days in Paris, if you like. While you're there, I'd like you to meet the new 004."

"What?" Bond's voice went cold.

"Don't be a damned fool, Bond. I told you when you were in London that the last man died in East Germany."

"Where do I meet him?"

"Go to the George V at seven tonight. Ask for

room five eight six. They'll be expecting you. It's just a formality. Press the flesh, say hello. And, Bond?"

"Yes?"

"Did you know Felix Leiter had been in on Pistachio?"

"Felix? No. What happened?"

"Bit of a crash dive. There was a problem with a man called Silver."

"Doesn't surprise me."

"He tried to stop Felix making contact. He turned out to be some kind of double. And, Bond, I'm afraid Pistachio himself . . ."

Bond heard the emptiness of the line. It meant only one thing. He swore violently.

"Take some time in Paris," said M. "Felix's passing through on Monday on his way back to Washington. I think he'd like to see you."

"I'll tell Moneypenny where to find me."

"That's all for the moment."

"Thank you, sir."

He replaced the receiver and walked down to the river. Darius had been a good man, but, like Darko Kerim in Istanbul and others before, he had always known the risks involved.

Bond tried to put the thought of him from his mind. His pockets were still full of new francs as he strolled along the *quai*, stopping occasionally to look at the cheap paintings, souvenirs and second-hand books that the stall-holders were displaying beside the river. It always surprised him that the padlocked green wooden stalls could contain so much when they were opened out. He picked up a miniature Eiffel Tower and turned it over in his fingers. Should he buy Scarlett a present? he wondered. Time enough to do that before tomorrow evening.

He contented himself with buying a suitably risqué postcard for Moneypenny and went to a small pavement café on rue des Bourdonnais to write it. He ordered an Americano—Campari, Cinzano, lemon peel and Perrier—not because he particularly liked it, but because a French café was not a place in his view for a serious drink.

It was surprisingly good, the zest of the lemon cutting through the sweetness of the vermouth, and Bond felt almost fully restored as he left some coins on the zinc-topped table and stood up. He would double back, cross the river at the Pont Neuf and walk slowly towards the Dôme. He had time to kill.

When he was half-way across the bridge, he noticed, about a hundred yards upriver, the Mississippi paddle steamer, the *Huckleberry Finn*, "on loan to the City of Paris for one month only" —the same vessel he had seen after his first lunch with Scarlett on the Île St. Louis. Cheerful tourists thronged her decks, and a minstrel band in striped blazers and white trousers played noisily in the bow. Bond glanced at his watch. He had nothing else to do.

He saw the boat moor at a stop on the Left Bank and went down the steps to the river. He bought a ticket and went up the gangplank.

There were empty seats towards the bow, and Bond settled down alone on a bench. It was a warm summer's day and Paris was *en fête*. He sat back as luxuriously as the wooden seat allowed, closed his eyes and let his mind picture what the evening ahead might have in store. The boat proceeded slowly down the river.

Bond's reverie was interrupted by a shadow blocking out the sun. He opened his eyes to see a tall, bearded man looking down on him. The beard was full and dark—too dark for the fair skin. It looked odd and unfamiliar, yet there was no mistaking the eyes—or their look of burning, zealous concentration, as though their owner feared that other people might corrupt the purity of his purpose.

At the same moment, Bond felt something hard and metallic being driven against one of his lower vertebrae through the open back of the bench.

"Do you mind if I join you?" said Gorner. "Forgive my childish disguise. My face is rather more widely known than I care for just at the moment. The press can be so intrusive."

"How the hell did you find me?"

Gorner let out the grunt that was his version of a laugh. "The fact that one of my factories has suffered a setback doesn't mean I have become impotent overnight, Bond. I have staff in London and Paris, as well as connections in Moscow. When I gathered that the plane had not reached Zlatoust-36, I had Chagrin fly to Moscow to keep an eye open. Just in case. Word reached me that you and the girl were bound for Leningrad. What else would you do but run for home? We found business cards in the handbag my men took from her in Noshahr, so we knew where she was based and we knew you'd head either for London or Paris. I had my men watch both airports. They've been following you. But in my mind there was no doubt you'd follow the bitch's scent to Paris. That's why I came here first."

"And what do you want?"

"I want to kill you, Bond. That's all. In a moment the minstrel band will strike up its noise again and no one will hear the sound of a silenced gun."

Gorner glanced behind him, where his hitman was leaning forward, the long silencer of his gun concealed beneath a folded raincoat.

"This is Mr. Hashim," said Gorner. "I did

business with his brother once. But that's another story."

"What happened to your desert factory?"

"Savak," Gorner spat. "With information from their American and British 'chums,' the Persian goons finally located it. The army moved in and closed it down."

"Was there bloodshed?"

"Nothing much. I told my staff to co-operate. I was in Paris by then."

"And the people inside, what happened to them?"

"The addicts? God. Who knows? Who cares? Back to their gutters, I imagine."

Bond could see the horn player in the band emptying spit on to the deck and the clarinettist turning the pages of his music on the stand. The drummer was sitting down on his stool again.

Then he looked at where Gorner held his gloved left hand with his right, both folded in his lap.

"Do you like music, Bond?" said Gorner. "It'll start again any second now. I'm not one of those idiots who looks for a protracted or picturesque death for their arch-enemy. A single bullet is good enough for British scum like you."

"Was Silver working for you?" said Bond.

"Who?"

"Carmen Silver. The man at General Motors. I hear he tried to stop the real CIA making a move."

"Perhaps he was being blackmailed by the Russians," said Gorner. "Perhaps he'd 'gone native' and thought he understood American national interest better than his bosses."

"Yes," said Bond. "Or perhaps he was just a man without qualities."

"There will always be such people in your world, Bond. Loose ends. Oh, do look, the conductor is coming back to join the band. Mr. Hashim loves negro music."

Bond waited while the conductor, in his striped blazer, looked round the twelve-man band, nodding and smiling. Gorner was watching with avid eyes, eager for this treat. Then, as the conductor lifted his baton to tap the music stand in front of him, Bond reached over, grabbed Gorner's left hand and tore the glove from it.

He had remembered from the crimson office at the desert lair that the deformity was the only thing that had the power to deflect Gorner's concentration.

With one hand, Bond hurled the glove as far forward as he could, almost to the feet of the conductor, and with the other he held up the monkey's paw in the sunlight for all the passengers to see. Gorner threw himself across Bond in his desperate attempt to pull his hand back. As he did so, Bond yanked on Gorner's arm, bringing the full weight of the man across him, thus dislodging for a moment the gun from his own back. The hitman hesitated for a second lest he shoot his paymaster. With Gorner's bulk across him, Bond lashed out once with his forearm into Hashim's face. Then, still with Gorner on top of him, he grabbed Hashim's hair, pulled his head forward and smashed his face into the back of the bench. With his right hand, Bond shoved Gorner down on to the deck where, on all fours, he searched frantically for his glove. With his left hand, Bond kept Hashim's face against the bench. He heard the sound of a silenced gunshot, but it went into the deck by his feet. Then he vaulted over the bench and took Hashim's right wrist between both of his own hands. The gun went off again, this time upwards through the striped canvas canopy.

Passengers had begun to scream as they saw what was happening. Two crew men were running towards Bond and Hashim. Bond had managed to get Hashim's arm behind his back and was twisting it violently. He could hear the elbow dislocating as the crew closed in on him. The captain sounded the alarm as the band stopped playing their Dixie tune. Hashim let out a grim, feral scream and dropped the gun. Bond grabbed it from the deck and ran forwards.

The *Huckleberry Finn* was approaching a low bridge as the captain killed the engines. Gorner, his precious white glove now back on his left hand, had climbed on top of the enclosed wheelhouse where the captain and the pilot stood. There were iron rungs let into the brickwork of the bridge that was slowly approaching them. By the time Bond had seen what was happening, Gorner was hauling himself up the side of the low bridge. Bond managed to catch the last iron handhold as the *Huckleberry Finn*, now drifting without power, slid beneath the arch.

With Hashim's gun in his waistband, Bond pulled himself up the dozen rungs and on to the parapet. Gorner had already crossed four lanes of traffic and was making off towards the Right Bank.

Weaving between furious, hooting cars, Bond steadied himself on the central island, planted his feet and fired once. The phlegmy cough of the silencer was followed by a scream from Gorner as the bullet caught his thigh.

Bond dodged through the northbound traffic. As he did so, he heard the rumble of the steamer below as the captain restarted the engines.

Bond ran towards Gorner, but when he got there he found that Gorner, bleeding but not disabled, had pulled himself up off the pavement and on to the brick parapet. Bond stopped and pointed the gun at Gorner's chest.

"I won't give you that pleasure, Englishman," panted Gorner. The black beard had come half unstuck.

Bond watched closely, expecting him to produce a second gun. But Gorner said nothing, merely turned, jumped and disappeared. Bond ran to the edge of the parapet and looked down. Gorner was still alive, floundering in the brown water.

The *Huckleberry Finn*, presumably making with all haste to a point where the captain could disembark the passengers and report to the police, had changed course and was now heading upstream, back beneath the same bridge. The wounded Gorner, splashing impotently with both arms, was directly in her path.

Gorner appeared stricken, unable to move, as the great paddle swept under him, lifted him up in its teeth, and rolled him round and back beneath the water. Bond watched in fascination as Gorner rose and circulated once more, leaving a poppy-coloured bloodstain in the river. A third time, the trapped body was swept up and revolved in the indifferent paddles, as the captain of the boat, unaware of what was happening, proceeded at full steam ahead.

The minstrel band began to play again as the

paddles turned—this time with no trace of Gorner. Then on the surface of the river there appeared, floating like a water-lily, a single white glove. It bobbed and turned in the wake of the boat for a few seconds, then filled with water and sank.

Bond barely had time to telephone Scarlett's office where he left a message—"Crillon lobby at six thirty tomorrow"—before the police were on the scene. He spent most of the afternoon explaining to them what had happened. A suicide, a bizarre accident . . . At five o'clock he persuaded them to call René Mathis, who was happy to vouch for Bond's good name in person.

It was six thirty by the time the paperwork was finished and the two men stood on the quai des Orfèvres.

"I would love to . . . But I . . ." said Mathis, looking at his watch.

"Me too," said Bond. "Business."

"Lunch on Monday," said Mathis. "That same place. In the rue du Cherche Midi."

"I'll see you there at one," said Bond.

They shook hands and went their different ways. Bond hailed a taxi—a black Citroën DS—which rolled him smoothly through the heavy traffic of the Champs-Élysées and on to the George V. It was five to seven as he crossed the great marble-floored lobby with its ornate tables groaning beneath giant glass vases of lilies.

"Room five eight six, please," he said to the clerk.

There was a muted telephone conversation.

"Yes, Monsieur, you are expected. The elevator is that way and to the left."

The George V was a witty choice for this meeting, Bond reflected, as he jabbed the number-five button inside the lift—named after the British king who had instigated the Entente Cordiale. How cordial would this meeting be? He knew most of the other double-Os by name or by sight, but contact was kept to a minimum for security reasons.

Ah, well, he thought, as he went down the softly carpeted corridor to room 586. The first few months in the job could be difficult. He would do his best to be polite. He knocked on the door. There was no answer.

He tried the handle, and the unlocked door opened into a darkened room. Everything was exactly as they had always been taught. What light there was shone into his eyes, leaving the rest of the room in shadow, but as he closed the door behind him Bond knew exactly what he would see. Without turning, he said, "Hello, Scarlett."

"Hello, James. We seem to have met a day early."

She stood up from the chair in the darkest corner, where she had been sitting, and turned the lamp away from him. She reached for a switch in the panelling, and the room returned to a normal, muted lighting.

She was wearing a sleeveless black dress, black stockings and a modest silver necklace. She had the red lip colour she had worn as Mrs. Larissa Rossi when he first set eyes on her in Rome. Her hair was glowing and clean on her bare shoulders.

Yet she looked, for the first time since he had known her, ill at ease. She looked frightened.

"I'm so sorry, James." She took a hesitant step towards him. "I didn't mean to fall in love with you."

Bond smiled. "It's all right."

"When did you know?" Her voice was tight with anxiety—the dread of one who fears the loss of love.

Bond sighed deeply. "When I walked into this room. But all along, really."

"Which?"

"Both."

Bond began to laugh and found it hard to stop. The tension of the preceding days seemed to pour out of him.

Then, with a deep inhalation, he controlled

himself. "I think the moment when you shot clean through the electric cable in the hangar at Noshahr . . . That was when I first suspected."

Scarlett pouted. "It was very close."

"Not that close."

"Oh, my darling, I'm so sorry. I'd spent the week before firing in two new Walthers on the range. My eye was in. Can you forgive me?"

"I don't know yet, Scarlett." Bond sat down on the velvet-upholstered sofa and lit a cigarette. He put his feet up on the coffee-table as he exhaled. "I'll have to forgive myself first. You gave me enough clues. The way you left no shadow when you hid outside the building in the boatyard. The way you smelt of fresh lily-of-the-valley when I kissed you in Noshahr—though you were meant to have come direct from the airport in Tehran in an overheated car."

Scarlett looked down. "I wanted to be nice for you. I'd actually been in Noshahr for a day. Oh God, James, I feel terrible. I hated misleading you, I just—"

"Why did M send you?"

"It was my first assignment as a double-O. He thought I might need help. He wanted to break me in easily."

"And he thought I might need help, too," said Bond, ruefully.

"Only because there was too much for one person to do. And you had . . . You'd had a bad time. Tokyo and . . ."

Scarlett took another step closer. Bond felt the light touch of her hand on his. "And after all, James," she said, "we made a pretty good job of it. Didn't we?"

"And the way you put on a parachute," said Bond. "Without training, people are all thumbs."

"I'm so very sorry, James. It had to be that way. Those were my orders. M knew you'd never consent to having me along if you knew. But he wanted you back. He needs you."

"No wonder the old man looked so shifty when he briefed me. And Poppy?"

Scarlett shook her head. "Every man's fantasy, James. Twins."

"How did you do the birthmark?"

"Tea and pomegranate juice."

"And the different eye colours?"

"You noticed! I wasn't sure men took these things in. Coloured contact lenses."

"I didn't know you could buy such things."

"You can't. Q section made them for me. It helped with the dissimilar twin story because identicals have the same eye colour. "

"And what did you do that afternoon in Moscow, when I thought you were at the embassy?"

"I just went to another park and stayed out of sight. I had to keep the story going till the end."

Bond smiled. "You're one hell of an actress. You were so like yourself . . . And yet somehow not. And Mrs. Rossi, too. Larissa."

"I know. I had two years at stage school from when I was twenty-one. It was one of the things that got me the job. That and speaking Russian."

"The way you turned your back on me in the cell when I told you we were leaving Poppy behind, so you could fake your sobs without me seeing your face . . ."

Scarlett was so close that he could smell her skin, the faintest scent of Guerlain. Her eyes were looking up into his, pleading, brimming with tears.

Rejecting an impulse to weaken, Bond stood up, ground out his cigarette and went over to the window. "What the hell was M thinking?" he said.

"I told you," said Scarlett, desperately. "He wanted you back. My predecessor was dead. 009 was acting up—close to a breakdown, they thought. M needed your experience and your strength. But he wasn't sure you still had the will, the desire."

"It's against all normal practice," said Bond.

"How much did he brief you? You seemed to know more about Gorner than I did."

"Most of it I just made up," said Scarlett. "M gave me a free hand with the cover story. He said he didn't need to know. He just told me to draw you in. He said I would find you . . . indispensable. And I did."

"And he mentioned my Achilles' heel."

"Women? Darling, everyone knows that. It was the first thing Felix told me. 'Mention the broad and the 'coon'll be treed.' What on earth does that mean by the way?"

"It's a raccoon, I suppose. Some Davy Crockett thing."

"It's even on your SMERSH dossier, I'm told, under 'Weaknesses.' "

Bond looked back at Scarlett's anxious face. "How much of the stuff you told me about Gorner and your father was true?"

"Some. Please, James, just—"

"How much?"

"My father was a don at Oxford at the time, but he never knew Gorner. My father taught music. Not a Gorner speciality."

"And his hatred of Britain?"

"I don't really know how that started. But I was delighted when he spouted all that anti-British stuff, of course."

Bond breathed in deeply and looked back across the opulent hotel room at this woman in her black velvet dress, the force of her beauty checked only by the anguish in her eyes. Then he thought of all they had been through and how she had never once flinched or let him down. He took two hesitant steps towards her and saw her upper lip stiffen in reflexive arousal, as he had first seen it in Larissa Rossi in Rome.

And whatever else was true or false, he knew this girl did love him. He reached out and wrapped his arms round her. She sighed and clamped her lips to his mouth while his hands slid down her dress and pulled her by the hips roughly against him.

When they had kissed for a minute, Bond said, "Now we're going to order dinner. Exactly as we described."

Scarlett went to the telephone. There were tears of relief in the corners of her eyes. "Shall we skip the eggs Benedict?" she said.

"Just this once. But I'd like a real drink first. A jug of martinis."

Scarlett began to order rapidly. "What year Château Batailley do you want?"

" 'Forty-five will do," said Bond.

"They're sending out for that vintage. Dinner will be up in half an hour."

"Time enough," said Bond. "Now come here. My boss told me to 'press the flesh' and I don't like to disobey orders."

The belle-époque furnishings of the room included mirrors on the doors of the many wardrobes, as well as one above the marble fireplace. Bond watched Scarlett as she undressed, slipping out of the black dress, the stockings and the black underwear. There were four, eight, sixteen of her. She was multiplied in reflection, stretched to infinity in the soft light of the warm hotel room.

"In the words of one of Felix Leiter's bosses," said Bond, hoarsely, "we are in a wilderness of mirrors."

Then he ran his hands over Scarlett's naked body and took her roughly, quickly, with the pent-up urgency of their long and chaste association.

Scarlett was in the bath when the dinner arrived, and Bond took a martini through to her.

"I also brought you this," he said, taking a bottle of Floris gardenia bath essence from his pocket.

"So it's just as we planned." Scarlett smiled from the bath as she sprinkled some drops into the water.

Bond tipped a glassful of the icy martini down his throat and sighed with happiness as he wheeled the room-service trolley to the bed. He took off his own clothes and put on the white towelling robe from the bathroom door.

He lay back on the plump pillows and sucked the smoke of a Chesterfield deep into his lungs, then exhaled in a blissful stream, while Scarlett, naked as she had promised, prepared the caviar and the sole meunière. She sat cross-legged at the end of the bed, looking at him with her wide brown eyes, as though she feared he might disappear.

Bond drained the Bollinger. "I miss Poppy," he said. "She was so . . . demure. Surprisingly so, for such a wild child."

"Whereas Scarlett, who as a banker you'd expect to be restrained—"

"Is anything but."

"And which one," said Scarlett, "would you like me to be tonight?"

"I think Poppy till midnight," said Bond, drawing the cork on the Château Batailley, "but from then on pure, uninhibited Scarlett."

They talked through the events of the past week over dinner. Bond told her of his final encounter with Gorner as she cleared away the plates and glasses.

Scarlett took the last of the champagne and slipped under the bedclothes, leaning back next to Bond against the pillows. "What will happen to me, James?"

"What do you mean?"

"My job. I mean, on my very first assignment, I've made the terrible mistake of having an office romance."

Bond got off the bed, stood up and walked to the window. He was aware of how much his body ached—his rib, his shoulder, his hip, almost all his muscles.

Beneath him he could see the City of Light stretched out from the distant place de la Concorde, up through the Opéra and Pigalle to the terrible tower blocks of the northern *banlieue*.

He pulled the curtains together tightly, thinking of M, and Julian Burton, the new psychological-fitness trainer, Loelia Ponsonby, Moneypenny and all the others.

"Some office," he said, returning to the bed.

"Yes," said Scarlett, smiling as she pulled back the covers to reveal her naked body—pink from the bath, clean, soft and waiting for him. "And some romance."

Acknowledgements

Hardware: James Holland, Mark Lanyon, Rachel Organ, Lt.-Col. John Starling, Rowland White. For the Ekranoplan, see auto speed.com and www.se-technology.com/wig

Software: Atussa Cross, Hazel Orme.

Elsewhere: Andrew Burke/Lonely Planet; Patrice Hoffman.

Bondage: Hendy Chancellor, Zoe Watkins, Simon Winder.

With thanks,
SF
London, 28 May 2008

About Sebastian Faulks

Sebastian Faulks began his working life, like Ian Fleming, as a journalist, working for national newspapers in London from 1978 to 1991. Since then, however, he has been a full-time author, and his novels have been among the most widely admired of their time. They include the epic *Human Traces* (2005) and the much-loved *Birdsong* (1993), which has sold more than three million copies. He is also the author of a triple biography, *The Fatal Englishman*, and a book of literary parodies of other authors (including Fleming) called *Pistache*. His most recent novel is *Engleby* (2006). He first encountered the Bond novels as a twelve-year-old; the books were banned at his school, but he read them by torchlight under the sheets.

About Ian Fleming

Ian Fleming was born on 28 May 1908 in London. He wrote his first novel, *Casino Royale*, in 1952—and introduced James Bond to the world. For the next twelve years, Fleming produced a novel a year featuring the most renowned spy of the age. He also wrote, for his son, a children's story about a car that flies—*Chitty-Chitty-Bang-Bang*—which has inspired both film and stage productions.

Fleming was educated at Eton, where he was a noted athlete. After failing to complete the officers' training course at Sandhurst, he spent a formative time in Austria and Germany, learning languages and gaining an enduring love for the Alps. He joined Reuters and learned to write accurately and fast. A further career in the City of London was cut short by the outbreak of war in 1939.

As assistant to the Director of Naval Intelligence throughout the Second World War, he found his niche, and his experience in Naval Intelligence was to provide many of the incidents and characters in the Bond novels.

Later, while working for the *Sunday Times* as foreign manager, he would spend two months each winter in Jamaica and there, at Goldeneye, he wrote his novels. His interest in cars, travel, good food and beautiful women, as well as his love of golf and gambling, was reflected in the books that were to sell in the millions, boosted by the vastly successful film franchise.

Ian Fleming lived to see only the first two films, *Dr. No* and *From Russia with Love*. He died of heart failure in 1964 at the age of fifty-six.